CW01090851

Other Prowler Titles

Diary of a Hustler
ISBN 0-9524647-64

Young Cruisers
ISBN 0-9524647-72

Slaves
ISBN 0-9524647-99

Corporal in Charge
ISBN 0-95246478-0

Hard
ISBN 1-902644-01-8

The Young and The Hung
ISBN 1-902644-07-7

Aroused
ISBN 1-902644-08-5

Shipmates
ISBN 1-902644-14-X

Feeling Frisky
ISBN 1-902644-15-8

Paradise Palace
ISBN 1-902644-18-2

Virgin Sailors
ISBN 1-902644-03-4

Active Service
ISBN 1-902644-06-9

California Creamin'
ISBN 1-902644-04-2

Brad
ISBN 1-902644-09-3

Going Down
ISBN 1-902644-12-3

Summer Sweat
ISBN 1-902644-10-7

Riding the Big One
ISBN 1-902644-16-6

The Captain's Boy
ISBN 1-902644-23-9

theinitiation david keane

prowler books

The Initiation by David Keane

Copyright © 2000 David Keane
3 Broadbent Close London N6 5GG. All rights reserved.

First printing January 2000. Printed in Finland by Werner Soderstrom Oy.
Cover photography © 2000 Prowler Press

web-site: prowler.co.uk
• ISBN 1-902644-17-4

British Library Cataloguing in Publication Data.
A catalogue record for this book is available from the British Library.

One

Paul Montgomery set out for school. Just another day of tedium, boredom and perhaps the chance to get a smoke. Paul had learnt through the time of his school career that if you kept your head down no-one would bother you. He was neither white nor black belonging to no group and therefore ignored by almost all. However, someone was keeping an eye on him unknown to Paul. The tone of his skin fascinated a fellow 18-year-old sixth former. For the past couple of months Paul had been watched. Every detail of his athletic, firm body encased in the well-worn T-shirt and tight, clinging, faded jeans was of interest. He was average height for his years with dark curly hair and deep-set, dark brown, brooding eyes. All of these details had been observed and taken in. Alex, the School Sports Captain, could not come to terms with these feelings. He had fantazied about Paul as he lay in bed stroking himself to a climax. If only he could find some way of speaking to this object of his desire. Perhaps if he spoke to him, the spell would be broken and he could continue to work his way through the girls that lined up for his attention. After all, he had everything: good looks, excellent body, was a natural sportsman and a gifted academic. Dark-haired and well-groomed, he was the only son of a financially comfortable middle-class family. Both his parents were doctors in practice in one of Birmingham's better-off areas. Everything was so neat and tidy: Sixth Form then on to University and perhaps follow the family tradition and join the medical profession. Alternatively, the law had its attractions. Now over-shadowing everything was this dark brooding boy who was totally unaware of the effect he had on a guy. Two 18-year-old students, same school but worlds apart. One full of pent up desire, the other naive and unaware of his latent power.

Paul travelled on the school bus each day and sat with the smokers at the back. This was the only group he felt any kinship with, as smoking transcended race. If you had a packet of twenty you always had friends.

David Keane

Systematically Paul had stolen cigarettes from his mother who made sure that packs of two hundred were the main priority on the weekly shopping list. She never bothered to wonder how she managed to smoke so many each week. Paul was always careful to steal them when she was out, or entertaining some boozed-up old geezer in the bedroom. All her men seemed to be drunk, smelly and once they had got what they wanted disappeared into the night. He hoped his father, who had disappeared when told of the pregnancy, was nothing like this constant trail of dead-beats. All he knew was that his father came originally from Jamaica and lived in Balsall Heath, Birmingham. There were times when Paul would have liked to have known more but on balance he decided against it. He had stopped asking his mother questions and she did not volunteer information. One thing did bother him and that was when his mother had any spare cash for extras such as a new pair of trainers, it also seemed to coincide with a visit from one of her better dressed male friends. He had been aware at school of some pointing and sniggering at the mention of his mother's name, but like everything else he just ignored them and they soon turned their attention elsewhere. There was one thing he was becoming aware of, and that was himself. In his bedroom he had an old pre-war wardrobe with a full-length mirror. After showers he had started to return to his bedroom and look at himself standing naked in front of the mirror. His skin tones owed more to his English mother but he liked the hint of darkness. For several years when getting changed after games at school, he was aware that some boys kept themselves well-hidden, and others exposed their equipment for the whole world to see. He had seen nothing that he would have swopped with, although he had not particularly exposed himself to the world. When at home he stood looking in the mirror and mentally compared himself to the others. Sliding his left hand down his firm stomach, he allowed his fingers to toy with his bush. As he did so his erection soon formed and he often turned sideways to admire the length. Before dressing he usually mastarbated and watched himself in the mirror, defeating the object of the shower. Afterwards, he dressed and made his way through to the living room of the sixth floor tower block flat he shared with his mother. Physically a man, sexually a defenceless child.

Two

Paul's mother had insisted that he went on the school camp to the Yorkshire Dales. Previously when any trips were mentioned, his mother soon put a stop to any ideas he might have harboured by simply pointing out they had no money to waste on 'bloody outings'. This dismissal was usually given through a cloud of cigarette smoke and she did not enjoy reminders from Paul that there might be more cash available if she gave up the weed. This time was different because there was a 'rich uncle' on the scene who wanted to take to take Paul's mum away for the weekend, without the 'youth' in tow. Paul came home with the letter from his tutor, explaining there was a place available as Philip Constance had fallen and broken his right ankle. For once in his life Paul was lucky, as that same evening his latest 'uncle' explained his plans to Paul's mother. No-one was more surprised than his tutor when Paul returned to school on the Monday morning with the acceptance form signed and £35 in cash. Friday lunchtime eventually came and Paul, along with 32 other students boarded the coach for the three hour journey to Yorkshire.

Paul was not high enough up the student hierarchy to claim a back seat place, but he was nearer the back of the coach than the front. As school trips went the journey was the norm. The anticipation of two nights away from home stimulated the group, who fed each other's excitement. Brief toilet stop at the Motorway services and no-one caught shop-lifting. Mr. Anderson, the member of staff in charge, was looking a little more relaxed now they were well on their way. The Lower School PE teacher had been persuaded to be in charge as a good career move. At twenty-four years of age, he needed a few 'Brownie Points' to kick-start his dormant career. For as long as he could remember he had been a sports fanatic, but only a moderate performer. Dearly he had longed for a career with a Premier League club, but early enough in life he realised this would remain merely a dream. Never would the twin towers of Wembley witness him scoring the 89th-minute Cup Final winning goal. Once he had accepted the situation, he worked his butt off to reach the standard required to train as a teacher and gain a sports science degree. It had been a struggle for him as he never enjoyed the academic world. Every moment of his life revolved around sport: football, basketball and swimming being his favourites when a schoolboy, but lately he had taken up golf. Not being academically-minded he empathised with the lads of the school who could see no purpose in lessons and exams. Popular as teachers go, he was determined that everyone on the trip was going to enjoy themselves, come what may! Although he was in charge he was the youngest member of staff on the trip. Just a few months older than John Anderson was Ms. Katy Pearce, history teacher and in charge of the girls. Strict but fair was how she wished to be regarded by the staff and students alike. Rightly she believed that she had attained this position. Older members of staff who came along to make up the supervision numbers were Jack Price, fifty years old, bald and never made a management position, so GCSE Maths with the "Terds"was his fate. Of course this situation was because of oppression by others as he readily told anyone who cared to listen. (Over the past couple of years nobody had voluntarily). His wife had gone off with a guy from work. He never really understood why, although many of his colleagues could have explained it to him. He had been press-ganged onto the trip as he had no-one else to worry about: a free agent, as the Head pointed out with crass insensitivity. Final staff members were the husband-and-wife-team James and Debbie Masterson, who met and married at the school. Both in their early thirties, they looked forward to the camp and being able to observe the students discovering themselves and their potential. Regarded by all the students as a pushover, they were oblivious to the scheming machinations going on around them, whether it be by the students, or their erstwhile colleagues.

For ten years the school had been using the private farm campsite for occasional weekend expeditions. Situated within a stone's throw of Skipton, it still had a farm's isolation, making it ideal for projects designed to test endurance and form character. This was the general scheme of things but the student perspective was one of crafty fags and as much groping of the opposite sex as could be safely carried out under the staff's noses without discovery.

The tents were already erected before the party arrived. Messrs Anderson and Price together in the latest Arctic Two-man, the Mastersons sited slightly away from the circle of tents in their trim lightweight, and finally Ms. Pearce close to the girls' tents in her backpackers' special. Over the years the site had developed to boast two toilet blocks, each with a wash-room and shower area. A new addition was a camp kitchen and a spacious but simple meeting hut that could be used as a recreational area, study cen-tre or wet-weather shelter.

The whole experience was new to Paul. Along with five other sixth-form students; Chris, Tony, Gordon, Shamir and Alex, Paul assisted in preparing the inside of their Giant Pearl tent. All, except Alex, were GNVQ students, unsure as to the future, especially concerning career prospects. Alex, the sporting academic, destined for University and a professional career, assumed leadership of the group. Each group was responsible for their own areas and there was an intense hum of excitement as sleeping bags were laid out alongside overnight bags. By chance Paul was to sleep with Alex on one side and Gordon on the other. Alex was to sleep next to the door. He told the boys that this was so they could not slip out at night to the girls' tents. The boys laughed and suggested that perhaps they would need to keep an eye on him. Already there was an easy relaxed atmosphere in the tent which could never have been achieved at school.

Paul's group, along with one other were on cooking duty for the first night. This was not too bad as the staff had done most of the work before they had presented themselves for duty.

"Sorry Mr. Anderson, but we had to get the tent right first," Alex apolo-gised.

"No sweat Alex. It's a good night to be on as we have salad first night with sausage rolls. Not much washing-up either."

John Anderson was right and the meal was soon consumed along with a variety of rabbit impressions that tested the patience of the Mastersons. Excitement can prove to be tiring and the students went to their tents for an early night. Paul was grateful for this as his eyelids were getting very heavy. In the tent, each boy with the exception of Alex, self-consciously undressed under the bright gaslight. Squatting on or alongside their sleeping bag, they removed their top layers and then just before getting in the bag slipped out of their trousers. Each boy seemed to have a giggling fit for no apparent reason other than someone else was laughing. Once they were settled, Alex stood before them and stripped down to his boxer shorts. Each boy glanced at him pretending at the same time not to. Looking at him they each admired his firm, well-developed frame and at the same time felt their own to be inadequate. As the others looked away Paul held his glance and Alex, well-aware of his actions, smiled at him. Paul quickly looked away and felt his cheeks redden. Their Common Room talk back at school had been of girl-shagging and boasting of imagined conquests. Together in a tent on a Yorkshire campsite the years seemed to fall away and they were mere adolescent boys, confused but relishing the comaraderie the enforced closeness brought.

The gaslight gave out warmth and cosy assurance as the boys lay in their sleeping bags. Paul was tired but the conversations continued, covering the usual laddish topics of what Chris would like to do to Samantha Beresford and what Tony was alleged to have done with Clara Dove. This was no great achievement as Clara was not a difficult lay if the lad provided the condom. In a nearby girl's tent Clara was telling her eager audience that Tony came as soon as he put the condom on. The next time they were in the kitchen at her house. No-one else was in and she wanted to give him a blow job. This was fine except that he shot his load in her face as she knelt before him. OK, he had a big cock but no control. Tony in his tent informed his enthralled companions that she gave a great blow job. Alex listened intently but like Paul made no comment. Before ten o'clock Paul had drifted into a deep sleep. All except Alex quickly followed. He reached up and carefully turned out the light which flickered defiantly before being extinguished. Alex settled down in his sleeping bag and as his eyes adjusted to dark night he turned towards Paul. He could see his outline as he lay on his side facing him but the deep, steady breathing told him that like the others Paul had drifted into another world. Reaching down inside his own sleeping bag, Alex grasped his erect cock but sleep took over before climax. It had been a long day.

It was light when Paul awoke. The sleeping bag belonging to Alex was empty and Paul could not recollect hearing him leave the tent. Perhaps the sound of the zip opening had stirred him from his slumbers. It clearly had unaffected the others who were dead to the world. More likely his reason for waking was the need to visit the toilet. Carefully, so as not to wake the others, he eased himself from the bag and reached across to the tent door and so cautiously eased the zip up. Stepping out and rezipping the door he faced a silent campsite basking in the bright morning with traces of dawn mist clinging to the nearby woodland. After the noise and bustle of the previous evening, the natural silence of the morning wrapped the site in an eerie presence. Only the dawn chorus filled the air, a sound that was alien to the city lad. Suddenly Paul was reminded of the reason for his early rising and he made his way to the toilet block.

Walking into the block, Paul was quickly reminded that he was not the only early riser. Through the doorway into the open shower area he could hear the sound of water gushing. After he hurriedly used the urinal Paul edged towards the archway of the showers. Two bodies were standing locked together, their mouths pressed firmly against the other as their tongues worked feverishly, probing the opposite throat. Paul was rooted to the spot, fascinated by the gentle gyrations of wet flesh lurching in and out of the steaming water. For a brief moment the couple were totally unaware of Paul's presence, then Alex caught sight of Paul. He broke free from his partner, at that moment Dale, his long, normally ponytailed hair clinging to his soaked neck and shoulders, turned to face Paul. The three boys stood in silence, each seeking an excuse for being there. Suddenly Paul turned and ran from the block, his mind racing, trying desperately to come to terms with what he had seen. Where to go? He walked across the site in the direction of the farmhouse.

"Morning. You're an early bird!"

"What?"

"Early bird... Oh forget it. Are you OK? You look dreadful"

"I'm fine... just a....."

The farmer reached out to Paul who stepped back. Paul knew there was nowhere to go but back to the tent. He stood in front of the silent tent, hesitating, reaching for the zip, his lips dry, his stomach churning and bile rising in his throat. Before he made contact with the door zip, Alex walked up behind Paul.

"Wait!"

David Keane

Paul froze. Now what?

"Let's take a little walk shall we?"

Paul knew it would be hopeless to resist. He was sorry for what he had seen but surely Alex would realise it had all been a mistake. What was he supposed to do? Yes, he could have gone in the trees but why should he? Oh how he wished he'd gone in the trees! They walked away from the group of tents. Alex seemed nervous and Paul was desperate for him to speak. Just get it over with!

"It wasn't what you thought. You know that, don't you?"

Paul felt the fear drain away from himself. Alex was scared of him. The school stud and super-star was shitting himself, and Paul knew it.

"Didn't know you shagged like that !" mocked Paul.

"Hang on! No-one must know! No-one must ever know! No-one would believe a shit like you." Alex gripped Paul by his shoulders and looked him straight in the eyes.

"Maybe. But you can't take that chance, can you?"

"OK. OK. What do you want?Whatever it is you must keep your mouth shut." Alex again gripped Paul by the shoulders. There was a build-up of intense pressure upon the top of Paul's arms. The intensity conveyed to Paul the menace in Alex who was now reacting to the fear of exposure. He could not afford to take chances. Paul must be silenced. After all as Sports Captain he had to keep up appearances and Sports Captains only shag girls. Don't they?

"What do you mean, what do I want?"

"Think of something! Make it quick!"

Paul would not be rushed. He was now gaining in confidence and realised there may be opportunities for him to exploit the anguish and guilt of Alex. Suppose he could blackmail him and demand regular payments. After all, Alex did own a car and was not short of cash. He would think about it.

"You'll have to wait. Don't hassle me."

"What do you mean wait? Alex the assured was now thoroughly rattled.

"Just like I said. Wait. I'll tell you tonight."

With that Paul turned and walked to the tent with Alex in tow.

"Hi there. You look a lot better now sunshine!"

"Yes I am thanks," responded Paul to the cheery farmer's greeting as each went about their business.

One hour after the shower block discovery, the breakfast bell rang across the site. Alex had not returned to his bed. Paul stretched along with the others, giving the impression of having just woken up. In reality he had lay in his sleeping bag turning over in his mind the events of early morning. Much to his surprise he did not feel any revulsion, but a surge of anticipation of what the future could bring. His early ideas had revolved around how much cash he could safely extract from the shamed Alex. Also what about Dale? He also deserved to pay the price. Dale was also a member of the Sixth Form and popular with the girls. He spent much of his spare time as lead vocalist with a wannabe band. Realistically he knew the chance of breaking into the pop world in a big way was slim, but he enjoyed the music and doing gigs. Sex was on tap for this 18-year-old who in all aspects of his life was excited by experimentation. Hence the session with Alex in the shower. Lead vocalists could always get a lay after a gig so why on earth had he put himself into this situation with Alex? It meant nothing to him emotionally, he just wanted to know what it would be like with a guy, admittedly a good-looking guy. Conversations laced with innuendo had occurred over the previous two months and had increased in intensity during the final week. A "dare" suggested by Alex had been agreed to on the journey north. They were to meet in the shower block at 5.30 am and prepare to streak naked around the site The run did take place and no other living being in the world knew of it. After the run a shower together seemed a good idea. Just one shared shower and mutual admiration of each other's assets. A touch leading to a caress, then a kiss, a sudden lurch from Alex and their lips met.

They were totally unaware of Paul's entry into the block. As passion heightened, Paul moved to the arched doorway and then Alex saw him. Hurriedly breaking from Dale to expose them both to the glare of Paul, it had all gone wrong. The sexual excitement had been raised by the thought of discovery, but that all disappeared in the reality of total exposure. No-one spoke and momentarily it all seemed so unreal. Dale was so hard and this boy was looking at him. Now what? Alex told him not to worry, just leave it to him to sort out. Good idea, leave it to Alex. He had a way with people, that's why they were in the shower in the first place.

Alex squeezed himself between Paul and Shamir on the bench at the breakfast table. Breakfast had been created by a group led by the Mastersons who were pleasantly surprised at the standard achieved. Sizzling trays of sausages, rubberised fried eggs, cauldrons of baked beans and tomatoes steaming, plus a dripping pile of fried bread, all washed down by stewed tea from a giant urn.

As Alex sat down, Paul took a deep breath, said nothing and was not surprised that Alex remained silent. All the boys piled their plates high and with appetites sharpened by the clear fresh air attacked the food. James and Debbie Masterson watched and felt gratified that their efforts were being appreciated.

"Something special about eating outside and perhaps we can remember the bacon tomorrow!" said Debbie.

"OK funny girl! One thing about outside fry-ups is that the you can get away with producing rubbish. This lot will eat anything!"

"Oh great, and here's me thinking we had produced a gourmet's delight and that's why they were eating it! "laughed James.

"Come off it. It's feeding time at the zoo and you know it."

"Anyway it's good to see them eating. I'm sure some of this lot think smoky bacon crisps are a breakfast food".

"They are aren't they? teased James, and Debbie pretended to hit him.

"Fight, fight", called out Chris and peals of laughter rolled around the recreation room. No-one noticed that three boys were not part of the easy laughter.

The day's programme was to involve orienteering, football and free time for shopping in Skipton. Once breakfast was completed, each group had to report to the control centre and collect their instructions from Jack Price and Katy Pearce. The whole party were summoned together for the safety talk imploring them to not deviate from the instructions, not take chances and to read maps carefully. If faced with problems stay together and blow emergency whistles to summon help.

"Any bugger blowing unnecessarily will be severely dealt with by yours truly. Is that clear ? "

"Yes Sir" the group chorused back in unison.

Tony and Chris grinned at each other, silently hinting to each other of some as yet unformed plan of mischief. The day had prospects. Some of the group, not just the girls, were unconvinced by the exhortations to teamwork, challenges and character building. They would have been far happier in HMV or Rackhams in Birmingham. Soon all that would be forgotten as each group were sent on their way. In reality, at no time would any group be more than one mile from base. Thankfully the weather was dry and the sun was winning its battle with the wisps of morning mist. Whoops of war echoed around the wooded site as each group set off on their way.

Alex gathered his troops together and authoritatively spoke to his men.

"Now you lot, no pissing about and we're going to win this. Aren't we?" Half-hearted mutterings of agreement did not inspire Alex to any great heights of confidence, so he tried again.

"Are we deaf? We're going to win aren't we? Not going to let that pouf Dale and his crew beat us, are we?"

The two groups were almost side by side and exchanged various obscenities that in a perverse way seemed to heighten team spirit and raise the temperature. At this moment Paul caught the eye of Alex and held his look for a significant couple of seconds. Both searched the other's expression for any clue as to hidden thoughts; none given, none assumed. Jack Price unknowingly broke the spell with a loud long blast on his whistle that sent Alex's group on their way.

Quickly but thoroughly, Alex checked the co-ordinates before leading the group forward. The course was not particularly difficult, fully in keeping with the idea of it being a fun day. At a steady jog, the group moved through the woods and soon overtook the group ahead of them. "V"signs aloft, plus youthful cries of "poufs "and responses of "bollocks", both groups wished each other well as they passed. Paul followed behind Alex, Chris and Tony with Gordon and Shamir close behind. The pace was comfortable for all and easy banter passed between them. Alex now seemed fully at ease after the trauma of the early morning. Paul found himself admiring the sleek body of Alex as he moved across the varied terrain tirelessly. Wearing black soccer shorts and a claret and blue Aston Villa top, Alex was in his element. Pausing briefly to check co-ordinates, he kept his group together and moving at a pace with-in the capabilities of all. Other groups were dismissed, almost with contempt, and the finish line was quickly crossed. Had Alex led them to victory?Shamir was jumping around excitedly as he realised that they were in with a real chance. Only Dale could beat them. The final group must cross the line with-in the next minute to win. No sight nor sound of Dale's group as the seconds ticked by agonizingly slowly. Suddenly the sound of shouting, yelling voices. Straining, urging for one final desperate effort. In sight and only seconds to go, Dale led his men to the line.5,4,3,2,1, NO, NO, NO. Seconds late, too late. Alex and the boys had won. Paul along with the others leapt into the air as the previously unknown joy of victory overwhelmed them. As Dale plunged over the line, he fell into the welcoming arms of Alex. Paul felt the knot of jeal-ousy tie in his stomach.

Returning to the campsite Alex beckoned Paul over to him.

"Thought anymore about you know...."

Paul looked Alex full in the face. "Might have".

"Well? Come on, if it's cash you want, how much?" Paul did not respond.

"You can have the cash now but remember the deal – you keep your gob shut".

There was a pause as Alex waited for a reply. When there was none a new tone of menace crept into Alex's voice.

"Now look here you shit! Don't try and be clever. You try anything and you can forget being a father! We'll talk in the shower block tonight then no-one will overhear. When everyone has settled down tonight, I'll tell you when, go to the block. Remember, I'll be next to you in the tent. Just remember that!"

The threat was implied but none-the-less clear. Paul did not feel fear, only pain that Alex could threaten him.

Tony, Chris, Paul, Gordon and Shamir listened intently as Katy Pearce explained to them which bus would return them to the site as they intended to walk into Skipton. All explained and the time of 5 o'clock ringing in their ears as the required time of return, off they went in high spirits. All that is, except Paul, who was wrapped in his own thoughts. As they exited the camp, they came across Alex and Dale sat on a dry stone wall. Alex, wearing only the black shorts, stopped them with his ready smile.

"Don't forget my present!" Alex laughingly taunted them. Paul was amazed at the thoroughly relaxed persona of Alex considering their recent conversation. As he looked at Alex, Paul became aware of the dark thin line of hair extending above the top of the shorts and that the firm inner thighs exhibited a slight covering of black hair. Alex was aware of Paul's gaze as he slid easily from the wall.

"Penny for them sunshine?" he remarked with just a touch of tease in his voice. Paul quickly looked away and tried to laugh but that knot had returned to his stomach.

The walk into Skipton was uneventful, the conversation revolving around sex, masturbation in particular and also which male member of staff had the biggest cock. Favourite for the latter award was James Masterson, due to the constant use it would be getting from satisfying Debbie. The logic being that being so often erect it must stretch, therefore increasing in size. The one dissenting voice for this theory came from Gordon, who took the view that the constant use would weaken it and it would not stand so erect.

"Do you reckon he's been giving her one while we've been here?" wondered Chris.

"Nah, he'll have to do wi'out here," was the considered view of Gordon.

"We could check 'em out tonight," speculated Tony.

"Get real!" said Paul.

"Why not ?" questioned Tony. All we have to do is wait until Alex is asleep, then take it in turns to get out our tent then keep a look out on their tent. If he's going to shag her it will be soon after lights-out I reckon."

"Yeah, but they're not going to do it out of tent are they? So how are..?" asked Shamir.

"That tent's so small we'll know!" was the final view from Tony, who was most determined for the operation to take place.

"We'll cut cards when we get back for a rota after me. I'll take first watch for one hour then we'll have a rota for the night".

"What, all bloody night?" said a horrified Paul.

"Of course, you dick-head. Some like to have it in middle of the night. So we need to be ready. Bet you've never had it, or else you'd know that!" boasted Tony.

David Keane

No-one was fully convinced regarding his experience, but nobody questioned the fact.

"OK then, tonight we do it. Cards cut as soon as we get back."

They walked on in silence for a short distance before Chris wondered if anyone in their tent had been masturbating the previous night. Tony was totally sure on the matter.

"Alex did! You should know, Paulie. You slept next to him so you should know. Did you wank him off? Has he got a whopper chopper?"

All except Paul roared with laughter. Paul could feel the colour rising up his neck and face as he fought to control the embarrassment.

"Ooooh look at him. He's doing a cherry. Hey, you didn't really wank him off did you?"

"Don't be daft," spluttered Paul who now forced himself to join in the laughter.

Paul hadn't touched Alex and he was puzzled why he had reacted in the way he had to Tony's jibes. OK, he had seen the scene in the shower and of course Tony could not have known about that. If he had, the whole site and miles around would have known by now! What really happened in the tent was much more straightforward. When both Paul and Alex had returned to the tent, Tony had been disturbed from his deep sleep, but he was unaware of what had disturbed him. He lay awake for sometime, trying to get to sleep. He reached down upon himself and prised his cock out of his shorts. Under the cover of his sleeping bag he gently stroked his solid tool. His pace quickened until he was interrupted by a whisper from Chris.

"Hurry up wanker and cum. You'll wake everybody if you don't hurry up!"

"Shit. Finish me!" pleaded Tony.

"Get stuffed," was the whispered response. Moments later Tony ejaculated onto the inner sheet. What he did not know was that Chris was about to grant his wish. They turned away from each other and sleep soon overwhelmed them.

Whilst in Skipton the boys teased the girls they saw, in particular Clara Dove. Although at school Clara gave the impression butter would not melt in her mouth, more than butter had slipped past her lips. This information had clearly not reached the staff. If it had, she definitely would not be on the trip.

Clara and her friend Samantha Beresford had separated from the others in their group to shop alone. Close to the Town Hall market a pensioner couple were taken aback when Tony yelled as he and the boys approached the girls.

"Hey look who's here! Give us a suck!" Tony thought he was impressing the others, but all were uneasy with the public situation. The pensioner couple tut-tutting moved quickly away.

"Lay off," suggested Gordon

"Why? She likes it!"

"Do me a favour," replied Clara indifferently as she and Samantha pushed by.

"Don't think she quite likes your style," mocked Gordon.

Tony ignored Gordon and pretended to be unruffled by the rejection.

"Let's get some booze for tonight," said Tony breezily.

"Easier said than done," observed Paul.

"No problem. I'll do a little shopping in here," commented Chris, and he quickly disappeared into the self-service off-licence. Moments later he reappeared with his hands across his coat front.

"Split! Now!"

With Chris leading the way, they hastened through the Market Place and up the main street away from the bus station.

"What you got? asked Tony

"Scotch. A big one."

"Great."

There was still some time before the bus back to the campsite. Tony announced they should leave town with their 'shopping' and stash it somewhere where the staff could not find it.

"Can put it in my stuff," suggested Shamir.

"They'd never think I'd have 'owt."

Shamir was pleased with the nodded agreement from the boys. He belonged. He felt accepted. Tony knew he was right. No-one would suspect Shamir of having booze and once clear of Skipton the bottle was carefully tucked away into Shamir's shoulder bag.

They were now committed to walking back to the camp, as they didn't wish to risk walking through the town to the bus station. The road wended upwards out of Skipton and the boys soon left the town behind. Climbing over a stile built into a dry stone wall the conversation soon reverted to the old topics. Crossing open fields, they were the only people in the whole world. They reached the brow of a hill and suddenly Chris released a piercing scream that took his comrades by surprise. He flung his arms out wide and let out a cry similar to a diving aircraft and sprinted downhill. Peals of laughter rang out as the boys joined in the moment's craziness and charged downhill to rejoin Chris.

"You dozy bugger", greeted Tony as they regrouped. All members were laughing in an easy relaxed manner. Tony sat on the grass and pulled from his jeans pocket a packet of cigarettes. He reached out his hand in a gesture of sharing. Chris, Paul and Gordon quickly extracted a cigarette each from the slightly crumpled packet.

"No thanks. I don't," said Shamir.

"No thanks. I don't," mocked Tony. "Bet his balls haven't dropped yet either!" Tony paused as the other boys laughed at his jibe and at Shamir's discomfiture. Paul joined in but felt uneasy at the mockery.

"You have got balls, haven't you? You lot do have them eh?"

"Cut it out Tone. That's no way to talk to a mate" said Chris.

"Yeah. That's right "agreed Gordon who sympathetically glanced at Shamir.

"OK. Sorry mate," Tony quickly responded. "Come on you lot. Light up".

The easy relaxed atmosphere returned and Shamir gave no outward indication of being hurt.

Tony's mind had returned to his seemingly favourite topic.

"You know that Samantha. I'd really like to give her one"

"You'd run a mile if she offered it!" confided Chris. Tony lay on his back with his left hand in his pocket, clearly fondling himself. Although all were aware of what he was doing, nobody seemed to care.

"Do you think she would?" asked Shamir.

"Do what?" enquired Tony.

"Well, er, shag?"

They laughed at Shamir's naiveté, but he did not mind. He was one of the group, that's all that mattered.

"She was only a virgin for two seconds when she was born! She fell on the midwife's finger when she came out! Since then everything's been up her!" Laughter rolled across the valley. Tony still lay on his back, fondling himself. The boys drifted into silence as they looked on. Four pairs of eyes fixed their gaze on Tony's jeans. Tony was aware of exactly what he was doing as he gently but obviously manipulated his now firmly erect cock. It was curiously exciting for Tony as he lay there knowing he was being watched. He needed to cum. With his right hand he started to slide the zip down on his jeans. No-one spoke as the boys leaned in over Tony. Partly to get an even better view, but also to protect him from outsiders. Paul looked around the whole area. No-one there. They were totally alone. Tony continued to open his jeans fully. He lay there with his tight blue Calvin Klein undershorts exposed. Still hidden from view, his erect cock strained against the stretched material.

"Come on, get it out!" gasped Shamir, astonished at his own outburst.

Tony smiled and allowed his head to rock back onto the grass as with both hands he eased his shorts down. His hands by his side, he lay there as he believed he was being admired by mates. The scene being taken in was of a complete cock with a clump of black pubic hair. His tool twitched untouched, as though beckoning, demanding attention. Tony gazed skyward as a hand clutched him and began steady rhythmic stroking. Suddenly his balls were being caressed. Slowly raising his head, he was astonished to see Gordon stroking him whilst Shamir cupped his sack in his left hand. He continued to look down and what happened next completely blew his mind. Suddenly and without warning Chris went down on him, knocking Gordon's hand away. Shamir stayed in place. Gasps of astonishment could be heard at Chris's action. Pleasure surged through Tony as he pumped out into Chris's eager mouth. Chris remained in place until every spurt was consumed. As Tony climaxed, Shamir's finger pushed between his legs thrusting to Tony's hole. When the climax was complete Chris raised his head and announced to the world.

"I've swallowed it! I've swallowed it all!" Chris's excitement was obvious. Shamir's hand lingered as Tony started to return to composure. Tony glanced up at Shamir and the smile thanked him. Paul who had not physically taken part, just watched, thought to himself after seeing Tony that Samantha

David Keane

Beresford would find more to entertain her between his legs. That was for him to know and the others to wonder about.

Incredibly, as they continued their walk back to camp there was no embarrassment between them. Their actions had drawn them together in different ways. Paul was amused by the whole situation but he was nervous about the plans for the night. He must meet Alex in the showers to cash in on his knowledge, but what about Tony and his 'Shag Watch'. Perhaps they would drink themselves stupid with the whisky and he and Alex would be able to slip away unnoticed. Gordon and Shamir had been stimulated by the whole event. They had never acted that way before but it seemed so natural at the time. Chris had on occasions when Tony had stopped over at his house always resisted Tony's implorings to give him 'a blow'. They had mutually masturbated each other which Tony always seemed to enjoy. For Chris the masturbation just made him cum, without any great satisfaction. It had begun between him and Tony when they had compared each other's erections. Tony had admired Chris's cock. He had a firm stomach and Tony told him he had a good body. He knew that for himself but the praise pleased him. Chris had been circumcised when a baby, and this was the reason he was assured by Tony that his cock was bigger than Tony's. Chris had always waited for Tony to make the first move but rarely resisted him. He could not understand why he had hesitated the night before in the tent and yet lunged down on Tony in the field, watched by an audience. The action had made his body shake and as the cum slid down his throat, his prick filled his pants. The moist warmth soon gave way to a clammy damp and he urgently wanted to change his gear. Yet the prospect of the night in the tent excited him although he wasn't sure about Paul and Alex. Paul especially worried him. He hadn't even touched Tony and yet he hadn't stopped them. Alex – now he was another matter. Caught a glimpse of him as they got ready for bed the night before and what he saw he liked. Tony had never before felt so out of control and it had been wonderful. All except Paul had groped him but perhaps that would change tonight, but what about Alex? Shamir without thinking had reached out for Tony. White boy's cock was OK. Little different from his own deep-brown shaft. Pity Chris swallowed the cum. Did that look different to his? Gordon had noticed that the general shape was the same, perhaps just a little smaller than his "black tor-

– 18 –

pedo". He did see that Tony's pubes were a little longer than his tight black curls, although he probably had a few more. Gordon suspected that Paul didn't have much to write home about, that's why he just watched. Anyway none of it meant anything and he wondered what Samantha might do to him sometime. He had heard from friends that she wanted a black knob up her, but he didn't dare even speak to her let alone ask her directly for a date. It all remained in his dreams.

As the walk continued no one refered to the action until close to the camp Shamir turned to Chris and whispered. "What did it taste like?"

"What?"

"You know. His, er, spunk! Eh what was it like?"

"Nothing. Just like warm salt. There were loads of it. I've never done that before you know." Chris truthfully explained to Shamir.

"I don't know why I did it then. It was weird, you know. First I was just looking at, at Tony." Chris hesitated and the two of them had dropped a little behind the others.

"Then I was down on him and he was coming. I couldn't lift off him." Chris looked down.

"The truth is I didn't want to," he quietly added.

"I know what you mean. I ain't done that before either. He just lay there didn't he. He knew what was going to happen didn't he?"

"Tony doesn't care about anything really. He just wants thrills, no matter how or where. He's always horny. Always."

They walked on a little further.

"What you gonna do?" asked Shamir.

"About?" asked Chris.

"You know about back there ?"

"Do? Do?" Chris looked at Shamir full-on.

"I'm going to screw him. That's what I'm gonna do."

Chris saw the shock in Shamir's eyes. Undaunted, perhaps even inspired by the shocked look Chris continued.

"I'm going to fuck him. I mean it. I know I want to, really want to. Got to fuck him!"

Shamir stood stock-still. Chris jogged on to catch the others up and flung

David Keane

his arms around Tony's neck making a whooping cry, then putting his hands around his throat in an act of mock strangulation. Tony responded by pretending to head-butt Chris then flung his arms tightly around his companion. Paul turned back to look down the track and saw Shamir start his fresh faltering footsteps towards the group. As they moved through the camp entrance, Tony raised his arms in the air and by gesture commanded the boy's full attention.

"Don't forget tonight. We'll catch those two at it. The Mastersons? Remember?"

"Well it's not fair is it? They are married you know," implored Paul. All except Tony nodded in agreement but Tony pressed on.

"We could sabotage the tent and really have fun. Oh come on you deadbeats. It's party time!"

Reluctant nodded agreement from the gang.

"Right, now I'll take first watch for an hour. Instead of cutting cards for the next watch, how about volunteers. What about you Paul?"

"Me? Why me?"

"Why not? Not scared are you?"

"No, of course not. Just seems daft to me." Paul hesitated.
"OK I'll do it."

"Good. That's that sorted. Bet we don't need a third shift. When they start I'll fetch you lot. If we have to wait for your turn Paul, come and get us when the action begins."

"What about Alex ?" asked Gordon.

"He'll be asleep with all that whisky down his neck. He did asked for a present didn't he?" Tony laughed.

"Oi! You lot over here sharpish when you've got into your football gear. Now. Not next week!" shouted Jack Price.

Alex and Dale had been put in charge of arranging the mixed football match. It seemed that each team would consist of about fifteen players at any one time. Alex and Dale being opposing team captains thought they were picking the teams, but unknown to them Clara had decided she was going to be in Alex's and Samantha in Dale's. The girls had discussed with some of the others the football game and how they could use the situation to target the boys. As the teams were selected, Alex ensured Paul was on his team. Eventually after some fooling around each team chose eleven players to start the match. Tony started to suggest a complicated formula for the number of girls in a team at any one time, but he was shouted down by the others. Mr. Price called the captains to the imaginary centre circle and tossed a coin asking Alex to call. He called correctly and chose to play downhill. The game began and it was not long before Dale set off on a mazy dribble through a not particularly committed defensive formation. Dale struck the ball firmly and it sped past Gordon to register the first goal. The game ebbed to and fro and when the score reached 12–10 to Dale's team, the first to score 15 was the agreed target. Few players were taking the game seriously although Mr. Price doggedly tried to keep some semblance of order. Clara and Samantha soon realised they were not going to get close to their targets via a football game and drifted away to lean on the stone wall.

"Looks like plan B," suggested Clara.

"What's plan B?" asked an intrigued Samantha.

"Don't know. Haven't thought of it yet!" laughed Clara.

As they chatted, goal 15 was thankfully tapped past Gordon to the immense pleasure of Dale. Most of the players were relieved that the game had ended. By the finish both squads had reduced in numbers to eight a side. Clara and Samantha had gathered some of the defectors to their wall and they chatted about the boys still playing.

"Hey that Paul's got a nice packet," announced Samantha and met with giggled agreement.

"Haven't really noticed him before but you're right. Nice legs too. Just look at them thighs," sighed Clara.

Paul was absorbed in the game and was blissfully unaware of the attention being paid to him by the girls. When the game ended he was disappointed that his team had lost and felt he had let Alex down. When the final whistle blew to herald the winning goal, he looked in the direction of Alex, but Alex did not appear too concerned as he moved towards Dale to embrace him as they left the field. That knotted feeling returned to Paul's stomach. Groups of boys and girls were making their way to the shower blocks. A good idea now the exertions of the early evening were fulfilled. When Paul entered his tent all the others except Alex were already there and gathering their towels and toiletries. That relaxed 'boys together' atmosphere had returned.

"No dropping the soap on purpose," declared Tony amid laughter. The laughter increased as Shamir asked,

"Why not?"

"Just don't," Paul told him as he caught a look from Tony. Noisily they made their way to the showers with Shamir still trying to understand Tony's remark. As they entered the block, the steam-filled atmosphere concealed the naked shapes as they allowed the hot water to caress away the aches and pains from the day's activities. Paul and the others entered the steam as Alex walked naked past them. Paul waited, looked and felt that knot once more as Alex greeted him.

"See you later," Alex smiled. It was a moment of knowing when two people accept the inevitable. Paul hesitated momentarily before mumbling a response and entering the steam. He bloody well knows thought Paul. My God he knows!

Evening meal comprising of a main course of sausage and mash was eaten with relish, as the fresh air had truly sharpened most appetites. The general atmosphere was mixed. Everyone had now settled into the pattern of camp life, yet tomorrow they would be returning home. The weekend had simply not been long enough. Clara and Samantha for example. Time seemed to be against them as they tried to complete the challenge of Alex and Dale. In reality more than time may well have been against them, but they were not to know that.

As darkness began to envelop the site, torches flashed about the night sky. The recreation centre was to be the place for evening entertainment provided by the staff. A thankfully brief cabaret involving the female members miming to a girl pop group followed by the male teachers doing likewise to an old Beatles tape was hardly likely to get them jamming in the aisles. Taken for what it was, a cheap way of confining the group to camp, the cabaret served its purpose. During the Beatles set, Alex caught the attention of Paul and gestured with his head for him to leave the hall. The attention of all had been held by the grotesque performance being enacted before them so it was not difficult for the two boys to slip away unnoticed. Paul was the first to leave and he walked a short distance away from the hall towards the shower block. The door of the hall opened and Alex was briefly silhouetted by the interior lights before disappearing into the night as the door closed. Paul watched as Alex paused and looked about him trying to spot Paul, when he eventually saw him. Then with a step full of purpose, Alex headed towards him. During the day Paul thought he had worked out exactly what he was going to say, now it seemed different. Quickly Alex was alongside him.

"Time for a walk don't you think?"

"If you like," Paul responded, trying to sound calm and nonchalant.

They walked away from the shower block and the recreation centre towards the small wooded area bordering the site. Neither spoke until they were at the wood's edge. The whole area seemed so different than in the daylight. Alex led Paul to a fallen tree which provided a surprisingly comfortable seat.

"If it's cash you want to keep your mouth shut, how much? Remember the deal? Cash for your silence. We were not really doing anything you know," said Alex trying to sound convincing.

"Perhaps not. But if I hadn't come along you would have. Anyway I don't want your money, so don't worry yourself."

"Well, spit it out then." Alex made no attempt to disguise the relief he felt in the tone of his voice. Paul did not respond.

"If that's it I'm off back inside" Alex made to move away but Paul restrained him by grabbing his left arm.

"Hey! Watch it!" Alex in the shadows of light was aware of Paul's apparent distress. Paul was quietly sobbing. Alex was taken aback. He had not expected this and was not sure how to react. It was not supposed to be like this from Paul's point of view either. Alex reached with his right hand towards Paul's face and as he touched his cheek Paul toppled forward onto his chest. Alex unhesitatingly put both arms around him in a gesture of comfort. Paul looked up at Alex's face then slightly stretched his neck and gently pressed his lips onto unresisting lips. They broke away and Alex was the first to speak.

"Well, you are full of surprises!"

"You don't mind do you? I'm sorry really, I don't know what to say... I just..." Before Paul could complete the sentence, Alex pulled him towards him and

David Keane

locked his lips onto his. Alex gently forced his tongue into Paul's mouth to be greeted with a stifled murmur. Paul became aware of a hand reaching up inside his sweat shirt and teasing his left nipple. Salty tears continued to flow down his face as Alex broke the kiss and began tenderly to wipe the tears away with his finger tips. Holding Paul's head in both hands, he then kissed the forehead, then gently took Paul's right earlobe in his mouth. Paul had never been happier. For the first time in his life he felt wanted for himself. He hadn't planned it to be like this. He could never have expected this before he came away. How was it possible for him to love Alex? Did Alex love him in return? As his mind sought answers, Paul became aware that a hand was trying to enter the top of his jeans. Although this was his first time, he knew what he was going to do. He stood up and stepped over the log and headed into the trees. Alex followed him and a short way in Paul stopped and turned to face him. Without a word he began to unbuckle his belt and open the top of his jeans. Alex mirrored Paul's actions and soon both stood with their jeans around their ankles. Alex reached for Paul's head and then coaxed him downwards. Paul allowed himself to slide down Alex until he was on his knees before his prize. A brief moment of a teasing pause and then Paul felt Alex's hand behind his head pushing him forward. Opening his mouth wide as Alex entered him, he then clamped his lips around the delicious shaft. Alex held Paul's head and gently thrust back and forth moaning slightly. Still holding Paul's head in place he stopped moving. Through the trees Alex could see a figure in the open doorway of the hall. The back lighting clearly illuminated Dale's ponytail . Alex gently moved himself free of Paul's demanding mouth. Paul began to topple forward as he sought to remain in contact.

"Come on, time to go. On your feet. Make sure your jeans are OK." Swiftly Alex pulled his boxer shorts and jeans up and lightly brushed them with his hands. Without a word he left the wood. Paul remained on his knees. Nothing could happen now that could humiliate him further.

Paul was unaware why Alex had left him the way he had. The campsite was in darkness, the silence of the night disturbed by the deep bass thump of the disco music, as he made his way back to the hall. A female scream of delight followed by laughter and loud "shushings"plus giggles surprised Paul as he nervously walked across the field. He stood staring at the hall door tak-

available. Her cunt must be that stretched it would be like waving in a cave !" Paul felt disgusted with them all, but overwhelmingly with himself.

"You know it all don't you! Well I could tell you something about our wonderful Alex. Really, really tell you something!" Alex glared at Paul as he spoke.

Before Alex could speak an excited Tony got in first.

"What, have you seen him at it? Yeah that's it", explained an excited Tony answering his own question.

"Wow, fucking hell! Where?"

Neither Alex or Paul responded for what seemed an age, but as the silence developed Alex felt safer.

"Forget the last five minutes of your lives if you know what's good for you – understand?" The threat was delivered with a smile by Alex, but his full meaning was known by all. "Now, I think Paul and me are going to take a little walk, even if it's just to sober him up." Without further ado Paul stood up with his head slightly bowed against the sloping tent roof and edged his way to the flap. Both left the tent and started to walk to the shower block.

"I'm not pissed you know".

"I know but they can still think that, can't they? It's better for all if they think that. OK?"

"Yeah I suppose so, but what now? You hate me don't you?" As he said this Paul suddenly felt tired, too tired to care any more.

"Of course I don't hate you. Why say that? After what you did over there I certainly don't hate you. Always remember it's just a game. Dale and me you know, it was just a bet, nothing more. I guessed what you wanted and as a favour let you give me a blow. I'm right aren't I, it's what you wanted? Look, you're a nice guy but what do you take me for. Don't for one minute think I was particularly enjoying it. I didn't cum did I? If I wanted it I would have cum wouldn't I? So get real. Forget it. I screw birds. Remember that. I screw birds !" They reached the shower block and through the shadows a figure was heading in the same direction. It was Dale. Exactly on time.

"What's he doing here?" asked Dale, his ponytail already untied and flowing free.

Alex was now taking deep full intakes of breath and seemed to be getting distressed. This surprised Paul who had on most contacts with Alex believed him to be supercool and in control. The scene being enacted totally astonished Dale who regarded Alex as ready for any challenge, any excitement, living for the moment.

Alex looked at Dale. "Give us five minutes will you? Go on! Please."

Dale hesitated before nodding in agreement and then wandered back in the direction of the tents. As he walked back, Dale could not help himself from questioning in his mind the events of the last two minutes, but perhaps unkindly he wondered what was Alex up to now. Anyway, he would soon find out as he intended to be back at the shower block in exactly five minutes. Glancing at his watch he wandered aimlessly through the tents.

Paul looked Alex fully in the face as Alex raised his arms and put his hands on his tense shoulders. Now smiling he seemed to have a complete mood change.

"Look Paul I'm sorry about what I just said to you. You know the business about the screwing. I just said it. I didn't mean to upset you."

"I wouldn't like to be around then when you decide to hurt someone, especially me!"

They looked at each other directly and it seemed an age before Alex spoke.

"Come on, let's go inside," and with that he released Paul's shoulders and stepped inside the shower block. Paul followed and as he thought afterwards he entered without considering any of the consequences. Once inside and out of range of any prying eyes, Alex reached out once more. This time lower, much lower and with his left hand gently stroked the front zip area of Paul's jeans. There was no resistance as Alex pulled Paul to him and gently kissed his cheeks with a tenderness that was completely out of Paul's previous experience. Paul was so hard he wanted to explode as Alex whispered in his left ear.

"Do something to show me you really care for me."

"What ? "

"Give Dale a blow,"

Paul did not reply. He could feel Alex's hand caressing his entombed cock, struggling to escape from his jeans.

"I suppose you're going to watch are you? What if anyone comes, apart from Dale that is?" Paul tried to laugh at his own inept attempt at a joke but Alex's face surveyed him with a hard stare.

"If you really want to be a mate you'd do it. Without question. But of course if you're not up to it... Take it as a challenge and do it. I'll make sure you're rewarded. Virgin are you? You know, your cherry ready for plucking. I'd love to do it for you. Just do this for me. Perhaps you want to screw me. Is that it? OK, OK, but first do me the favour. Do it for Dale while I watch." Before Paul could reply they both had become aware of Dale's approaching footsteps.

"What's he still doing here?"

"We're all going to take a shower, aren't we Paul" With a flat tone Paul eventually replied, "Suppose so." Dale shook his head as he quietly laughed. "Am I thinking right about this? Are you mad Alex?"

"Come on. Let's blow our minds. Literally. Blow our minds."

"Agh, fuck it. What the hell? You only live once!"

With that, Dale walked into the actual shower area, turned to face the others and began to unbuckle his belt. Paul and Alex followed into the shower. Dale was slowly removing his T-shirt. Paul watched in silence as Dale lifted his arms as he removed the top and in doing so revealed under arm bushes of moist hair. Paul was surprised to see wisps of chest hair. Gently Alex pushed Paul towards Dale. With only a slight glance backwards, Paul reached forward and took hold of the top of Dale's jeans. With a little effort, Paul, with both hands pulled the loosened jeans open and slid them down to Dale's feet. Dale pulled his trainers from his sockless feet and stepped out of his jeans. Standing only in his mini-briefs it was obvious to the observers that he was totally ready for action. None spoke as Paul turned to Alex as though questioning if it was OK to continue. Dale broke the silence.

"Is that it?"

Alex roughly took hold of Paul and pushed him to the floor in front of Dale. Forced into a kneeling position his face was almost touching the stretched briefs. Alex grabbed his hair and forced Paul's face to touch the briefs as Dale's hand pulled them down across his thighs. As he did so his erection hit Paul across his nose and mouth. A hand reached from behind Paul to hold Dale's cock, whilst the hand clutching his hair pulled his head back. The cock was then pushed against his lips. He opened his mouth fully to accept Dale.

David Keane

Paul was vaguely aware of laughter that he believed was coming from Alex. Hands now held his head firmly and it was impossible for him to move away from Dale who was thrusting to and from the back of his mouth. Suddenly he was thrown to the shower floor by Alex, causing him to involuntarily dig his teeth into Dale who gasped in pleasant surprise as he stepped back.

"What you doing Alex? Come on, leave him. Let me get dressed and that's enough. We've had our fun."

"We've only just started," yelled Alex. From his position on the floor Paul could see the full erection of Dale and for a moment the whole situation appeared so ridiculous. Then without warning Alex was pulling at Paul's jeans and they offered little resistance.

"Leave him, leave him!" Dale begged Alex.

"Shut up and help me!" demanded Alex.

Momentarily there was silence and Paul lay waiting for what he expected to be the inevitable.

"Do it Dale! Do it Dale! Do as I say if you know what's good for you!"

Dale knelt beside Paul and started to put his hand inside Paul's open jeans. As he did so he leant over him and whispered, "Sorry, I got to."

"Just get it over with quickly," was Paul's whispered response.

The talking was over. Dale encountered no problems as he pulled Paul's jeans and shorts down. Infact, Paul slightly arched his back to make the act easier. At the same time Alex pulled Paul's T-shirt over his head . Paul stretched himself out fully on the floor wearing only his white socks and cheap trainers. Perhaps they would just wank him off, he could cope with that, especially if he closed his eyes. No such luck. Dale moved so that he lay alongside Paul but facing his feet. Paul knew exactly what was expected of him and turned his head to accept Dale. With his tongue he played with Dale's demanding shaft, his mind urging Dale to shoot quickly to get it over with.

"Go on Dale, 69, 69!" urged Alex.

There was no verbal response from Dale as he first stroked Paul's now eager shaft and then slowly took him up to the hilt in his mouth. Both boys were now sucking feverishly and toying with the other's balls. Dale was fully on top of Paul and each murmured appreciation of each other. Both were unaware that Alex, whose eyes had never left their writhing bodies, was stripping frantically before stepping across to stand naked astride them. Paul was aware that Dale's sucking was becoming more and more frantic and he soon knew why as hot salty juice filled his mouth. Lying on his back he felt a choking sensation as he desperately tried to gulp the juice down. As he struggled, Dale suddenly released Paul as he lifted himself clear, leaving Paul on his back with his erection still clearly in evidence.

"You bastard Alex. You bastard!" Dale muttered quietly.

The tight expression on Alex's face was unchanging as he turned the shower on. The water warmed quickly and cascaded down onto Paul's inviting athletic body. Dale moved out of the shower as Alex still stood astride Paul. Alex looked down at Paul below him and beckoned him upwards. Paul awkwardly sat up as the shower now blasted him. Silently he took Alex; the shaft bigger than he thought.

"Good boy! Good boy!" muttered Alex.

Paul gripped Alex's thighs from the rear, pulling the firm legs apart as water trickled over and through his fingers. Simultaneously, Alex put his hands on the back of Paul's water-sodden head and pulled him towards his body. The solid cock sought to gain further entry to Paul's throat, causing him to retch. Alex showed no mercy as he furiously shagged the tightening mouth. Paul's teeth gripped the throbbing shaft as he knelt unmoving in front of the ecstatic Alex who rushed to a massive climax, his gushing spunk pulsating violently into the welcoming throat. The climax brought an exultant cry from the depths of Alex's throat as he cried out, "Yes! Yes! YES!"

Dale had dressed himself and kept a nervous watch on the entrance to the showers as Alex appeared to collapse upon climax. Alex withdrew from Paul, who was frantically pulling his own shaft. Alex reached down and knocked the hand away before grasping the well-endowed virgin, apparently helping him to reach orgasm. The shower was still pouring out its warm comforting water as Paul groaned slightly. Before rocking a little sideways, his head slumped forward and then flicked upwards as his shaft throbbed and shot its load into Alex's waiting hands. As Paul tried to catch his breath, Alex smeared the mess across Paul's face and thrust his fingers between the sore, tired lips. Paul had no strength to resist. There would never be enough water to wash him clean. He felt humiliated and ashamed that there had been moments of pleasure through the ordeal. Paul tried to stand but slipped back to the shower floor. The water cascaded upon him.

"Get up you whore. Got what you wanted?" Alex gestured as though he was going to urinate on the prostrate Paul. "Don't! Don't!" pleaded Dale as he pulled away the naked Alex. A manic laugh echoed through the block. The sound of singing could be heard outside from one of the tents. The toilet block next door was being used and Paul still lay motionless on the floor. Dale put his arms around Paul and looked him directly in the eyes. He wanted to beg for forgiveness but he just helped him to his feet and said nothing. Alex had slipped his clothes back on and he switched the shower off. The sudden silence of the block in its own way was deafening. The outside noises continued and Alex was now smiling and his face had relaxed into the charming handsome youth of earlier in the day. Paul quickly dressed under the nervous and concerned gaze of Dale.

"What have we done?" Dale seemed to question himself as he bit nervously the back of his hand.

"Come on, time to go." was the casual response from Alex and the three boys left the block.

During the short walk back to the tents, Paul's mind was in overdrive. Alex casually bade Dale goodnight at the entrance to his tent and the two remaining boys moved towards their tent. You will pay. One day you will pay for tonight was the overriding thought in Paul's mind as his eyes fixed unsmilingly upon Alex.

The smell of scotch met them as they entered the tent. No-one was awake and the invasive light from Alex's torch did not disturb anyone. All were in a deep sleep induced doubtless by the amber nectar. Alex and Paul without speaking stripped down to T-shirt and underwear before sliding into their sleeping bags. The light was extinguished and Paul lay there in silence gazing upwards into nothing. "Hey, you asleep?" asked Alex. "Remember our little secret?" Alex continued. "How can I forget," thought Paul as he drifted into the comforting escape of sleep. The nightmares were for another time and place.

The morning was bright clear and crisp. As Paul awoke he realised that Alex had already left the tent.

"Hey, what were you and Alex up to last night ?" Tony's voice boomed across the tent with accompanied giggles from the others who were fully awake.

"Nothing. Why ask ?"

"Well, when we went to sleep you weren't here and neither was Big Boy. What are we supposed to think?" More giggles. "I mean, you missed our little games and the booze." Laughter this time. Paul glanced at the Scotch bottle. "Well you didn't drink much looking at that bottle. It's nearly half-full."

"We had enough. Anyway we had other things to do Little Boy!" More knowing laughter that can only be shared by intimates and Paul was not one.

"If you want to be with us there is a little ceremony you have to do," Tony announced to Paul. "But you're probably too chicken," and Tony made a loud clucking noise and wafted his arms up and down in the manner of a chicken attempting to fly. More laughter from those wishing to maintain Tony's patronage.

"Well, what is it?"

"Show us your cock!" was Tony's announcement.

"Is that all!" mocked Paul.

"Yeah! And I expect we'll need a magnifying glass to see it !" More appreciative laughter from Tony's followers. Without any hesitation Paul unzipped the sleeping bag but did not reveal the contents. "Chicken!" mocked Tony. Then Paul casually peeled back his sleeping bag. There was an appreciative gasp from the onlookers but Tony remained silent and he realised his authority and influence had diminished.

This was the final morning and as they breakfasted, Mr. Anderson lectured them on the need to leave the site tidy, and thanked them for their responsible behaviour during the camp. This final remark brought wry smiles to the lips of two girls in particular as they looked in the direction of Alex and Dale, who did not notice as his head was bowed. Camp was soon broken and small groups waited to board the coach. Paul stood with Gordon and Shamir; just a little to one side were Tony and Chris. Permission to board was given by Ms. Pearce and the first to move were Clara, Alex, Samantha and Dale. The two couples; arms entwined, Clara with a triumphant look on her face, were laughing as they approached the coach. Alex saw Paul standing near the entrance, looked directly at him and then broke free of Clara's clutches.

"Just want a quick word with Paul," Alex spoke easily in a reassuring manner. No-one questioned him. With a light touch on Paul's shoulders, he guided him a short distance from the group who continued to board. Alex's face was smiling broadly but the words he uttered did not match the outward look.

"Remember shit, I screw birds. Remember! Nothing happened between us. Remember!"

"If you say so." Paul quietly replied. "But just remember that I know who I am, in every way. And I know you, really know you, better than you know yourself. You don't frighten me but I bet you frighten the shit out of yourself!"

Before Alex could reply Clara shouted,

"Come on you two. We're ready for the off!" Alex rejoined Clara. As Dale boarded the coach, he turned unsmilingly to Paul and looked him directly in the eyes. Paul with his head held high gave no indication of even recognising him. Rejected, Dale continued to climb aboard and slapped the rear of a giggling Samantha.

"What was that about?" asked Shamir.

"You don't want to know, I promise you."

Both took their places on the coach and it was not long into the journey that the songs began. A group of youngsters singing songs as they devoured the motorway miles. Ten green bottles soon became nine and so on. One boy did not join in. His mind concentrated on revenge as he watched Alex's hand grope an unresisting Clara. As he watched, he was reminded of a salty juice in his mouth. Warm and pleasing he had to admit to himself. His thought processes were broken as Tony leant over the headrest from the seat behind.

"Hey Paul, my Dad's picking me up when we get back. Want a lift?"

Paul allowed a small smile to crease his lips.

"OK. Why not? Why not ?" Then Paul closed his eyes to the world.

Three

The first few days back at school following the trip took on a surreal aspect for Paul. It was as though nothing had happened. No-one mentioned the sex, just kept their comments to how great the trip was without ever being specific. No-one looked anyone directly in the eye. Paul had not seen Alex for almost a week after their return, although Alex had watched Paul from the Common Room window. Whether he was awake or in his dreams, Alex was constantly in Paul's thoughts. He wanted so much to see Alex again, but would he feel the same? Maybe they would meet and they would hate each other. When they met again for the first time it was sudden and to have far-reaching consequences for both of them. On such chance encounters are lives regulated and charted. Fate decides, and for Paul fate decrees that decisions are taken from his control. His body was to be his fate, his arbiter of decisions and the means to an end.

On the Friday, after returning to school the previous Monday, Paul decided to make a toilet call before going to the bus bay. As he stood at the urinal Paul was aware of someone entering after him.

"Well, hello stranger. Been looking for you all week."

Zipping up as he turned, Paul responded more sharply than he intended.

"You couldn't have looked very far. I've been around."

"What do you do with yourself on a Friday night?"

"Not much. Probably watch telly as my mum will be out. That's it really. Anyway what's it to you?"

"Like a lift home?" Alex surprised Paul with the question. He wondered what had happened to Alex's fan club for him to be offering him a lift on a Friday night. Paul had heard the gossip about the 'Shagmobile' as the girls called the Fiesta, but this did stop the seemingly endless girls who were prepared to giggle their way through the apparent danger. Perhaps Alex was going to make more threats. When was he going to realise that there was no threat? Paul had mellowed during the week. On their return to Birmingham there had been a problem as Paul struggled to find answers to questions he could not understand. After all, despite the aggression, he had brought him physical pleasure of a previously unexperienced intensiy.

"Well, do you want a lift. Dale's waiting?"

"Yeah. Why not ? "

They left the building and as they headed towards the car park, Paul felt a surge of excitement as he walked alongside Alex. Tony and Chris ran past them, with Tony making loud whooping noises in celebration of Friday. Chris would be going round to Tony's later in the evening. Tony's parents would be out late, and Chris hoped for a little more experimentation. They usually watched one of Tony's dads porno videos, often loudly encouraging the participants to greater efforts. Tony usually commented on the size of the women's breasts and positively drooled at the crutch shots. Chris particularly liked the cum shots, especially if they lasted for several seconds out of big cocks. Both pondered the question if some of the men were wearing large plastic tools, as surely no man could really be that big. Chris usually stayed over and they mutually masturbated each other on a fairly regular basis. What really amazed Chris was that Tony's dad didn't seem to know that Tony knew the 'secret' hiding place behind the set of bedroom drawers.

Dale was waiting beside the Fiesta and Paul felt a knot of jealousy tightening in his stomach as they approached the car. The walk alongside Alex had strangely excited him. These were feelings he had not experienced before and he felt proud that other students had seen them together.

"You two know each other I believe," teased Alex. Dale and Paul tried to avoid each other's gaze, but only succeeded in blushing rapidly. Just the reaction Alex expected. He was in control and would exploit his two companions mercilessly if given the opportunity. Alex unlocked the car and gestured Paul to get into the rear. No-one spoke as they entered the Fiesta.

"Cat got your tongues?" mocked Alex, clearly enjoying his companions' discomfort. His sarcasm did in fact break the tension between the boys as Alex drove out onto the main road. Now that there were no observers or eavesdroppers, Dale and Paul's tension evaporated. Dale turned in his seat to face Paul.

"How you been since Skipton?"

"Fine," was the one-word response from Paul. As he sat back in his seat he wondered why no-one talked about "it". No-one mentioned the sex, the gloriously ecstatic moments they shared together, that for each of them had had a different meaning. Paul had realised that to most people it would seem that Alex had abused him, raped him. Dale if asked would probably claim he was a victim too, taking part because he feared Alex, his mate. And what would Alex claim? Did it all just for fun. Just a game. Lying bastard!

"Hey! Are you on this planet?" Alex broke into Paul's thoughts.

"Sorry I was miles away."

"I gathered that. To give you a lift home I need to know where you live, so can you give me a clue?" The three boys shared the joke with light laughter. Suddenly Paul was overcome with feelings of embarrassment as he didn't really want the others to know that he lived in a tower block, on a run-down council estate. Alex probably knew already, but there was no need to confirm it.

"Elm Street on the Grove Estate."

"Christ, I've not got my bullet-proof vest. What about you Dale boy?" Only two boys laughed this time.

"Bollocks!"

"Touchy! Touchy! No need to be like that," chided Alex.

"Lay off him Alex."

"Perhaps you'd rather lay on him!" taunted the unrelenting Alex. The two in the front of the car laughed loudly, but Dale's efforts sounded forced. Paul did not give Alex the satisfaction of a reply. Moments later they turned onto the estate. It was a sick tribute to the sixties, an exhibition of graffiti, boarded-up ground-floor windows, faulty lifts and stairways perfumed by the stench of urine. Paul lived on the sixth floor and he hated every living moment he spent there. Dale tried to ease the perceptively growing tension. Alex's comments had been so unnecessary and Dale wondered why he had these uncalled-for moments of unpleasantness.

"Existed here long?"

"Long enough! Hey Alex, Why did you give me a lift? Was it just so you could take the piss, or was it check if I'd told anyone that you like to shag boys! Remember, do you? Last week? "

For just a fraction of a moment Alex was taken aback, but he soon regained his outward composure, by spreading a broad smile across his face.

"No. I don't really mean any harm. I'm just a sorry bastard," replied Alex in an almost inaudible whisper in the direction of the rear view mirror.

"You can say that again," muttered an increasingly agitated Dale.

"OK you two. I'm sorry. My mouth runs away with me sometimes. I offered you a lift because I think you're an OK sort of guy. I really do. So can we start again, and if we bump into each other, just don't think I'm going to stitch you up. OK?"

"OK?"

Paul was happy to accept this version of an apology, although like Dale he knew that sincerity did not figure highly in Alex's characteristics. Alex was a user, so stand-by to be used sometime soon Paul!

Alex brought the Fiesta to a halt at the start of Elm Street and opposite the entrance of Elm House. Neither Alex or Dale made any move to release Paul from the rear of the two-door car.

"Bet you can buy some interesting stuff around here," suggested an unsmiling Alex.

"Don't know what you mean," Paul replied, not sure what to make of the remark. Alex and Dale were outsiders and at least one of them could be dangerous. After a momentary pause Alex gestured for Dale to let Paul out from the rear seat. As Dale got out of the Fiesta, Paul pushed the front passenger-seat forward. Alex reached across a restraining arm and spoke quietly.

"Bet you don't pay with cash for anything. There isn't anything you wouldn't do to escape from here, is there?" Paul did not respond and he stepped out in front of a grinning Dale.

"See you around," smiled Dale.

"Yeah, see you both," replied Paul as he involuntarily bent down to gesture his thanks to Alex for the lift. Dale got back into the car and it was soon speeding away, leaving Paul with his confused thoughts, and an embarrassing protruberance in his trousers.

Already on the third floor of Elm House were Tony and Chris. Chris had come round for his tea and he would stay overnight with Tony. After tea,

Tony's parents would take an age getting ready to go out, but out they would go eventually, not returning until the early hours, leaving the boys to their own devices. By their return, the boys would be fast asleep in Tony's single bed. His mother would peep around the door and see her little boy lying there with his pal, sleeping the sleep of the innocent. She would not see two late-teenage boys who had just enjoyed each other to the point of ecstatic orgasm. They had shared the same single bed since their early teens. Nights of experimentation had led not much further than groping to orgasm; the towel at the foot of the bed stiffening as the boys' juices dried upon it as each had spat out the other's cum after completing a very pleasurable, uninterrupted 69.

Paul had watched the Fiesta disappear from view before taking the short walk to the tower flats. He stood looking up at the dirty grey concrete and glass monster. Paul vowed to himself that he would do whatever was necessary to escape from this prison. What had Alex meant when he suggested that he would do anything to escape. How did he know? On second thoughts, he knew no-one had to be a genius to realise anyone in their right mind would want to escape that hell-hole. Paul trudged up the stairs as yet again the lift had been vandalised. As he progressed upwards his mind toyed with the problem of escape. He would be leaving school as soon as he completed the NVQ course without a certificate in sight. What would his future be? Perhaps Alex knew something he did not. Paul decided he would engineer a situation where he was alone with Alex, and try and question him as to what he was hinting at. After all he spoke in a way that was private between the two of them, not for Dale's ears. As he unlocked the door of the flat, a strange surge of excitement rushed through his body once more. The same feelings he'd experienced whenever he'd thought of Alex since the Sixth Form Farewell Camp.

At 3a.m in the third floor flat Chris awoke. He was aware of Tony's hand resting against his crutch. In the small bed, he could feel Tony's warm breath against his cheek. Gently, he pressed his lips against Tony's forehead. Not truly a kiss, just a moment of tenderness. Tony began to stretch so Chris moved quickly away.

"You awake Tone?"

David Keane

"Mmmmmm...."

Gently, Chris began to stroke Tony's bristling pubic hair. There was no resistance, just a murmur of quiet contentment. Encouraged, Chris grasped Tony's throbbing erection, stirring him to full consciousness. Chris lay on his back contemplating his next move. His whole being wanted to have its first full shag with the most wonderful boy, his friend, in the whole world. Tony sat up and looked down in the shadowy darkness, sensing Chris's desire. He gently bowed his head and carefully placed his lips upon Chris's pleading lips. With a suddenness that took Chris by surprise, Tony's tongue forced its way into a receptive throat. Tony forced his body onto Chris who flung his arms around him. As demanding fingernails scratched into his back, Tony broke lip contact to almost scream his pleasure, aware his parents would now be home, suddenly afraid of waking them. How ridiculous! Tony could never believe his overweight father ever had this pleasure between the sheets. As these thoughts invaded his mind, Tony became aware that Chris's fingers were beginning to probe and invade him. Pleasure was mounting and both their needs were about to explode.

"Tone! Tone! I want to shag you!" Chris gasped out. There he'd said it!

"No, no you perve, wank or blow – that's it! God are you queer or what?" Tony pushed himself clear of Chris.

Although desperate at the rejection Chris shot his load.

"Not on the sheets you prat."

Chris was now horrified. Did Tony really think he was gay? After all, they were mates and mates do things for each other. But gay! No way! Tony had deliberately, even in the tiny bed, managed to manoeuvre himself free of any part of their bodies touching.

Tony shot his spunk onto his bare stomach. Chris was asleep, unaware of Tony reaching over him for the stiffening towel. Before drifting back to sleep, Tony wondered what it would be like to have a cock inside him.

Friday night for Alex and Dale usually meant a visit to a pub just a few miles from home. Friday and Saturday nights usually meant leaving the Fiesta at home and travelling to the pub by bus, and then into town for a night clubbing, and eventually returning home by taxi. Alternate weekends were spent at each other's homes. Both sets of parents admired their son's choice of best friend: two academic achievers working hard for success so they could tread the traditional path through 'A' levels to university, and then into law or medicine. All planned out and seemingly inevitable. Their parents were so proud of their handsome boys. These were the same two lads who liked to pop a few pills, smoke weed, and more. These two 'inseparable boys' who on occasions shared the same girl and each other. If the girl was unwilling to be shared, they tried to ensure that the one left out could watch. Tonight may well be such a night. Alex was in such a mood and if the girl, whoever she may be, was not willing she could be persuaded by force if necessary. He loved seeing Dale's face as he shot his load into some total stranger, his eyes closed, his mouth wide open, gasping with pleasure. Alex sometimes shot his load just watching and listening. Dale enjoyed watching Alex as he increased the tempo of pumping just prior to ejaculation. Sometimes Alex became violent at the point of orgasm, clenching his teeth and his well-formed neck muscles tightened and stretched as he pulled his victim's hair and thrusted unceasingly into the girl, ignoring her pleading with him to be more gentle. The more she pleaded, the more excited he became and greater the orgasm. Dale, as he watched, his own excitement rising, sometimes feared that Alex would go too far, but once he had come, Alex always quickly released his victim and became momentarily caring, and then dismissive and disinterested. At least the girls agreed at the start, so far that is.

Usually in the pub they would meet up with other members of the Sixth Form, before they decided which club it was to be for the night. On this particular Friday there were few friends arriving and Alex wondered if there was a party going on somewhere that he did not know about. This was quickly dismissed as being too ludicrous to be considered. It was just one of those slack nights that occurred for no apparent reason that can occur during the summer months. Two couples came in but they were part of the 'Virgin' set and not really part of the boys' scene. Both girls had rejected Alex's advances at the Christmas Rave and he genuinely could not understand their reasoning.

"Come on, let's split. There's nothing here for us tonight." Dale nodded in agreement and quickly finished his lager. Leaving the pub they decided to head to town by bus. On the way out Alex diverted into the gents' and made his usual Friday night purchase from the machine. Flavoured and ribbed were

David Keane

the choice to cover all possibilities. Once in the city centre they strolled towards their favourite haunt, 'The Noise,' appropriately named as the loudest spot in town and very popular with the younger set, plus being good for one-night stand pick-ups. No problem here in getting a little extra whether it be pills or sex. After midnight the nearby alleyways were popular for up-against-the-wall-sex. No-one seemed to care. They just got on with it. Progressing from heavy petting to full stand up sex, the discarded condoms told their story as daylight broke each Saturday and Sunday morning. It was here about a year ago that Alex and Dale had completed their first side-by-side shag. The girls were not particularly memorable, but the fact they were performing together was what made the orgasm wonderful and knee-bending. Later when they were discussing the merits of each shag, they both agreed that the thrill came from being mates together. It was not long before they were picking up a girl and sharing the spoils. They had surprisingly few knockbacks and the first girl to agree was very quickly on the same wavelength. Alex performed first, as Dale watched closely. Other couples were in the alleyway but too absorbed in their own facefucking or wallbanging shag to care what anyone else was up to. The girl had her skirt pulled up and Alex did not bother to drop his designer jeans. All he had done was to open them fully and undo his belt. Through the slit of his designer boxers stood his firm cock and he asked Dale to roll a condom into place. Dale eagerly obliged and then stood back as without further lubrication Alex forced his cock into the willing hole. Dale verbally encouraged Alex and then began to rub his hand around on the inside of the boxers across Alex's soft-skinned bum cheeks. With fingers searching for Alex's hole, Dale used his free hand to undo his own jeans and release his aching throbbing cock. As his probing index finger entered Alex, Dale felt the full throbbing release of Alex as he repeatedly shot into the condom. Suddenly Alex pulled free and simultaneously the girl dropped to her knees and filled her mouth with Dale who obligingly filled her throat with warm salty juice over and over again. When it was over the two boys quickly adjusted their jeans and left the girl retching, trying to clear her throat whilst still on her knees. Later, when discussing the event, they could not agree as to the colour of their first victim's hair. It was not long before Alex was suggesting that they might not always need the assistance of a girl every time. Tonight may well be such a night.

Alex had seemed very unsettled all evening and although Dale had point-ed out several potential targets, Alex appeared distracted. There were some of their previous conquests there but it was always regarded as a last resort to go with one already sampled. Even this option did not seem on tonight as Alex gazed around him distractedly. Just before midnight he announced that he was not in the mood and that they should go home. Dale agreed because without the involvement of Alex, sex lacked that special something. They were lucky in finding a taxi and they were at Alex's home before 12.30. The house was silent as his parents were always in bed by 11.00, even at weekends. Usually Alex's mother drifted in and out of light sleep until she heard the front door open and two whispering boys enter. Tonight was no different and once she had heard those comforting sounds she soon slipped into a deep slum-ber.

The boys faced each other in the kitchen.

"Beer?"

"OK."

Alex opened the fridge door to reveal a well-stocked store. He passed a can to Dale and they sat at the large breakfast unit. Alex filled his mouth with the frothing beer and some escaped running down his chin. The significance of the act was not wasted on Dale and he mimicked Alex. Suddenly they laughed out loud and then loudly shushed each other, so as not to wake the rest of the household.

"Come on, let's go up. I'm tired tonight."

"Can't stand the pace?" teased Dale.

With no further hesitation, Alex, still clutching his beer can, moved to switch off the kitchen light. Dale, also with can, followed him up the stairs. Alex's bedroom was situated the furthest away from his parents' room in the four-bedroom detached house in the middle-class area of Edgbaston. On entering, Alex switched on the small lamp close to his single bed. The soft light cast shadows across the boys. Alex closed the door and then the cur-tains before moving purposefully towards Dale. They reached out to each other, reading the other's mind perfectly. With certainty as their arms wrapped around each other, their lips met with tongues thrusting with desperate urgency. They fell to the bed locked together and their hands sought to gain frantic entry to each other's jeans. Breaking free simultaneously they stood up and undressed themselves with unrestrained urgency. When totally naked they faced each other, both standing proud, fully aware of each other. With tenderness Alex reached to Dale's ponytail and released the dark hair allowing it to cascade across its trembling owner's shoulders. Alex lay on the bed with his arms raised to welcome Dale. This was no boy, as his manhood stood proud demanding Dale down upon it. Slowly and tenderly Dale filled his mouth with Alex. His tongue teased the totally receptive shaft and Alex moved in harmony with Dale as pleasure surged through his expectant body. Gently he lifted Dale's head from him and willing lips sought more. Eagerly Dale moved up Alex as his tongue searched the surface of his lightly-tanned skin. Resting upon a firm nipple, lips gave way to biting teeth that sent Alex into a spasm of gasping ecstasy. Reaching upwards, Dale put a hand over Alex's quivering lips as he turned his attention to a second pointed nipple. Releasing the nipple, lips replaced hand on mouth; simultaneously hands grasped the now demanding magnificence of Alex. Breaking free, Alex leaned from the bed towards his discarded jeans. Stretching fingers sought the packet of condoms. Quickly one was passed to Dale who tore the packet open, removed the contents and deftly rolled the rubber down Alex's shaft, who removed from the bedside cabinet a tube of lubricant. As Alex smeared liberal amounts of lubricant, Dale rolled free and on to his back, opened his legs wide and brought his knees upward. Trembling slightly, his dark highlighted ponytail splayed across the pillow he waited to receive Alex. A lubricated finger teased the entrance to his hole, then entered him to prepare the way. Alex gently placed himself between Dale's legs and unhesitatingly entered him. Dale, with eyes closed, received him with joy. Lips met, tongues entwined, their experience of each other providing ultimate pleasure. Lovers for several months now, they did not speak of their love for each other. They just pleasured each other, and words seemed unnecessary. Words would mean facing reality. That could come later, if ever. Alex surged into Dale and they exploded to climax together.

"Paul! Paul!" was the cry from Alex's lips.

Sleep refused to blot out the humiliation felt by Dale. As Alex slept beside him, Dale could smell the remnants of a designer aftershave mingled with raw sex-generated male odour. Eventually daylight overcame the darkness. No matter how Dale tried to shut out the light of morning and the distress he felt, sleep had not come to protect him. Alex lay alongside, his breathing steady and unconcerned. "How could you?" thought Dale. Did he really want that working-class yob? Was it just a slip of the tongue? Don't kid yourself, thought Dale. Perhaps there is another Paul, but that thought was no real comfort and it did not make it easier to bear. Did it really mean that as he was shafting him, Alex, was mentally coming into that Paul? Dale continued to look at the sleeping Alex before he had to rush to the en-suite bathroom to throw up.

Breakfast time was difficult in two very different areas of the city. In the tower block there was little conversation between Tony and Chris, unlike their usual Saturday morning banter. Tony's mum assumed there had been a little disagreement and unless asked she was not going to interfere. These two never fell out for long, so leave them to it. Probably all over some girl.

Alex floated around the dining kitchen of the large detached house. Wearing a vivid-multi-coloured dressing gown that had been a free gift with some expensive toilet water, Alex assaulted the toaster. Dale studied Alex across the central diner and came to the conclusion that Alex had no idea of what he had shouted at the moment of orgasm. Dale found this comforting and began to relax. Alex had wondered if Dale was unwell when they got up, but as Dale now looked more at ease he didn't mention the matter. Plans needed to be made for the day and as no-one else seemed to be stirring there probably would be time for them to share a shower. Alex handed Dale a plate of hot buttered toast.

"Ta mate," and with that Dale crunched into the thick, dripping semi-burnt offering.

"Wonder what that Paul's doing today. Can't begin to imagine what it must be like living in a shithole like that. He seems different from the other morons." Alex failed to notice that Dale had stopped eating his toast.

"And you want to find out do you?" snapped an increasingly angry Dale.

"What's biting you?"

Wearing just his boxer shorts, without speaking Dale leapt from the high breakfast stool, rushed out of the kitchen and charged up the stairs to the

David Keane

room of his humiliation. After a moment of hesitation brought about by shock, a bemused Alex followed, taking three steps at a time. When he entered he could see the now naked Dale at full stretch across the bed, lying on his back with his hair almost covering the Manchester United pillow case, that betrayed Alex's early teenage loyalties. If the truth were to be known, these had not changed, only it was not cool to discuss these matters with the trendy set he wished to hang out with these days.

"Not enough for you? Not big enough? Eh? Eh? Stretched my hole too much! Not tight enough for you now, is that it?" Dale yelled with a force that frightened Alex. He had no idea what Dale was so upset about.

"What's all the noise about?" was the enquiry from along the landing.

"I wish I knew," was the muttered response from Alex, as Dale sobbed with his face buried deeply into the pillow. Alex closed the bedroom door and stood looking at the naked form before him. Dale's smooth skin with the thin traces of dark hair on his legs excited him. Dale turned to face Alex and revealed the line of hair from his navel to crutch. Alex wanted him, but he wanted someone more. As his mind cleared sufficiently to remind him of something he may have said last night, Alex strode to the shower dropping the dressing-gown as he went. Dale slowly rose from the duvet and calmly got dressed.

Paul decided to have a lie-in. Nothing else particular to do so he began to fondle himself, but his cock did not seem interested as it was only half-hard. He looked down at himself and pondered briefly the question of why when he woke up his cock was rock-hard. Now it was softer, but still admirable. Comforting himself with that thought, he decided to get up to face another Saturday on the estate. Did life have to be that boring? The choice seemed to be shoplifting in the estate newsagents, or taking a day-trip to town and lifting a few choice items in the Bull Ring Centre. He checked his mother's bedroom, carefully opening the door, not sure what he would discover. There had been occasions when he had seen his naked mother next to some grotesque man, usually fat, ugly, old and snoring. This time the bed was empty and had not been slept in that night. Returning to his own room he gazed out of the window over the city. Wonder if it was the same guy who had made it possible for him to go on the school camp. He hoped so as he was a considerable improvement on some of the trash that had passed through recently. At least

– 46 –

he did not stink of booze like some of them did. Opening the window to let out the stale air, he leant out to take deep gulps of the morning air. He looked down onto the parking area and was surprised to see a Fiesta there that looked very much like the one belonging to Alex. As he looked idly down on the scene, Paul saw Alex step from the car and look up towards the sixth floor.

"What the fuck does he want here?" Paul muttered to himself and the clear fresh morning air.

Alex had agreed unhesitatingly to take Dale home. Their short journey was memorable for the lack of conversation. Dale explained that he might have a bout of 'flu coming on and probably would not be going out again for the rest of the weekend. Alex felt a rush of relief that they may not have to talk again that weekend. He told Dale he would see him at school on Monday if he was OK, and that perhaps his 'flu would not really develop into anything. The words were spoken politely like a stranger, giving no indication of the intimacies exchanged only a few hours before. Alex had not set out when taking Dale home to return via the estate, but he did. Now sat in the car park, he desperately wanted Paul to walk out from that tower block that contained him. If Paul did appear what excuse would he use for being there? His thoughts drifted back to the orgasm in the shower block that sent his cum gushing with such intensity. Dale had always been fun; moments of experimentation, but this youth; a couple of years his junior excited him. His firm, young, well-developed body, with its light brown soft skin and tightly curled dark pubes had dominated his thoughts since their return from camp. Sitting in the car Alex could feel the uncontrollable surge of blood to his hardening cock. It was a response he could not cope with. Why me? I'm not gay! I can't be! I'm Alex! The guy who could have the choice of virtually any girl at the school was getting a hard-on thinking about a GNVQ male student. Not something he felt he could chat to his mates about. Then there was that thought in his mind that he might have shouted Paul's name out when he was shooting into Dale.

"Oh God! Surely not!" Alex said out loud. His thoughts were confused, but there was that nagging doubt. Impossible to believe, but undoubtedly true. His relationship with Dale was surely over, but what really surprised him was that he didn't care. Alex was brought back to reality by a sharp tapping on the side window. Despite his efforts to keep a constant eye on the entrance to the flats, Paul had somehow evaded his gaze. Alex turned to see Paul crouching at the side of the Fiesta, and was horrified that he may have seen his hard-on. Winding down the window he gave a confident smile that belied his true feelings.

"Hello. Just thought I'd pop round and see if you were doing anything today."

"Why?"

"Do I need a reason?"

"As I said, why? What do you want from me? Are you scared I'll tell the world about last week? Don't worry, quit shitting yourself."

"Thanks for that... I think. Look, get in the car will you for a minute?"

Without replying Paul moved around to the passenger side, and as he did so Alex leant over and opened the door. Paul got in and once seated he felt at ease and a feeling of power swept through him. Alex was nervous and this communicated itself to Paul.

"Look my mum's out, so do you want to come up to the flat? Then you can perhaps tell me what you want, or leave me alone... OK?"

Alex did not answer immediately. He turned to face Paul and knew instinctively what he wanted and that he must talk to this guy, or at least try.

"Yes."

Once in the flat Paul was on his own territory and he had a strong feeling of power over the school's superstar. Handing Alex a mug of cheap supermarket brand coffee he waited for Alex to come clean. There was no response and Alex just looked at him over the edge of his mug. Paul held his gaze determinedly.

"You fancy me don't you?" Paul still held Alex's gaze, as he waited for an answer. Despite the thoughts Alex was harbouring, he was taken by surprise.

"Get real will you? Me fancy you? Do me a favour!"

"That's exactly what I thought you wanted me to do! Please yourself, but if you don't, what the fuck are you doing here?"

The silence was deafening and both knew the answer to the question. Even more importantly, the moment of acceptance had probably arrived.

Tony's mum left the boys alone in the flat as she set off for a morning's shopping. His dad had already left despite the late night. A day at Warwick

Races would not be overcome by a hangover. The fresh air would either be kill or cure.

Tony took a deep breath.

"Were you serious, you know, what you asked me in bed?"

"Why, what difference does it make now? Expect you'll blab at school. I didn't mean it really," Chris lied chosing not to look at Tony while he did so.

"Oh! That's a shame!"

Chris turned to look at Tony who was smiling broadly as he made his way back to the bedroom. Pausing briefly he enquired of Chris.

"Well, are you coming?"

Both laughed at the unintentional double meaning and Chris needed no further encouragement. Once inside the bedroom they undressed silently but with broad expectant smiles on their faces. Chris stepped forward and wrapped his arms around Tony. Both were now trembling slightly as their lips, at first lightly, brushed against each other. With a sudden fervour Tony pressed himself against the throbbing Chris. Breaking free momentarily they then fell onto the duvet. Tony knelt before his now expectant lover. Moving into position behind Tony, Chris shuffled up to his target. Tony rose to meet him. Before attempting entry Chris, reached around Tony to take his cock in his hands, as he gently stroked the receptive Tony. Chris leaned forward with his lips caressing the nape of Tony's neck. They stayed in this position of intense tenderness a few seconds before Tony pleaded.

"Now do it now! Please! Please!" As he pleaded he slipped a condom to Chris that he had pulled from below his mattress. It had been bought from a machine in a gents' toilet some months before. Partly as a dare and partly for the day it might be needed. That day had arrived. Chris fumbled as in a trembling peak of excitement he rolled the rubber down his expectant shaft. Chris inhaled deeply before using his left hand to try and guide himself into Tony. Pushing himself eagerly now in an attempt to penetrate, he felt his cock bending in response to Tony's gasped urgings.

"It's no good. It's no good!" pleaded Chris with a pained voice of disappointment.

Tony broke free from Chris's desperate efforts to penetrate, grasped him by the hair and flung him onto the duvet on his back. Swiftly he took Chris in his mouth, and the strawberry flavour of the condom stormed his taste buds. Chris thrust himself deeply to the back of Tony's throat. The explosion came quickly into the condom, the depth and length of the orgasm astonished and pleased them both.

"Hey that was brilliant!" enthused the ecstatic and breathless Tony. "I'll get some oil or something for next time, you know what I mean."

"Yeah corse I do." replied the slightly embarrassed but ecstatically happy Chris. He had the most exciting and fulfilling few minutes of his young life. Nothing could possibly surpass that moment of coming. In his mind he couldn't wait to try again to see if it could be matched or beaten. The hardening between his legs was proof, it any were needed, that his body was preparing to give it a go. Although he had failed to enter Tony, the pleasure felt by Chris was far greater than any pleasures he had ever felt before. The two boys lay naked side by side for over an hour, occasionally stroking each other and then fading into a light sleep. They were disturbed by the telephone with its insistent ringing. Tony moved naked from bedroom to living room and picked up he phone with Chris following.

"Hello Tone, it's Clara. What took you so long? Who you got there then?" Clara laughed down the phone. Tony gestured for Chris to go down on him and he willingly obliged.

"Hey! You still there?"

"Yes. 'Course I am," responded Tony as he looked down upon Chris lovingly caressing the demanding shaft with his tongue, then taking him urgently.

"Yeah what can I do for you that's legal?"

Tony held Chris's head in place as Clara droned on about some party at her house that night. She would appreciate it if he would tell Chris about the party and he promised he would. As he replaced the receiver, Tony grasped Chris's head with both hands and did not release him, with his knees buckling under the weakening, mind-blowing moment as his spunk rushed out to find its way to Chris's gagging throat. Once free of each other, Chris savagely pulled at his own pleading cock, and as Tony leant down to him he fired his load into his Tony's face. Tony rubbed both hands across his sticky face and then licked his hands clean of the white love juice.

"Party tonight at Clara's," both boys spontaneously exploded into laughter at the irrelevance of the remark.

"Hello love. Back early."

"Not feeling too great mum," Dale tried not to make too big a deal about the situation. There was no way he could tell his mother the real reason for his return home early on a Saturday morning.

"Pity. That Clara girl rang about fifteen minutes ago. Wants you to ring her back about some party tonight."

Grabbing the cordless phone Dale moved to go upstairs.

"I'll ring her from my room." He took the stairs three at a time on his ascent.

"Glad to see you're better," was the smiling response from his mother who continued the ironing unhindered.

From the privacy of his room Dale telephoned Clara and soon established details and no he didn't know that Alex was not at home, and he didn't know if he'd see him that afternoon. Reluctantly he agreed he would try to contact Alex. Dale stayed in his room until lunchtime playing a random selection of C.D.'s. His moÙher called him downstairs and offered him beans on toast. He thanked her and told her he was feeling much better now and would go to Clara's party. This pleased his mother who thought that Clara was a 'nice' girl, along with her friend Samantha. Just right for Dale and Alex. Not very subtle with her hints, his mother. How little she knew. Best that way. The party would probably get a bit wild and there would be stuff available. After that he might be able to get a quick screw to prove to himself he was wanted for himself and not just because he was a friend of Alex. He had all the necessary equipment and knew how to use it without any help from his so-called friend. Plenty to drink and smoke would keep Dale happy. Help him to forget his humiliation and prove he was a man. Dale smiled to himself as his mother went on and on about his 'nice' friends. Tonight he would blow his mind and his bollocks. Fuck the lot of 'em he thought. He really was past caring. Start a new life that would not include Alex. Alex could take a running jump, preferably from the top of a multi-storey car park. Persuading himself was difficult though, as a feeling of emptiness swept over him.

Four

Alex and Paul moved from the small kitchen through to the equally meagre living area. They sat uneasily together on the two-seater settee. Suddenly Alex spoke.

"Fancy a ride out?"

"I don't get you. Why take me out? What's in it for you?"

"Look, stop looking for answers to questions that do not need to be asked. Do you fancy a ride out? A simple question. Yes or no? That's all."

"OK. Surprise me!"

"Right, let's go now. We'll see where the car takes us. Come on."

With a sudden urgency Alex leapt up and headed for the door. Paul was excited at the prospect and agreed to leave immediately. The drive out of the city was uneventful and Alex was still debating in his mind where they would head for. Paul saw a sign for Stratford and yelled out he'd love to go there as he had never had the chance before. Alex was surprised by the choice but was happy to oblige, so Stratford it was.

They laughed a lot at nothing in particular. A kind of kneejerk nervous reaction. Occasionally Alex's hand brushed against Paul's leg as he changed gear. Paul did not make any comment regarding the touching and neither did he make any attempt to move away. First port of call was the McDonald's close to the Marina and the theatre. Alex bought two large cola drinks and they perched on high stools to drink them. Paul's mind was in a whirl. He never expected to be visiting Stratford, today or any day, as people from the Elm Estate did not visit 'posh' Stratford. But here he was! His attention was firmly fixed on the seemingly easy, matured Alex, who being the clever person he was had passed his driving test first time just a few weeks ago. Was there nothing this strangely attractive dark-haired, A-level student, with a firm well-developed body of medium height could not actually do! No surplus fat and with high cheek bones that encased dark,deep-set eyes that held Paul in their gaze, Alex was stirring those feelings he had suppressed the previous week. Alex smiled and allowed his head to loll back with his more normal self-assurance that was surfacing now they had arrived without any disasters, either on the road or in the car. All words carefully chosen. No more silly nervous jibes. As he pushed his fingers through his hair Alex gazed into Paul's limpid-pool eyes. Here is this youth sitting there drinking cola and causing him a chronic ache in his groin. Why were they there? After the rape of the previous week, because that's how some people would interpret the events at the school camp. How could he expect anything but hatred from this beautiful boy? Same age, different backgrounds, one academic and sporting, the other so young and drifting. Sitting in the burger bar Alex realised that the subject of the camp must be discussed sometime, and soon. Now was as good a time as any. Reaching to touch Paul on the arm, Alex became aware that Paul was staring in a blatant way at a group of four American female students. Perhaps now was not the time, but too late he realised that his hand was resting lightly on Paul's arm. Paul wanted to talk to Alex so much, but chose to look at the Americans instead, amazed by their accents and the fact they were there, and so was he. He had never seen real Americans, live ones, before. They must be loaded to be able to travel so far. As these thoughts teased his mind he became aware of a hand resting on his arm.

"Penny for them?" Alex asked as he tried to decide how to approach the subject he so desperately wanted to mention.

Paul glanced down at the hand before replying.

"Sorry, I was in America!"

"Can we talk about school camp? You know all that happened there...the shower...you..." Alex tightened his grip on Paul's arm. Paul raised his free arm in a gesture of requesting silence before speaking.

"Look, stop it Alex." Paul spoke in measured tones. "There's nothing to say. Last week was last week. Understand? History." The grip tightened before release.

"Thanks for that...It means a lot to me...It really does..." Alex's voice was barely audible. Paul nodded his understanding, it was enough.

"Come on, let's get this Shakespeare dude sorted," yelled Paul as he leapt from his stool, much to the relief of Alex. They left the burger bar side by side and there was a little skip in Paul's steps. Crossing the road, they made their way to the river bank. Alex pointed out the Memorial Theatre and Paul gazed at the edifice with silent admiration. Glancing sideways, Paul was aware that Alex was looking at him and he felt himself begin to blush.They progressed on to the Theatre Terrace and Paul astonished an elderly couple sat in the Terrace Cafe when he sucked in his cheeks and hunched his back. The sudden action also astonished Alex who joined Paul in a burst of easy laughter as they sprinted to the end of the terrace. Leaving the terrace they entered a small riverbank park where Paul stopped and without hesitating, as Alex came alongside he flung his arms around him. Alex did not object. but responded by wrapping Paul in his arms. They were blocking the narrow path, much to the annoyance of a middle-aged couple who 'tut-tutted' their way past by stepping on the grass alongside the gravel path.

"Theatricals!" Was the couple's exclaimed response that answered all middle-aged prejudices.

Alex allowed his forehead to brush against Paul's cheek before release.

"Come on! We're going to do some rubbing!"

"What?" exclaimed Paul.

Running through the park they headed for an old Victorian Chapel, now reincarnated as a brass-rubbing centre. Alex explained to Paul that they could choose their brass to rub and all the necessary implements would be provided. Paul chose Henry V111, whilst Alex went for a knight in shining armour. About one hour later the rubbing was complete. With care, Paul added colour to his work. Alex was appreciative of Paul's efforts and the assistant rolled their efforts into tubes. Walking back towards the theatre, Paul clutched his work with pride.

"Thanks Alex. I'll pay you next week."

"No, you won't. You've paid me already with the look on your face. Please accept it as a special gift...a very special gift." As he spoke Alex looked into Paul's entrancing eyes and an ache snatched at his groin.

They made their way to Shakespeare's birthplace, but did not stay long as Paul had caught sight of the open-topped tourist buses.

"Come on, Alex. Let's have a bus ride!"

Boarding the bus, Paul rushed upstairs and sat at the front, making whooping noises as it rolled into motion. Alex lay a restraining hand on Paul. They stayed on the bus for the complete round trip. Ignoring the various drop-off points, Anne Hathaway's and the Arden cottages did not match the attraction for Paul of being able to try and stand up, allowing the force of the wind to put him back in his seat. Another joy was to mimic the droning commentary given for the several-hundredth time by the obviously retired school teacher, much to the pleasure of the increasingly enamoured Alex. For Paul it was the rushing wind, the open air, the freedom, and the one he was with, that excited him.

Returning to Stratford they made a bee-line once more for McDonald's. As Paul devoured his Double Cheeseburger, Alex watched him intently. He could not really believe the exciting spontaneity of the day. Here he was in Stratford with a youth he adored. They were from totally different backgrounds and aspirations. There was no way that Paul would go to university like himself. Watching Paul lick his fingers aroused Alex in a way he could not control. Turning away from Paul he suggested they ought to be heading back to Birmingham. Paul sighed as he responded positively but reluctantly as he did not want this day to end. As they approached Elm Estate he pointed out that his mother would probably not be at home, and that if Alex liked the idea they could pick up some cans of lager from an 'offy' and take them to the flat. Alex did like the idea. At the first opportunity Alex stopped the car and headed for the first 'offy' that came into view. Paul shouted from the car window,

"Bring some smokey bacon crisps and dry roast nuts."

Alex returned to the car with twelve cans, plus four bags of smokey, along with the same number of nuts. While Alex was in the shop Paul had idly opened the glove box and immediately wished he hadn't. Confronting him was a packet of three, with two missing. Paul found himself jealous of someone he probably had never met, unless it was Dale. He hated the idea that Alex had shagged in this car, in the car they had shared a wonderful day. Before he could jump to any more conclusions, Alex returned and they continued on the remainder of their journey. Alex was confused by his own actions. He was now going to spend a Saturday evening supping from lager cans, eating crisps and nuts, no partying, probably watching television. Suddenly, the prospect seemed attractive and his groin twitched in anticipation. As they arrived at the flats it began to rain, making the boys run to the entrance. Much to Paul's surprise, the lift was working. This had to be a lucky omen. Unlike the morning there was no unease between them as they spread themselves on the settee.

"Get your arse off the remote." was the casual comment from Paul as he reached for it behind Alex. Paul searched through the TV channels before settling for a Saturday gameshow. Part of Alex wanted Paul's mother to return but the major part desperately wanted her to still be out. The major part was satisfied. They supped their lager and conversation was easy. Paul explained to Alex how he had never really known his father, and that his mother could never get it right regarding the men in her life. Very quickly Paul was telling the silent but attentive Alex things he had never discussed with anyone else. The evening took on a warm, calm feel as Paul opened up to Alex. He explained that he really wanted to 'get somewhere' in life, but knew it would have to be through some route other than exams. Alex agreed but suggested eventually he could work his way through a college course and catch up on lost time. Paul laughed and told Alex he sounded like his mother. Alex was angry with himself for sounding so patronizing. The evening passed by, they had drunk eight lagers between them, and Paul had also consumed two bags of crisps and a bag of dry roast nuts. Paul glanced up at the cheap wallclock and saw it was nearly 11.30. He immediately regretted the glance. The last thing he wanted to do was for Alex to think he wanted him to go. Alex had seen the glance and checked his own stylish watch.

"Can I ask you a favour? Sunk a few lagers tonight and it might not be a good idea for me to drive home, so can I crash out on here and go in the morning. I really would appreciate it?"

Paul had difficulty in keeping his enthusiasm under control as he tried to reply in an off hand manner.

"Yeah. I think that will be OK."

"Good. Pass me another lager." Paul duly obliged, and took one for himself. As he snapped the ringpull, the lager frothed up and Paul took it in his mouth, allowing the excess to run down his chin. Alex ruffled Paul's hair and met with no resistance. A surge of warm contentment washed through Paul that stirred his young innocence. If only the clock could stop and the moment would last forever. Through the evening Paul had continued to tell Alex about matters he had not breathed a word about to any other living soul. There was no embarrassment and they continued to drink the lager. Alex did not tell Paul any secrets, and this was a fully-conscious decision. He just listened and felt himself once again attracted to this fellow student who he had discovered to be sensitive, caring but insecure and craving his own version of love. Often hurt by those who should have loved him, Paul was reaching out. He related to Alex the time when one of his mother's lovers had beaten him on several occasions with a leather belt. There did not have to a reason, he just did it. Paul was about to take Alex completely into his confidence and tell him that on two occasions he could see the man's cock stretching his trousers as the assault took place. He turned to face Alex and was immediately aware that he had slipped into the protection of sleep. Slowly and carefully Paul stood up and reached out to tenderly touch Alex's face.

"Thanks pal for a wonderful day. You're not such a bastard after all." he quietly whispered as he withdrew his hand. On tiptoe he went into his bedroom and returned with a blanket that he carefully placed across the now deeply asleep Alex. Before he had slipped into the alcohol-induced sleep, Alex had fantasized that Paul was about to push his huge cock inside him. The pain would have been magnificent. Sleep took over all too quickly. Paul, in reality, after a quick visit to the bathroom went to his own bed, and as his grandmother would say, he was asleep before his head hit the pillow.

Earlier in the evening Dale had made his fifth attempt to contact Alex on his mobile phone. On each occasion an electronic voice informed him that the phone was switched off, and that he should try again later. How much later, thought Dale as he wondered what the hell the shit was up to. Alex always had his phone switched on so he could pose with it. After all, all he wanted to do was to tell him about the party. Useful for a lift. No need to sleep with him. No, draw the line at that. Still no reply. Go by bus. Dale was still feeling bitter about Alex calling out Paul's name as they were climaxing. But on reflection perhaps it wasn't that bad. Of course it was and he hated Alex for it. Dale could feel the hate and anger twisting and gouging away inside him. He would show him. Alex couldn't treat him like that and expect him to get away with it. He would go to the party and find some easy lay and screw the night and his

David Keane

cares away.

Samantha made a bee-line for him as soon as he arrived. He didn't want the amphetamines that Samantha had brought, but what the hell. As Alex was falling asleep on the settee, Dale was trying to get a hard-on to do the business with Samantha. Eventually he succeeded and thrust forcefully into the tight hole. His teeth bit into her neck as he shot into her. Samantha tried to push him away but he realised too late that he was coming. The orgasm had been swift, brief and not particularly satisfying. Dale withdrew from Samantha's tightness and rolled onto his back across Clara's parents bed.

"Sorry," Dale gasped as he tried to regain control of his breathing. He had promised Samantha that he would pull out before shooting as neither had a condom. There had been no foreplay, no tenderness, just a fuck.

"You bastard!" was the only response he got, as he muttered his apologies once more. He really had intended to withdraw but the tightness of Samantha had gripped him and his climax had taken him by surprise. Stupid bitch he thought. She should be on the pill, the number of times she spreads her legs. Anyway, it was not much better than a wank. Neither had been naked, just removed or lifted enough to do it. Dale returned to the party leaving Samantha wiping herself with tissues by the handful. As he left the bedroom he bumped into Chris.

"Get yourself in there for a quick shag." Chris was standing talking to Gordon, who peered round Dale as though trying to see through the closing door.

"Go on, get yourselves in there. One can shag her and the other could choke her with a good cock. Perhaps a great big black one !"

Both boys stood in open-mouthed silence as Dale lurched downstairs, just as a tearful Samantha rushed from the bedroom in the direction of the bathroom. Chris and Gordon burst out laughing as Tony joined them at the top of the stairs.

"What's funny?"

More laughter but less controlled than before.

It was six o'clock when Alex woke with a stiff neck. Stretching carefully he gradually remembered where he was. Alex wondered where the blanket had come from and realised his reason for waking had been his desperate need to visit the bathroom. On his return he hesitated outside the door to what he correctly assumed was Paul's bedroom. The silence was deafening. Cautiously he opened the door to reveal in the early morning light the sleeping figure of Paul. His lower body was covered by a duvet, but his upper torso was naked. Paul's head was resting on his upraised left arm. Alex was surprised by the amount of moist black underarm hair. The smoothness of the skin on his gently heaving chest caught his eye. He wanted so much to pull off the duvet to see if he was totally naked.Why had the events at Skipton taken place messing up everything, before anything had even happened?

Alex was unaware how long he had been standing there before Paul began to stir. Slowly stretching each arm in turn he became aware of a presence in the room. Before he spoke, Paul, To Alex's disappointment, pulled the duvet up to cover his body.

"What time is it?"

"About six." answered Alex.

"Well, don't just stand there – you make the place look untidy." replied Paul as he turned the duvet down to reveal a naked left side. Alex removed his shirt but paused to wait for a reaction, before undressing further. The answer was an encouraging smile. Trousers removed, Alex checked the smile once more before dropping his boxer shorts and stepping out of them onto the hessian mat. Without further hesitation Alex slipped into bed alongside the clearly excited Paul.

"This time is because I really want to," then his arms engulfed a slightly startled but expectant Alex. Searching lips began to smother Paul, starting with his forehead and across his eyes to his ears. Alex's tongue forced its way into each ear before lobes were sucked and nearly swallowed by the now fiercely excited prefect. Paul whimpered as lips found his mouth and fingers probed his inner thigh before moving to his moist hole. Alex's tongue was violating Paul's mouth as a finger entered him, probing deep inside and his mind screamed with desire as his body arched to accept more. A hand grabbed his hardness and just three pulls later spunk cascaded from him and he let out the cry of a hunted animal. Paul's spunk hit Alex across his stomach and some lay on the duvet. Paul breathed in rapid desperate gasps as a second orgasm took them both by surprise, but Alex was quick enough to take Paul in his mouth and enjoy the final spurts. They lay in silence for several minutes on the bed. Alex continued gently sucking and licking Paul's cock as it regained hardness.

"I don't usually come that quick" Paul informed the still licking, sucking Alex.

Alex raised his head.

"Oh, you've done this sort of thing before have you?" jested Alex.

"Yeah of course," said Paul and he immediately regretted the needless, unfounded boasting. Alex just smiled and did not believe a word. Paul drifted back into a contented sleep and Alex became aware of a clammy stickiness on his hand. He smeared some of the mess onto his thick seven inches before thrusting his fingers into his mouth, reminiscent of Paul in the burger bar. With this thought in mind, a few urgent pulls and it was over. A body-convulsing climax followed as cum arched through the air to fall on his already spunk-smeared stomach. Two juices mingling as one. When the convulsions had subsided, Alex thought to himself that Paul was not the only one shooting rapidly today.

Tony and Chris enjoyed the party, especially the performance of Dale and Samantha. Enough there to gossip about for ages. A good laugh, even if everybody knows she's a whore. No time for oil. Just a quick 69 and sleep for the two lads. It had been a long night.

Upon his return downstairs, Dale had to answer several persistent and annoying questions regarding Alex's whereabouts. He explained he didn't know where he was and just managed to prevent himself from adding that he didn't care either. In the crowded party he managed to avoid Samantha and force himself onto a girl, also in the sixth form, called Lynn. She had fancied Dale for some time but suspected he had something going with Alex, so she had not pursued her feelings. Her doubts were confirmed when he failed to rise to the occasion. After several minutes of futile fumbling against the garden shed, she made her apologies and left. Dale decided it was time to leave and without saying goodnight to anyone left and walked home. Once in bed his tool came back to life but was ignored by the desperately lonely, exhausted, and bewildered youth.

"What we doing today?" shouted Paul as he leapt around the bed prodding wildly at Alex. Paul had never been happier and there was still a large chunk of Sunday left. Please mum don't come back until later, much later, were the words dominating his thoughts. Alex flung the duvet from the bed in an exaggerated gesture. What Paul could see told him exactly what they would be doing for most of the day.

Soon after ten o'clock, Dale was disturbed by his sister playing her latest CD. He decided he would try and raise Alex once more on his mobile. Alex's mum had insisted she set him up with the phone in case he had an emergency in the car. He was delighted to be given the phone as it boosted his street cred. Dale persuaded his sister to turn the sound down on the CD player while he tried once more to contact Alex, only to hear that automated message once more. When he telephoned Alex's mother she was surprised to hear Dale asking if Alex was at home as she assumed he was staying overnight with Dale. She promised to ask Alex to ring when he came in. He wanted to get something sorted out before school on Monday. Dale replaced the receiver and verbally abused his sister who ran through to the kitchen to complain to their mother. For the rest of Sunday Dale stayed at home, had a family lunch, and filled the afternoon preparing notes for a history essay. He waited in vain for a phone call.

Chris and Tony irritated Tony's mother as she tried to do the weekly chores. After a sandwich lunch they went to the park for a kick around with their mates. Later they relaxed over a stolen cigarette and chatted about the party. Eventually each returned to their homes to rush through some unfinished coursework and prepare for another tedious week at school.

Paul and Alex eventually left the bedroom at 11o'clock. The morning had been spent drifting in and out of sleep, enjoying tender caresses, and gentle stroking that brought Paul to another explosive climax. He had never known that his body could provide him with so much mind-blowing joy. Paul was beginning to became edgy as he thought his mother could return at any time. He explained his fears to Alex who agreed that all good things come to an end, if only temporarily. Alex showered quickly, returning to the bedroom to dry off. Paul lay naked on the bed observing Alex's firm body, with its little teasing chest hair and the thin line from crutch to navel, plus the darkness on his inner thighs. Alex's flaccid cock swung freely and he gently rubbed his pubic hair dry, before caressing his cock to dryness. Throughout all of this enticing action, Alex was fully aware of his every movement and the effect it was having on Paul's appealing nakedness.

A brunch of toast, beans and egg was eaten in relative silence as each knew they must part soon. Each explored their memories of divine sex; Paul desperately wanted to ask Alex when they could meet again, but was afraid in case he was refused. The impasse was broken by Alex.

"Don't get me wrong, but it might not be a good idea for us to be seen together at school. I hope you can see the sense in that?"

Yes, he could see the sense in that,and now for the big brush-off. Now the goodbye and thank you. Thanks for the blow, but no more if you don't mind as it should not have happened in the first place. Didn't mean anything of course and of course you won't say anything to anyone, will you?

"What you doing Wednesday after school? Monday got to see grandparents and on Tuesday got an athletics meeting after school. So how about Wednesday? You know the video shop near school? Well, meet me in there at say four-thirty and we'll take it from there."

"Oh yes that would be great. I'll be there!" Paul was annoyed with himself for showing so much eagerness. Before he could say anything further Alex kissed him full on the lips and pushed his tongue into an unresisting mouth. The moment lasted just five seconds before Alex broke away and moved to the door.

"See you Wednesday." With that he was gone. Paul suddenly realised that he had not thanked Alex for Stratford or for the weekend.

Paul's mother returned mid-afternoon.

"Been good love?"

"Yes mum....very." Paul allowed himself a small smile of self-satisfaction, and triumph.

Five

Monday mornings were the same for Paul, as for thousands of people around the world. Regardless of colour, age or gender, that sinking feeling grips the gut: it's that morning again. Monday is such a star that songwriters have been stirred to sing its praises, or condemn its existence. For Paul, one Monday, the one after the weekend with Alex, was very different. He couldn't wait to get to school. Just seeing Alex would be enough and he would respect his request that they wait until Wednesday. As he lay in bed it was easy to make these decisions, but would his resolve hold if they met? Paul slid both hands down his body as he stretched his legs. The mist of sleep was being replaced by the clarity of a bright sunlit morning. His hands met an obstruction on their downward journey. Paul gently massaged his cock, appreciating its outline, its hardness and its stickiness. Only then did his mind clear enough to remind him that the drying evidence on his tool needed attention.

Standing in the shower, his mind was reflecting a kaleidoscope of images: the shower at Skipton when he was straddled by Alex, through to the moments of pure ecstasy in his own home. The water gushed over his head and down his firm youthful body. Paul used a shower gel that he brought to full foaming by stepping out of the torrent and massaging it into his pubic hair. The foam increased rapidly and he stroked his hardness gently, along the shaft and then caressing the tenderness of his tip.

Paul was about to discover his own assets and to realise their potential. Stepping back into the caress of warm water, Paul enveloped himself in his own arms, imagining Alex was crushing the breath from his surrendering body. Taking his cock in his left hand he gripped tightly and tugged viciously at its shaft. He was soon rewarded by his shaft throbbing and the heavy spurting from his cock easily matched any amount he had shot before. Paul was impressed with his own performance as he recalled the torrent of spunk he had fired in the previous twenty-four hours. He completed his shower and

David Keane

made sure that no evidence remained of his pleasure. After all he didn't want his mother to know what he was up to. Mothers don't understand these things.

"Come on Paul. What time do you call this? What's kept you? You'll be late for school?"

"No I won't." Paul grabbed a slice of cold burnt toast and stuffed it in his mouth as he picked up his coat and headed directly to the door.

"Bye mum."

"Paul!" yelled his mum, but he probably never heard the final word.

Alex parked the Fiesta in his usual bay and hurried to the Sixth Form Common Room and stood by the window. He was unaware that Dale had moved alongside him as he watched Paul stride along the path.

"Have you fucked him yet?" Dale whispered to Alex, but he was startled.

"Piss off! Don't be so stupid! And don't you ever dare to say that to me or anyone again or I'll...I'll..!"

"Or you'll what?"

Alex moved towards his locker leaving Dale where he was, gazing out of the window in the direction of Paul who was about to enter the main school building, unaware of the spat he had unintentionally caused.

Alex was telling the truth when he told Paul that he would be visiting his grandparents after school. He would only stay for an hour and could easily have seen Paul later. The truth was that he wanted to see Paul, but at the same time he wanted time to clarify his thoughts and feelings. Although attending some of the same lessons and having free time simultaneously, Alex managed to totally ignore Dale, who had kept close and tried to attract his attention. Dale hurt, and he could not conquer the powerful destruction that rejection and humiliation brought.

Alex''s visit to his grandparents went well. They were so proud of him and wished him all the best for the athletics meeting on Tuesday. They had no doubt he would win and were probably right. After cups of tea plus scones, clotted cream and strawberries, Alex told his grandparents that he had an essay to write and they fully understood he had to go. He returned home for a couple of hours. His busy parents did not notice that their son seemed to be distracted and that their questions about school, his grandparents and the weather were answered in a desultory manner. Eventually Alex showered, then dressed in designer jeans and body-hugging black T-shirt, drove into the city, knowing exactly where he was going. For some time he had wanted to visit a particular bar. He had heard about it from a group of Upper Sixth students who for an end-of-term prank earlier in the year had been to the bar to try and make a pick-up. They had been successful in making contact but had not had the courage to leave the bar with their trophies. One boy would have done, but he would not have admitted that to the others.

Alex parked in the multi-storey car park and sat for a few moments before taking the final decision, buying a ticket and heading for the gay bar of his choice. Once more he hesitated outside the bar, carefully checking that there was no one around who he knew, then with a confident, determined stride, he entered the flock-walled bar. A combination of Monday and the comparatively early hour meant that there were few punters in the bar. Nevertheless Alex caused more than a ripple of attention upon entry, and unknowingly stirred a few crotches as he strode to the bar.

"Pinta bitter please."

The barman looked at Alex without speaking for what seemed an age. The reason was that he fancied getting to know this new punter better, and thought this might be a more interesting Monday than usual. Apart from Alex and the barman, the rest of the occupants were middle-aged businessmen in regulation suits, looking to score before returning home to wives, partners or an empty house. The empty house dwellers would stay on longer hoping for some company, those that were married or with partners departed earlier after furtive attempts at finding easily cooperative male company. Later the bar would come alive as the younger, less inhibited men arrived, to do some drinking and partner-hunting before disappearing to a nearby gay club. Although he had been apprehensive before entering the bar, Alex now felt comfortable with his pint, and as he caught the eye of the barman, he was aware of the smile toying at the edges of the man's lips, and his body, that was clearly toned by working-out. Like Alex he was wearing a body-hugging T-shirt proclaiming the power of a particular beer. Tall, blond and clean-shaven, he had crowded a lot of experience into his twenty-two years. Recently separated from his partner of two years, he liked what he saw in front of him. His partner had been his lover and also introduced him to a lifestyle of sex, more sex and money – money from his body, hiring him out to business associates of all ages. Some only wanted to talk, others wanted the works; in him, in them, it was all the same to Andy. The business had been going on for almost all of the two years but had come to an end when he wanted more of the take. He now had enough cash to set up his own pad, select his own clients, work in the bar and meet the guys he would share his body with for free. Two weeks before he had walked out on his middle-aged partner for good after paying the deposit on the small but exclusive city centre flat. Things were looking good and he adored the apparition before him.

"You're new in here? Bit early for anything worthwhile, unless your looking for the older dude."

Alex was shocked by the directness of the barman. He wondered if he looked gay, whatever that was. Although shocked he had to admit to himself that he was looking for sex, looking for a man – any man, just to see what it was like with someone who was experienced. To know if it was only Paul. Yes there had been Dale, but that had run it's course. Although he suspected Dale was in love with him it was time to move on.

"I've just come in for a drink.That's if you don't mind."

"OK, OK, if you say so. Don't get uptight. We get all types in here from leather to glam, get my drift. You're in here for a reason, but that's your business."

"Yes it is."

"Right. The name's Andy. Didn't mean to annoy you, bad for business!"

"Fine. Mine's Alex."

Andy offered his hand which Alex grasped, feeling his firm clasp and noticing the downy fair hair on the well-toned arm. The handshake lingered as Andy deliberately refused to release the still perplexed Alex. Both had experienced a steady hardening as the contact lingered and desire took over from reason. They were disturbed by a 'suit' wanting his glass refreshed and Andy filled the pintpot whilst looking constantly at Alex, who felt his face reddening and his cock straining the designer jeans. Everything was happening too quickly. It had taken Alex a few moments to realise he was being chatted-up by Andy. As this thought sank in, he felt the touch on his leg by the suit. His mind raced and pleaded please don't, but his body did not object.

"Can I refresh your glass?"

"No, I'm OK thanks." As Alex declined the offer the hand moved from his leg and patted his backside and the suit moved smilingly to a table away from the bar. Andy and the suit had exchanged meaningful glances that added to Alex's confusion. Andy silently polished glasses and alternated his looks between Alex and the suit.

"Pays well that one."

"Pardon?"

All this was beyond Alex's comprehension, but he wanted to know more.

"You know exactly what I mean! You don't have to do a lot. Just strip slowly while he wanks himself. Sometimes he likes to be wanked but he doesn't touch you. As soon as he comes it's get dressed and pay time."

Before Alex could respond another suit wanted a drink, and this time there was no touching, except by yearning eyes.

The time taken to pull the pint gave Alex time to gather his thoughts.

"Are you serious?"

"Sure, fifty quid serious. Interested?"

"Maybe, but I think I know someone who may be. He needs the cash. Does age matter?"

"Well yes. That punter likes young cock. That's why he pays well........He's married as well! Tell you what, I'm finished here in half an hour. Hang around and we'll go to my place and I'll fill you in on the details, if you get my drift!"

Alex gulped the last of the pint before pushing his glass forward for a refill.

"Half an hour you say. Can't wait!"

When Dale arrived home from school it was to a mercifully empty house. His sister had stayed at school for school play rehearsals. His father would be trying to financially bail out some floundering company, and his mother would be drinking tea at one of her friends', analysing some poor unfortunate's life, or lack of it. He had never felt such a depth of depression before. Dale decided to give Alex one more chance as he saw it. Try his home first. Dale in his confusion had forgotten that Alex always visited his grandparents on Mondays. In truth, Dale had forgotten it was Monday. Alex's mother pointed out the day and time and she would ask Alex to phone him when he returned.

David Keane

Dale then tried the mobile only to discover it was switched off again. Uncontrolled tears began to seep from his eyes as he drifted upstairs to rid himself of the clothes he had worn to school. After the initial relief of finding the house empty, he now desperately wanted to communicate with another living being. His stripping continued until he was totally naked and free, unleashing the pony-tail in a final act. Lying on his bed he decided he would punish Alex. Hanging from the back of his bedroom door was his dressing gown and attached to it was the cord. Suddenly it was all clear to him, the ultimate punishment for Alex. Reaching across to his bedside cabinet he found a pen, paper and a photograph of a smiling Alex, taken about a year ago. The message he wrote was simple. 'Hope you're satisfied now.' Pausing momentarily he addressed it to Alex and placed it on the bed. Picking up the photo he at last became aware of the erection he had been carrying for several minutes. The left hand began to masturbate him, whilst the right held the photo. It was no good, despite his hardness, the sensations were not there. Slowly he stood up, his tears now dry, his mind made up, he crossed to the dressing gown and as he removed the cord his cock ached and throbbed. From his earlier days in the Scouts he remembered how to make a slip knot and carefully slipped the noose over his head. It tightened easily and comfortably into place. Dale felt such power as he controlled his destiny. A little music would be nice and he selected heavy metal to accompany him on his final defiant journey. Alex would never forget him that was for sure. He made sure the door was shut tight and knelt. Taking up the loose end of the cord he tied it firmly to the door handle. No turning back now and he felt a comforting calm. Slowly he pulled at his cock and unlike a few minutes earlier the sensations were intense. The pulls at his swollen cock increased with intensity, until he saw the wardrobe rail. He stopped, and reached up to untie the cord from the handle. Moving over to the rail he had to reach up to tie it into place and as he did so the noose tightened further around his neck. His cock was about to explode and he saw Alex's photo lying there with the smile mocking him. Suddenly he knew he was about to come. One last look at Alex and his cock fired its juice across the room as Dale flung himself to the floor and the cord ripped into his neck. Orgasm and darkness arrived together as Alex, just a few miles away in the city centre, was asking for his second pint.

Samantha had missed school that Monday. Afraid of what the consequences of Saturday night could be, she had told her mother that she had a
headache and stayed in bed. Her mother set off to work after being convinced
that Samantha would be fine on her own. The day progressed but no phone
call from Clara. This both disappointed and surprised Samantha. After all
Clara was supposed to be her best friend and surely she wondered why her
best friend was not in school. If it had been the other way round she would
have phoned, she would have cared. As the morning progressed Samantha
managed to plunge herself into a deep depression. She showered hating her
body, her dirty defiled body. Over and over again she asked herself why she
had allowed Dale to screw her uncovered. And what was with him on
Saturday? There was something strange about him, not like the other times.
Thinking about Dale she realised she didn't particularly fancy him any more,
although he did have a lovely cock. Yes she liked the cock, but not the guy
attached any more. Yet she'd allowed him to ride bareback. She had always
been so careful, now she would have to wait and hope for the best. Could be
pregnant and what if he'd given her something else? There were those at
school who were jealous of that Alex and tried to spread rumours about him
and Dale. Probably jealous of his car, his brains and his body. After all, Clara
reckoned he was a mind-blowing shag, and he could keep going for ages. To
be on the safe side Samantha decided to have another shower and wrapped
her fingers in a face flannel, before pushing her fingers inside herself in the
mistaken belief this would solve any problems she may have.

The phone eventually rang towards the end of the lunch break. Clara
explained it had been difficult to ring earlier, and anyway why wasn't she in
school. It had been a great party according to Clara. Samantha calmly
explained that she had a headache, and Clara didn't believe a word.
Suddenly Samantha gave up the pretence and told Clara that she had had
unprotected sex with Dale. She was scared out of her mind. Clara told her she
was a stupid bitch, then told her there was probably nothing to worry about,
and that she would come round after school.

Clara kept her promise and by the time Samantha's mother returned from
work, Samantha was feeling more reassured, but not entirely convinced.
Clara stayed until late evening. After tea it took Clara some time to bring

David Keane

Samantha up to date with all the latest news, even though it was only one day at school. By the time Clara left her, Samantha had promised she would be in school on the Tuesday. Before finally going to bed Samantha had another shower.

Andy and Alex left the bar soon after the relief barman had arrived. This was no surprise to the new barman who gave Andy a knowing smile that suggested he thought Andy was well-fixed for the night. Arriving at the small city centre flat, Alex was surprised that it was an apparently exclusive area. It was a flat of contrasts. The walls were white and units black. Several black-framed brightly-coloured prints hung from each wall. Not many, just enough to give that dash of colour, including Van Gogh's Fishing Boats, plus The Yellow House. The whole place had a Mediterreanean style, and style in abundance. Compact, but still seemingly spacious. Alex looked around and realised that the flat with its kitchen, lounge, bathroom and two bedrooms, was surprisingly large and above all comfortable with a masculine feel. Andy read Alex's thoughts and as they sank into the white leather settee, he told Alex that there were ways of earning cash that were extra to pulling pints. Alex wanted to know more but before he could ask, Andy stood up and started to remove his work T-shirt. Slowly he lifted his arms and tugged the body-hugging shirt over his head, revealing a firm, relatively hairless body, apart from moist fair tufts of under arm hair. When Alex realised that Andy was aware he was being watched, Alex began to colour up in embarrassment.

"All this is a bit new to you, isn't it?"

Andy casually loosened the leather belt that held his jeans to his trim waist. Teasingly he flicked the buckle and jeans studs open, but tantalizingly the jeans stayed in place. Throughout Andy was fully aware of his actions and could see the effect they were having. An obvious straining bulge was visible on the outline of Alex's jeans, and he made no attempt to conceal it. Slowly wiping his armpits with his T-shirt, Andy suggested that Alex could get them a can each from the fridge.

"Were you serious about the fifty quid?"

"Well it's not always fifty quid, but if someone is prepared to pay you to come, why not? Never mind how much. Of course if I arranged dates for you, I'd want a cut."

Alex was trying to gather his thoughts. The idea of being paid for sex excited him, despite the fact he didn't really need the money.

"Who said I was interested?"

"Well, that's why you're here isn't it?"

Andy's smile was soothing and disarming. Alex knew why he was there; of course he was interested. He had set out that evening to pick up a man for sex. Just to see if he felt the same as when he was with Paul. He had to know himself better. A total stranger to do the business with, yet he was now confronted with a career opportunity!

"What would I have to do?"

"First you'd have to audition."

"What?"

Andy was not smiling now. He stood in front of Alex with his jeans clearly full. He walked over to his music system and selected a heavy metal rock CD. The music filled the room and assaulted the ears.

"Strip. Nice and slowly."

Alex moved to the room centre and picking up the beat of the music felt for his belt buckle. Just as Andy had done, he loosened the buckle and stud, but added to the performance with gyrating hip movements. Crossing his arms and maintaining the movements he took hold of the bottom of his black T-shirt and raised his arms. With his arms in the air he changed the gyrations to increasing hip thrusts. Tugging the shirt over his head, he felt free and the performance was for himself, not the totally aroused Andy. Alex was unaware that Andy was lying on the leather settee with his left hand thrust inside his jeans from the top.

Alex with his eyes closed was building to a frenzy as he ripped the belt from the holding loops and flung it away. By chance the belt hit Andy across his chest. Andy's hands were now still as he watched transfixed as Alex maintained thrusts and then gyrations as he slowly unzipped. The fall of the jeans bypassed his solidly erect cock that had freed itself through the front of his boxers. Opening his eyes he pulled both jeans and boxers downwards and quickly stepped from them. Trainers were kicked free from sock-free feet and Alex began to stroke his inner thighs to the strong rhythm of the CD.

"Come here!" demanded Andy. As Alex moved to him, Andy stood up and

with urgency stripped his jeans, shorts and trainers from his body with an effi-
ciency that suggested great experience. Andy displayed the biggest cock that
Alex had seen in his young life. The veins stood out on the fair-skinned shaft.
His purple head twitched in anticipation.

"Can you take it?"

Alex looked at the monster of perfection and desperately wanted to say
yes, but the idea also terrified him. Before he could answer, Andy grabbed
Alex's head and pushed him downwards. On his knees Alex was confronted
with a magnificent cock. Andy's hands held the back of Alex's head who
opened his mouth as wide as it would go. He closed his eyes as the purple
head made its way to his lips, then hands forced his head onto the shaft. Alex
reached up and grabbed the shaft to prevent himself from choking and held
it tightly. Andy began to thrust in Alex's fist. Alex held the shaft with one hand,
whilst the other sought Andy's ball bag. His mouth could not take all that was
offered but as he held Andy's balls, Alex could hear above the throbbing
music a moan of pleasure. This pleased him and he teased the offered shaft
with his tongue. Andy suddenly pulled clear and picked up the leather belt that
Alex had cast aside. He gave the belt to Alex and then walked to the doorway
between the living room and kitchen. Andy turned his back on Alex and
reached up to the top of the door frame.

"Punish me. Punish me now!"

Alex did not react immediately.

"Come on. Come on."

Alex stepped towards Andy and could see the clear muscle tones on the
firm body. Wielding the belt he lashed at the white buttocks before him.

"Hit me. Not tickle. Punish me now!

Once more closing his eyes Alex lashed out with power and purpose. The
sound of leather on flesh mingled with a piercing scream from deep within
Andy.

"Yeeeeees! Yeeeeees! Give me more! Three more."

Alex was delighted to oblige and with each lash his own cock jerked and
threatened to spurt. Each time it just held back despite Andy's cries were
deep searing pain. After the third lash Andy turned to face Alex who stood with
the belt hanging loosely by his side. The purple-headed monster mocked him

and Alex knew that his moment had arrived. Without speaking, Andy opened a draw and pulled out a condom and a tube of lubricant. Fear replaced pleasure for Alex as Andy rolled and stretched the rubber over his twitching cock.The rubber just met the tufts of fair hair at the base of the shaft.

"Turn round. Open your legs and bend over." The command was quietly delivered and Alex obeyed. He felt the cold moistness of Andy's fingers teasing his hole. The coldness turned to warm pleasure as the fingers sank in inch by inch. Then the fingers left him as his muscles tried to keep them within.

"Legs wider!" Silently Alex obeyed the command and reached forward to hold onto the dining table and braced himself. He could feel the well-lubricated rubber teasing at his hole and a hand reached under him and sought out his erect left nipple. Alex was distracted as fingernails dug into the brown mound and then searing pain ripped through his body as the rubber-coated purple head forced its way past protesting flesh. Inch by thick inch the serpent moved in him. Alex was aware of Andy, the sweat dripping onto him as he desperately tried to maintain consciousness through the invasion. He opened his legs even wider and another inch was taken. Now Andy was grunting and thrusting, grunting and thrusting, as Alex's pain-racked body gripped the table. Please let it end, please, was Alex's unuttered plea. Without warning Andy pulled himself free of the straining hole and swiftly removed the slime-coated condom. As he did so the relief-ridden Alex slid to the floor.

"Stand up!" Alex did as he was bid. To his surprise Andy went down on him and teased his trembling cock with his tongue. Andy's body was coated with sweat and the aroma aroused Alex and he knew that his body would climax soon. Andy held Alex's pleading cock and slipped it into his mouth as his tongue taunted the head. Alex gushed his juice in rapid spasms down the throat of the ecstatic Andy. They both let out simultaneous cries and as Andy released him, Alex uncontrollably collapsed to the floor, his body spent.

"You'll certainly get the fifty quids! Consider that an audition passed. Initiation complete."

Alex lay quivering on the carpet and his body felt ripped and torn. The area around and in his hole was numb in parts but the numbness elsewhere was being replaced by a throbbing deep ache. He forced himself to sit up and his cock was semi-hard but began to stiffen as he imagined himself and Paul making love and being watched by Andy. He was fully hard again as he imagined Andy having Paul. Swiftly he wrapped his lips around Andy's shaft. Andy held him in place as he fucked his mouth. Pain was still there and it felt as though Andy was going to ram his way through the back of his head. Alex ignored the pain as juice flowed from Andy into his mouth in a seemingly never-ending torrent. He gulped repeatedly and still his mouth seemed full. Andy made cries to his god at the peak of firing, then it was over.

"Switch that bloody music off!" was all Andy could say as Alex lay on his back still swallowing and rolling his tongue around his mouth to ensure every drop was enjoyed. Alex tried to sit up but at first could only get into a crouching position with his head tucked between his arms. As he rested, he felt a toe toying the rim of his fuckhole. It felt as though Andy was still inside him. Andy was standing over him and his manhood was poised for more action. Alex did not normally pray but on this occasion he made an exception. Please, no more. Viciously Andy kicked the cowering figure at his feet onto its back. Alex lay there waiting to be shagged once more and unable to resist.

"Shall I ring a friend to come round. You'd like him, and he'll pay. Because of his job it's difficult for him to find company, if you know what I mean."

"Why?"

"Well his face is rather well-known, and it wouldn't do his macho image a lot of good. He pays very well. Look around you. Most of this has come from him and his friends. You're talented so bloody well use it."

Despite the pain Alex was fascinated, hooked. Anyway the pain was subsiding and his cock twitched at the possibility of someone famous at his beck and call. They couldn't be bigger than Andy, that was impossible, and he had coped with him, if only just.

"How old is he?

"Twenty-two, same as me."

Andy lay on the deep pile carpet beside Alex and whispered a name in his ear.

"Really! Fuck me! Really!"

"Yes and he will!"

Alex was astonished at the name but was suddenly jolted back to reality as Andy posed the question.

"Well?"

"Er, not tonight, You're enough for one night."Alex tried to adopt a jokey tone.

"OK. But when. Make it soon.Think of the cash! My night off is Wednesday so...?"

"I'm seeing my mate Wednesday."

"Great! Bring him along too.You won't regret it."

As he spoke, Andy reached across Alex and lightly stroked the coarse hair around his rapidly stirring cock. Another condom was in Andy's hand and the pain returned to Alex at the thought of being ripped apart once more. Before he spoke he felt the rubber carefully being rolled down his shaft. Andy kissed him for the first time, a fact that astonished him. He had been butt-shagged by a giant, yet their lips met now for the first time. Andy's tongue sought a companion and each tried to swallow each other's spit. Alex's spit still contained traces of Andy. Breaking free, Andy held the tube of lubricant and squeezed a generous amount onto Alex's expectant tool. Lifting his head slightly, Alex watched as a deft finger spread the gel over the latex surface. Andy his preparation complete, straddled Alex and lowered his athletic frame down onto the eager cock, pausing to push his oily fingers in himself. Removing his fingers from his hole, he then supported himself on his shins and hovered temporarily above Alex. Then down he went, and Alex slipped easily into the receptive hole.

"Don't worry, I'll do all the work."

Andy smiled down on him and Alex could clearly see the pleasure etched upon the fair-skinned clean-shaven face hovering above him. Andy moved up and down, his strong well-developed thighs allowing him to thrust powerfully up and down the shaft. Alex saw that Andy's eyes were closed and that his head lolled back as he slid further down Alex. Fingers sought Alex's lips and they parted to receive and suck two probing digits. Andy was now riding fervently and Alex listened to his companion's cries rose to a crescendo. His own cock was now throbbing as his body prepared to climax. Alex reached up and took two light-brown erect nipples in his fingers and squeezed furiously. This brought a scream from Andy followed by a gasp and he fired his load hitting Alex's chin and mouth. Thrusting out his tongue, Alex could taste Andy

David Keane

once more and as he did so his body convulsed upwards in short fast spasms and he filled the condom tip to near bursting point. The throbbing spurting within Andy brought a final flurry from his balls and Alex received the final tasting of the night. Alex felt muscles alternately grip and release his still hard cock. Andy lifted himself from Alex and rolled on his back on the welcoming,soft,deep pile.

"You're quite a boy aren't you," gasped the breathless Andy.

"Do my best." smiled Alex as he rolled the spunk-filled condom clear of his still semi-erect shaft. Andy looked at the wonder before him and leaned across Alex and began to lick the spunk-covered shaft clean of the sticky mess. As he did so, the cock twitched once more and a pea-sized final spurt presented itself out of the tiny slit and was immediately taken by Andy on the tip of his tongue. Giving an acceptable impression of a snake with a fly, the tongue shot back into the mouth.

"Tasty!"

Alex was suddenly jolted by the thought of the athletics meeting tomorrow after school. Running two hundred metres could be interesting but this totally shagged-out body was the thought dominating his mind.

Alex and Andy showered separately. The small shower room was tidy with expensive gold fittings and designer label lotions, creams and soft luxuriant towels. Alex enveloped himself completely in a cream, thick, soft bathtowel. The intense pain in his passage had by now eased to a dull ache. He had achieved what he wanted. To have a man. He had given and received and he wanted more. The pain from Andy's throbbing cock had seared through his body and shattered his mind. All he could see before him was that huge purple head on that long thick shaft. He had adored the wispy bush of pubic hair and he tingled with anticipation of those downy arms holding him, crushing him before that shaft thrust deeper into him next time. Next time. Wednesday. But there was Paul. Had he really loved that lad? Now all he wanted was Andy. What was wrong with him? Was it normal to crave a shaft up him that would tear him, and enjoy the pain that that brought? It was impossible, but his cock was hard again, stimulated by the thoughts racing through his mind. He began to pull his cock gently as it felt a little tender after what it had endured for the past hour. He knew he could come again as his shaft responded by gently throbbing. As he increased the speed of his strokes, the door opened and in struggled a naked Andy, his tool hung low and long from his bush, caressed the inner thigh of his left leg.

"Naughty! Naughty! Naughty boys must be punished." Alex could clearly see Andy's rising expectation.

"No, please not again! Not up me. Save that till next time, please."

Taking yet another condom from the bathroom cabinet he also took a small brown bottle. Unscrewing the top he held the small open top in front of Alex's nostrils. With his free hand he closed Alex's right nostril and gestured for him to breath in. As Alex did so, his mind focused on the object of his desire and so desperately he suddenly wanted the pain. The left nostril was closed and this time he breathed deeply in and allowed the fumes to increase his desire to raging point.

Alex walked from the shower room and lay on the living room carpet, its deep pile warming him and heightening his desire. Andy stood over him furiously smearing the gel onto his fuckpole that was stretching the condom to its limit.

"Bring your legs up as far as you can. You do accept you have to be fucked. Only dirty little boys do what you were doing in the shower. Tell me you agree. Now!"

There was menace in Andy's voice. Alex was a little scared but the feeling of desire overcame all other thoughts.

"I know. I understand. Just do it now."

"Bring your legs higher." Alex responded and he opened his legs wide to receive Andy as he brought them higher. Andy lowered himself into the space offered and guided his cock towards its target. Resting on Alex's arse lips he paused to increase the younger man's desire. He got the response he wanted from dark, deep-set eyes that were pleading for him to penetrate. Slowly at first the huge latex-coated purple head pushed against the wet arse lips which loosened slightly as the head penetrated by an inch and then another. Alex gasped at the moment of penetration and his body convulsed as the aroma from the brown bottle wafted by his nostrils once more. Two more inches slipped down the tunnel. Just another four to go. Suddenly the remaining four inches entered and the fair bush was soon slapping against the dark, soft arse cheeks of the screaming Alex. Andy grabbed a T-shirt and forced it into Alex's open mouth. The pumping continued but Alex was having difficulty breathing and desperately flung his arms around and then clawed at Andy's back. This only heightened Andy's intense pleasure and just as Alex was losing consciousness, Andy's cock exploded in the condom more and more white love juice. When his thrusts and spasms subsided, Andy ripped the shirt from the barely conscious Alex. Huge gasps of air forced their way into Alex's lungs and although he didn't want to go through that again he knew he would. Nothing would keep him from this animal. No matter the cost. Should he offer him Paul? Yes,he would and he would deliver him on Wednesday.

Six

Dale lay on his bedroom floor and there was a slight movement of his naked legs. Reaching up, he grasped the knot in the cord as blood desperately tried to reach his brain and air, his lungs. There was a thumping in his head and violent colours flashed before his eyes. He was alive by virtue of the fact that the wardrobe rail had snapped as he plunged downwards. The horror of the thought he was alive terrified and disappointed him. Death had done him no favours. Rejected by death he knew he must go away for a time. As he removed the cord he thought about trying to complete the job by trying again, but the damage to his bedroom wardrobe would be difficult to repair and if he was to hang he needed to find something strong enough to hold him until the task was complete. No-one had arrived home yet, so he stood up rubbing his aching neck. Looking in the mirror he saw the burn marks of the cord. That settled it. He would pack a few essentials and go. Must leave a note for mum. The strange thing was, although blood had difficulty reaching his head it had no difficulty reaching his cock. He felt a heightened sexual desire, but he had no time to relieve himself. Still naked he sat on the bed, took more paper from the drawer and briefly explained to his mother that he was going away for a few days and not to worry. He needed to sort some things out and would phone in a day or two. Finally he wrote that he loved all his family, even his sister. Dressing quickly he put on a cotton rollneck sweater to conceal the cord burns and the bruising. Packing the smart, multi-pocketed weekend bag he ensured he had a complete change of clothing and toiletries. He packed the cord that he had allowed to slip through his fingers into the bag. Before leaving the house, he hacked away with scissors at his pony-tail. The strands fell into his hands and he stuffed them into a large envelope before stuffing the lot into his bag. When the time was right he would post them to Alex. Cutting his hair had brought back the tears but he soon regained his composure and left the house. Ensuring the door was locked he posted the keys back through the letterbox. He wouldn't need them again. Safely in his pocket was the photograph of Alex and the scribbled note he had written for him. He had left the note for his mother on the kitchen table. Walking briskly away from his home he did not look back. His mother only failed to see him walking along the tree-lined road by a matter of a couple of minutes. Enough time to decide the fate of a family.

Tony's mother found the note almost immediately. On her way in she had picked up the bunch of keys, not realising their significance. Moving into the kitchen, the note beckoned her from its resting place. Frantically she telephoned Alex and of course only got as far as his mother. No, neither boy was there, in fact although she had seen Alex, Dale had not been with him. Alex's mum gave her the number of her son's mobile. Desperately she punched the numbers in and only got the sorry, this phone is switched off message. She did manage to contact her husband on his mobile and he would be home when he could and she was not to worry. Hastily leaving the house, she headed to school, just failing to see Dale as she manouevered the four-wheel drive aggressively up the school drive. If she had taken the slightly longer route she would have seen her shorn son waiting for a bus to take him into the city. Rushing to the school theatre, she located her daughter who had not seen Dale all day. No, he had not told her anything. He wouldn't have, would he? She returned home. Perhaps Dale had done so as well. Disappointed and alone, she awaited the return of her family.

Dale headed by bus for the city centre and then for New Street Station. Before buying a ticket for anywhere he realised the cost of train travel was high, and anyway his family might check the station. Unlikely he would be remembered but he could not be sure. Checking his wallet he had about £15 in total. Not a fortune to start a new life with. Crossing to the bus station he chose the Solihull route. From Solihull he headed towards the M42, thumbing as he went. A car stopped fairly quickly and gave him a lift to the M42 junction as the driver was heading to Knowle. He asked no questions and Dale offered no information. After all, he wanted to remain low key and not attract attention to himself. This was certainly difficult as his strange hairstyle must eventually provoke comment. He thanked the car driver who sped away. Dale now had to decide on which direction. Nottingham seemed anonymous enough and he thumbed vehicles as he headed for the slip road. Standing at the top of the slip road in fading light his thoughts began to check through his predicament. Alex, he realised, was not the only reason for his desperate actions. His father had always been distant, and his mother shallow. Two years ago his father had expressed his opinion of gays following a TV programme, not a trace of understanding and this was at a time when he was struggling with his sexuality. Dale for sometime had felt an attraction to his fellows. Alex was not the first. In the school shower he had watched fascinated as he noticed the different stages of development his friends were going through. There was one boy who was ahead of everyone else. His black bush surrounded a well-developed cock that stiffened in the warm shower. Dale had watched fascinated as the well-endowed boy brought himself off in front of an audience, in response to the encouraging cheers. On one occasion, Dale noticed one of the PE staff watching the performance from the staff changing room. Later that day he saw the boy and teacher deep in conversation. They parted and the teacher patted the boy. Then there was Alex. He had tried several girls. Yes he could come with them, and he was popular, but he only felt intense desire towards Alex. He had tried to ignore the fact, but over the past week he had accepted that if he was anything, he was gay. Then, as he made love with Alex, he faced the truth, he was gay and he really loved that bastard. Then that boy's name was screamed. Paul. Damn them both. He had used Samantha and Lynn. He knew that now and he bitterly regretted it. His plan had been to tell Alex that he loved him, now he could not even pass the time of day with him. A father he could not approach and a lover lost. Leave it all behind. He had foolishly done the thing with the dressing gown cord. Best forgotten, head away for a few days. Nothing else mattered, not home, not school, just himself. To get himself together he needed to escape. Standing with his thumb thrust out he elicited a response from the driver of a large horsebox. The passenger door opened and Dale stepped up to look directly at the driver.

"Where you heading mate?"

"Harwich."

"That will do me."

A strong hand reached out and pulled Dale and his weekend bag on board. The driver smiled and tapped Dale's leg before he checked his mirrors, put the engine into drive and moved down the slip road and onto the M42. Night fell and so did Dale's defences.

The horsebox swayed and lumbered onto the M42 in the direction of the M1. Dale was surprised by the size of the interior: room enough for three up front, and between the seats there was a gap through which Dale could see a spacious caravan style living area. The driver, once he had built up to his cruising speed, turned to look at Dale. He had strong, heavily-tattooed arms that were fully exposed as he was wearing only a vest on his top half. As he casually turned to face Dale, chest hair brimmed over the singlet front. He was thirtyish and had more hair on his body than on his closely shaved head. His jeans exhibited evidence of the wearer having worked with horses.

"What you running away from?"

"Nothing. What makes you think I'm running away? Can't someone thumb a lift these days without people assuming they're running away?"

"It's just that if I had said I was going to Edinburgh, it seemed to me you would have said that was OK for you."

Dale chose to look out of the passenger window and not answer.

"Fine, so I was right. So what? Hey, what happened to the back of your head? Your hair?"

Still silence as the countryside sped by. Just as Dale was feeling comfortable as the miles sped by, the speed began to drop and the driver indicated to turn off to what was a huge service area. Coming to halt in the lorry park, but putting as much distance as possible between them and the next vehicle, the driver turned to explain his actions.

"I know I've not brought you very far but I do have to stop for several hours' rest, to be legal and safe! So it's up to you but I bet you've no bed lined up for tonight and as you can see there's plenty of room back there."

He turned his head to direct Dale's attention to the living quarters. Suddenly Dale did feel tired and he really had been in such a state, he had given no thought to sleeping. With surprising agility the driver left his seat and leapt into the rear. Dale followed and when he saw the two settees that converted into beds, he gladly accepted the offer.

"If you're sure it's OK, that would be great."

"It's OK if you know how to boil a kettle and make tea."

A smiling Dale moved to the kettle.

Later, when drinking the tea from chipped mugs, Dale relaxed and his eyes became heavy. Making a real effort to stay awake, he asked the driver about the horsebox and his route. He explained to Dale that in the rear there was room for two horses in separate stalls and that his eventual destination was to pick up two horses from a Hungarian stud farm. He may well have told him more but sleep enveloped Dale.

In his dreams he felt his jeans being unbuckled slowly unzipped and a hand reaching inside his shorts. It was OK because his cock was hard and he felt the warmth of a mouth slipping over its head and gentle slow sucking taking place. A hand was running up his inner thigh and his hardness increased. The hand slid down the inside of his jeans and he raised his leg. Another hand was inside his jeans and fingers were prodding his hole. In his dreams he felt a finger making entry and he arched his back to receive more. The finger obliged and slipped in, past the knuckle to its top. The sucking increased in fervour and as teeth sank into his shaft he awoke with a start to see a shaven head devouring his willing cock. His cock may have been willing but the rest of him was not.

"What the fuck do you think you're doing?" yelled Dale as he tried to escape from the teeth of the driver, who tried to push a second finger into him. His arms felt weak as he tried to push the animal from him. He made no impression and he tried to force himself to come so that it would end. Paul must have felt like this in the shower at camp. It was no good, his spunk would not leave him. As he began to despair he tried to relax to see if that would help. Lying back, he felt the teeth dig into his shaft and the head jerk violently up and down. Suddenly the driver stopped, lifted his head and removed his fingers from Dale. He stood up and for the first time Dale realised his assailant was naked, apart from his socks. Dale, perhaps partly through hysteria, began to laugh at the ridiculous sight the man posed. He was silenced as by a heavy slap across his face that knocked his head sideways. At that moment the driver saw the marks on Dale's neck.

"See you like it rough. So take this you little girly tart!"

A relatively short but thick, smelly cock, slapped against his face and at the same time a strong hand grabbed his sore aching neck.

"You pay for your rides around here. There's no such thing as a free ride.Get it?"

Dale got it all right and lay on the settee and opened his mouth. Do as the man says and it will finish. The unpleasant smell from the unclean cock made Dale retch as it entered his mouth. Dale closed his mouth and the man began to fuck. Keeping his head and tongue still, Dale lay there hating his very being. The man began to pump faster and faster. Please come thought Dale. Then the man did, gushing an enormous flow of seemingly never-ending cum. Dale through his lips felt the five great pumping surges fill his mouth and he desperately tried not to swallow. To no avail. The sheer volume and his position overwhelmed him and the juice found its way down his throat as he tried to take in air. The strange thing was, his rapist tasted the same as Alex. With that thought in mind Dale swallowed the remaining spunk. Once the man was off him he would make a run for it. The man couldn't follow as he had no clothes on. Sure enough the man lifted clear and Dale leapt for the door but it was centrally locked.

"Oh you shouldn't have done that. Oh no. Now what are we going to do with you? I might be able to forgive you if you show me your spunk."

Dale was now frightened as the man's eyes stood out in a wild blue anger.

"Take your clothes off. All of them girly boy. Show me the lot." Slowly Dale obliged, aware that his semi-erect cock was already exposed. First he removed the shirt and jacket. then his jeans and shorts, but kept his trainers on.

"Everything I said."

The man was lying on the settee pulling his stumpy tool that seemed to pop out from a dark forest.

Dale did as he was told and stood naked before his tormentor.

"Do it tart!"

Taking his cock in his left hand, much to his relief he soon hardened and pulled with increasing ferocity. This was unreal, inhuman. As he performed, Dale decided he would return home when this was over and beg Alex to take him back. He didn't mind sharing him with Paul. After all, they did share girls. At last the spunk flowed and the gentle ejaculation seemed to please the driver. When the last drop had flowed he walked to the man and spat his spunk-stained spit in his face. The anger overwhelmed the driver who leapt to his feet and grabbed Dale by the throat. The pain of the grasp on his self-induced injuries seared through his brain. He knew he was going to die and the thought he was going to die naked, by the hand of a stranger made him angry that he had failed to kill himself. 'I love you Ale, was his last conscious thought as blackness took over. No more pain as the man shook his now lifeless body over and over again. Eventually the driver stopped shaking the doll-like corpse in his hands and as he let go, the strangled broken-necked body fell to the floor. Dale would never know, but his spinal cord had dislocated and ended his life before strangulation succeeded. The effect was like that of an efficient hanging.

Calmly the driver looked at the corpse at his feet. He knew what to do. Lifting a section of the floor a very useful storage area was revealed. He rolled the body to the edge of the space and then with his foot toppled Dale into the storage chamber and quickly closed the lid and replaced the carpet. The driver talked quietly to himself.

"You boys never learn. All I wanted was a little fun with your beautiful bodies. You had a lovely cock. Now look, you've wasted it. It's all your fault, girly boy. You can be in France with the other one. So there."

Calmly he dressed and checked his hours carefully before resuming his journey to Harwich after a full English breakfast in the service area. No need to worry about the vehicle as he had someone to look after it now.

Dale never knew the name of the man who took his future.

Seven

One good thing about the Skipton camp was how new friendships were forged, and how they often transcended racial barriers. Such was the case with Tony, Chris, Gordon and Shamir. After the fun they had had on the walk back from Skipton to camp, there was bound to be some reaction. Fortunately, no-one was disturbed by the performance of Tony with the eager assistance of Shamir and Gordon, plus the extra-special assistance of Chris. It had been a good laugh but did pose some unanswered questions that whirled through the boys' minds.

Firstly, although he was with them, Paul had maintained his distance, both at the camp and in school. Always a bit of a loner that one, although each boy would have admitted that would have swapped equipment with him. He did spend a lot of time with that Alex, and each boy did wonder about that. Once back at school each got on with their own lives but much to the delight of Gordon and Shamir, they were acknowledged by Tony and Chris. Previously Shamir and Gordon had kept within their own racial friendship groups, and to some extent that remained the same after the camp, but time was spent in each other's company. That Monday was to be one such occasion.

They met prearranged in the kiddies' play area and were the only ones around. Tony was trying, without success to make the swing he was on swing over the top. Despite his claims, no-one had succeeded in completing the circle, but it made a good story for Shamir who pretended to believe the exaggerated claims. It was a calm, pleasantly warm evening and Tony explained the wind conditions were not quite right so they squeezed together on a graffiti-etched park bench. Tony had assumed the position of group leader and they'd waited expectantly for him to announce what they would be up to that evening.

"Who's flashing the ash then?" As the group leader it was natural for him to expect gang members would provide the smokes. Reluctantly Gordon produced from his jeans pocket a slightly crumpled pack of twenty.

"Great!" Tony snatched the pack from Gordon and offered the pack to each boy in turn. That is, with the exception of Tony who took three, much to the unexpressed annoyance of Gordon, before returning the rapidly emptying pack. Tony did pull from his pocket a disposable lighter and with a flourish offered to light his friends' cigarettes. When lighting his own, he inhaled deeply to show maturity and immediately convulsed into a coughing fit. His three companions laughed inwardly but maintained dead straight faces, so as not to annoy their leader. Tony regained his composure.

"Next time you nick some fags, nick some decent ones!"

"I bought those!" protested Gordon.

The four sat in a line with their regulation baseball caps reversed. Three different cultural backgrounds; one position for baseball caps. They spent a long time discussing the party, and each had heard incredible stories about what happened, who did what to whom and with what. Surprisingly, of the group only Shamir was not there on Saturday. Most of the party's events had escaped their notice, except those involving Samantha and Dale. The evening drifted on and they stayed on the bench until nightfall, when Tony made his announcement.

"I'm going home for a wank. Anyone coming?" Gales of laughter greeted the weak pun, which Shamir thought very clever.

"Seriously. I am."

"You could do it here, like in that field." suggested Shamir.

"I don't think so my little curry paste, not with all these flats above us. You can, if you like!"

"Perhaps not," giggled Shamir.

Nothing more was said and with his little troop of followers, Tony headed home. His father was on nights at the car component factory, and his mum at her sister's. Once inside the flat, Tony made no attempt to carry out his exhibition, until Chris rubbed his hand against Tony's crutch and felt a response. Tony stepped back and knocked Chris's hand away.

"I reckon one of these two," nodding in the direction of Gordon and Shamir, "should do it."

"Not me!" yelled Gordon, "I had one before I came out!"

David Keane

Shamir looked from one expectant face to another. All gave the same unspoken answer. He also wanted to be part of the group and this felt like an initiation ceremony. His left hand moved towards his zip, and as he walked towards the bedroom his audience parted before him. Shamir hesitated in the doorway but received an encouraging push from Tony. Once in the bedroom, the door was closed and the trio stood against it as Tony nodded towards Shamir's crutch, as though in instruction for him to get on with it. There was silence as Shamir dropped his jeans and briefs before lying on the bed. Gingerly he reached for his semi erect cock and slowly started to pull. As he did so, the audience moved forward as one to take a close look at the rapidly hardening brown shaft. A trim tight sack with wisps of black hair hung from five inches of smooth, brown, excited cock with a small black bush.

"What colour's your come then?" was the blunt question from Chris. Before Shamir could answer he was rapidly becoming aware that what he was doing was fun. Then they all heard a key entering the flat's door. Shamir leapt from the bed pulling his briefs and jeans up in one movement. It felt as though his tool was snapped from his body as it slapped back against his hairless stomach.

"Hi Mum! We're in here!"

She made no attempt to enter Tony's territory, which was exactly what he expected would happen. The others were not party to this information and scrambled around guiltily, especially the terrified Shamir. Leaving the bedroom, Tony explained they were looking for an overdue video to return to the shop. Each made their excuses to leave and did so, all within three minutes of Tony's mum's arrival. His mum was too busy to notice as she was trying to digest the fact that her sister had just confided in her that she was having an affair and didn't give a damn!

Eight

Dale's mother by the time her husband arrived home was approaching hysteria. Sandy, her daughter had not been able to add anything further and Alex's mother had promised twice to get Alex to phone when he came home. Dale's father became concerned when he saw the note and he could not understand the damage to the wardrobe. It was clear some clothes and his weekend bag had gone, but not best trainers, so he would be back. Seeking to reassure his wife, but not entirely convincing himself he suggested it was one of those teenage things. No it would not be a good idea to involve the Police, as he had clearly left the house voluntarily. Perhaps Alex would be able to help. Alex did phone and he had no idea where Dale could be. He had been out with another friend that they didn't know. Dale had seemed OK at school he lied. Yes if Dale contacted him he would get him to phone and he would also phone them. Not to worry. He'll be back.

A mother's instinct told her that Dale was not all right. In the early hours as she phoned the Police, her son's neck snapped.

The horse box driver returning from his breakfast, checked the storage compartment. It was as though he was checking, just in case what his memory told him had not happened. There lay this naked youth without a name. Pale, cold almost transparent flesh, apart from the bruised throat and neck. Silly boy, he should not have done what he did. If only he had done just as he was asked and not done that silly spitting business he would have been OK. Youngsters of today have no respect. The driver was annoyed with Dale for causing him this problem. The maddening thing was that he was not the first. Even more annoying was that he gave a good suck, thought the driver. So take him to the other one that struggled in France. That one did most of the things asked but made that dreadful noise when he tried to enter him. The nasty youth had hit him

David Keane

hard as he fought him off, and he was not having that. That first one took longer to die. He had his hands around his throat but he still kept kicking and lashing out. Then he just stopped, as though he had learnt his lesson. Left him in a wood on the old road between Calais and Paris. Pity about that one too because he had a nice big juicy cock. He was so ungrateful, because he was going to have a ride deep down into Germany. No respect these youngsters was the constant over riding thought of the driver as he left the service area. Now he was going to do the clever thing he thought. Forget Harwich and head for Dover. Then through Calais and he can leave this youth with the other one. Wonder how he got those first marks on his neck, pondered the driver. His mind drifted back to seeing him in that storage area. Next stop must put his clothes in with him, and that bag. Driving along the M1 after leaving the M42, he thought how peaceful the youth had looked. Bet he was a nice lad really. Should just have more respect.

The Police had been little help to Dale's mother. Surely she was aware that lads his age did this sort of thing, and that it appeared he had left home voluntarily. No, noone fitting Dale's description had been involved in an accident or incident as far as they knew, but she could further check with the hospitals herself if she wished. They would let her know if they got any further information. They assured her he would be home soon. It was happening all the time.

08.30 Dale's mother rang the school and asked to speak to John Anderson. Dale had spoken of this particular teacher and perhaps he would ask Alex and other students if they knew anything. Perhaps they would talk to him. John Anderson duly promised to do all he could and that she was not to worry.

John Anderson approached Alex in the Sixth Form area. Alex was surprised that Dale had not returned home. He promised to have a word with people but was sure that if Dale was planning anything he would have told him. They both agreed to keep enquiries low key as there was no point in alarming people unnecessarily. After all the bugger would be home soon, and all the fuss would have been for nothing and embarrassing. After John Anderson had returned to the staffroom, Alex stood looking out of the common room window. Although he had not said anything he was worried about Dale's mental as well as physical safety. This was totally out of character. His thoughts soon changed as he spotted Paul coming up the drive. Coming along very nicely. Hope Andy and his friend like him. These thoughts only reminded him of that dull ache that still occupied his tunnel. Run it off tonight.

Nine

As Paul wandered up the school drive on Tuesday morning, his mind was already made up. Get through the day as best and as quickly as possible, and although he had not been invited as such, he would go and watch the athletics match after school. Hopefully he would get there before Alex's events.

The day inevitably dragged for Paul, with no great events or achievements to record, but surely as night follows day, 3.45 arrived and away rushed Paul. Making his way out onto the sports field, he discovered that one of the three competing schools was late arriving and that there had been a delayed start to the inter-school event. Then he saw him. Alex was loosening up with his arms outstretched, twisting and turning at the waist. Paul immediately felt a tightening of his chest and slightly restricted breathing. He had thought about this moment all day. He kept a distance between them, but closely observed each movement. Alex's white shorts shimmered in the late afternoon sun, and his blue and white vest clearly exposed his lightly tanned arms. Alex was warming up at the start of the 200 metres and Paul moved around the trackside towards the finishing line. The starter called the runners to their blocks. From a distance, Paul could see Alex go down on his blocks, and as he did so, stretch each leg in turn. With each athlete settled, the starter seemed to keep them waiting an age, before the crack of a pistol brought the small group of spectators to life to cheer on their favourites, sending the sprinters surging around the top bend. Even as they cleared the bend it was unclear to Paul who was leading, as he mentally urged Alex on. All six competitors seemed to be in with a chance. As he peered down the finishing straight, Paul focused upon the clearly swinging cock in Alex's shorts and this transfixed him, so that he was unaware that Alex was run out of it at the last to finish third.

Alex was pleased with his decision to request he be left out of the 100 metres as he told John Anderson he might have a stomach problem, but requested to run just in his favourite event, the 200 metres. Crossing the fin-

ishing line the tight pain in his back passage was quite strong, but as he con-
soled himself over defeat he thought it could have been worse. After crossing
the line, he bent down and put his hands on his knees, his breath coming in
rapid bursts. Standing up he became aware of Paul just a few feet away. Alex,
much to the relief of Paul, smiled.

"What you doing here?"

"Just passing."

"Thought you might have come to see me. Pity, I lost."

"Don't flatter yourself!"

They laughed easily together as Alex removed his spikes and went to a
box on the ground to retrieve his designer trainers.

"Only doing that event, so that's me done for today. Come back into school
with me and I'll get changed and give you a lift. That's if you're ready to go?"

"Maybe," teased Paul.

They walked back into school and headed for the Sixth Form block where
Alex had got changed. He hadn't changed in the PE Block because he didn't
intend to stay for the whole event and the changing rooms would be locked
until the end of the meeting.

The Sixth Form area was deserted when they entered. Alex sensed Paul's
hesitance and as he smiled at him he put his arm around his shoulders.
Immediately Paul felt a stirring between his legs and found it difficult to keep
his excitement under control. Alex stepped aside and as he walked towards
a pile of clothes he did two things that Paul took to mean he would not have
to wait until Wednesday. Firstly Alex dropped the Yale lock and then moved
to close the Venetian blinds.

"Fancy a bit of privacy?"

Alex lifted his vest clear of his head and then removed his trainers and
socks. Paul watched entranced as Alex slowly and teasingly pulled down his
shorts, allowing his cock to spring free over the top. Without a word being
spoken, Paul moved forward. Alex finally removed his shorts and stood totally naked. Still in silence Paul knelt before Alex and leaned forward and began
to lick the rapidly rising cock before him. Quickly the purple head hardened
under Paul's teasing tongue. Alex ran his fingers through Paul's hair before
grasping his head with one hand whilst the other took hold of his cock and

guided it towards Paul's mouth. As Alex was taken, there was a whimper of pleasure issued from deep within Paul. Alex gripped the pleasuring head and began to furiously fuck the offered mouth. Moments later spunk filled Paul's grateful mouth and he eagerly swallowed the juice of the youth he now believed to be his lover. Before he released Alex, he made sure that he had taken every drop. The cock was still firm so he continued to tease and pleasure. The hardness was intense and Alex tugged at Paul's dark hair as he thrust deep into his throat. This was an unexpected pleasure and the better for it. This was not the first time that Alex had been pleasured in the Common Room. On one occasion he had gone all the way with Dale; part of a mutual dare with the door unlocked. Foolishly dangerous, but that helped a massive climax. Today the door was locked but the climax was as good and unbelievably about to be repeated. Briefly Alex wondered where Dale was but his thought processes were disturbed as an index finger surged inside him and he splayed his legs wider to take more.

"More fingers...... More..." gasped Alex and Paul duly obliged with four fingers clasped together. The grateful Alex shot once more into the mouth that had refused to leave him. With knees beginning to sag, Alex stroked Paul's hair lightly and pulled himself from the reluctantly releasing mouth. Paul stood up and fumbled with his zip before pulling it successfully down and tugging free his solid expectant cock.

The size of Paul's dick still astonished Alex. Standing with his firmness fully extended, Paul needed release and looked to Alex for satisfaction. Although tired by all the afternoons exertions, he took Paul in his hands and caressed him to orgasm. Both were astonished by the distance Paul fired. He stood with his legs open wide and Alex's deft fingers worked miracles. Huge globules of spunk were sent soaring through the air before landing in splats on the carpet. Paul took in deep gulps of air.

"Wow!"

"Wow indeed! We both needed that!" replied Alex. The sports captain quickly dressed and with his trainers rubbed the evidence into the carpet.

"Come on, let's go. See you tomorrow, remember, in the video shop. Get restocked for tomorrow and I've got a nice surprise for you. I'm sure you'll love it!"

"What surprise?" asked Paul, now excitedly anticipating Wednesday.

"Wouldn't be a surprise if I told you would it?" teased Alex.

They left the Common Room and Alex gave Paul a lift home. The athletics continued and Paul told Alex a joke about a cucumber and a teacher, but missed a vital piece of information out. The joke became funnier due to Paul's ineptitude and the laughter became easy and personal. Paul promised he would not be late on Wednesday and Alex drove home.

Alex rang Dale's mother immediately he got home and she tearfully told him that there was no news. He then showered and his thoughts drifted in anticipation of the following night's activities. Dale did not figure in those images.

Ten

End of school could not come soon enough on Wednesday for Paul. He had told his mother he was going for tea at a friend's from school who she did not know. He would be staying late, and may even stay overnight. This was enough information for his mother, but if he was going to stay overnight she asked him to telephone. No problem.

Stuffed into his sports bag was a change of clothes for the evening. Even the thought of getting changed in front of Alex excited him. When he walked into the video shop, he was a little disturbed to see that also in there were Tony, Chris, Gordon and Shamir browsing through the video covers in the adult section. At the counter, Barry, the store manager, was thumbing through a girlie mag, indifferent to their activities. Deciding the best way was to be bold and front-out the situation, Paul easily evaded Barry's attention and crossed to the group.

"Won't find good porno on the shelves. You'll have to ask Barry. Got some under the counter," advised Paul.

"I know that," lied Tony. "What you looking for?"

"Oh, something out of the latest releases."

Paul turned as Alex entered the store, and felt himself colouring-up. Alex, by a stroke of good fortune went straight to the new release section, and Paul moved to join him. Alex nodded a greeting and as he reached for a video star-ring Tom Cruise, he whispered to Paul.

"Five minutes. Meet me at the car. It's just along the street to the right." Without replying, Paul selected a video, browsed the cover, and then returned it to the shelf. Still without speaking, he turned and left the store without any good-byes. Alex took the video case to the counter and took Barry from his dreams as he completed the hiring formalities. Under Tony's watchful gaze, Alex left.

"Now, that is interesting." Tony muttered. He moved to the door and just opened it far enough to look down the street. Tony was rewarded by the sight of Paul getting into the Fiesta.

"Well! Well! Well! Guess what I've just seen."

"The Queen doing her shopping?" joked Gordon.

"Almost", was the cryptic comment from the grinning Tony.

"Bit of a treat for you tonight."

"Why, where we going?"

"Well I met someone the other night and he's invited us around tonight to meet a friend of his."

Disappointment swept through Paul at the thought of being with other people. How could he? Paul almost asked to be taken home. He couldn't face the idea of being with friends of Alex. What could they talk about? They would be all A-Level and university, whilst he was GNVQ and not sure where he was heading. He was so sure he would be completely out of his depth. Just as he was turning confused thoughts over in his mind he thought he heard Alex mention a guy called Jeff Manners.

"What's he got to do with it?"

"Aren't you listening? I just told you. He's going to be there. We'll meet him. OK?"

"What, you mean the real one?"

Alex laughed as he replied. "Yes the real one!"

"Right! What we waiting for?"

Jeff Manners was a twenty-two-year-old black Olympic hopeful. A 100 and 200 hundred metre runner who was heavily sponsored by those who expected a good return eventually from their investment. Unfortunately he was out of action for the season due to strained stomach muscles, but still in the public eye through TV appearances on chat shows and advertising sportswear for his main sponsors. A BMW with a sponsor's name on its side had been his most recent acquisition. Now all he needed was his fitness, and this would please the money men, and he could go out and beat the world. He often wondered if the money men would still be as keen if they knew they were investing a fortune in a black gay athlete. They needed him to sell to a vast, young, impressionable market, black or white, straight or gay, but would they draw the line at a black gay icon? Money had probably been the main reason why he stayed in the closet and shared some of his ready cash with Andy for services rendered. Discretion seemed to be best, and safest for the time being. After all, not many twenty-two-year-old black guys from Ladywood would earn in a lifetime what he had earned in the last twelve months. Now injury threatened the future, there was no need to take the added risk of coming out.

As the Fiesta came to a halt outside Alex's house, Paul was still unsure as to whether he was being lied to. Surely not, because what would Alex gain? After all, he would have to produce Jeff Manners, or make face-losing excuses for his non-appearance. Excited at the thought of meeting a famous, if yet to be successful sportsman, Paul still deep down wished he could be alone with Alex for the evening. He came to terms with the situation and reminded himself that there was plenty of time fo that later.

The house was deserted as usual with Alex's parents being at work. Alex gestured for Paul to enter. Paul bowed in an exaggerated manner, revealing his cheeky sense of mocking humour.

"You've not said anything to Tony and his mates have you?" Alex revealed his nervousness by asking the question that had gnawed away at him for the journey from video store to home.

"Don't be fucking stupid!"

"Well, it's just that although we said we wouldn't see each other at school, we did yesterday you know, like people could have seen us leaving the field together, and then there were those goons in the video shop."

"Let them think what they like."

"It's not that easy, Sunshine." But although Paul waited, Alex explained no further.

"Hey, is it right? I heard today that Dale had gone walkabout."

"Yeah, something like that." But again no further explanation.

"Can I get washed and changed somewhere?"

Alex disappointed Paul by suggesting he nipped upstairs to his bedroom, whilst he revealed his cooking skills with beans on toast. Paul longed to strip in front of Alex, but clearly the idea had not occurred to Alex. Perhaps later.

Paul returned refreshed and changed to a blue T-shirt with a big red number five on a white background, and tight, revealing jeans. As Paul ate the beans on toast, Alex went upstairs to prepare for the evening. Stripping off, he wondered what the evening would bring. As he showered he thought that perhaps he should have offered Paul the shower. Too late now. Alex dressed in white body-hugging T-shirt and the usual designer jeans, plus equally expensive trainers.

Paul was a little nervous as they set off in the car for the city centre. By the time they arrived he must have communicated his nervousness to Alex.

"Come on, loosen up. We're going to have fun, even if it kills us!" Paul laughed at Alex's ridiculous remark and felt better for it.

Parking was easy in the private car park and they both made their way towards the flat's entrance. A bit different from his place thought Paul and immediately the nervousness returned. Alex's thoughts went back to Monday night and the excruciating pain that went with it. He also became nervous as he rang the doorbell wondering if Andy would still like him and what would they, Andy and Jeff, make of Paul. Jeff was already in the flat, lounging casually on the white leather settee. Wearing a white sleeveless top that was tight across his well-defined pecs, he remained seated as Andy introduced Alex, and then Alex introduced Paul. Gradually the tension of unfamiliarity disappeared with the opening of lager cans. Paul was transfixed by the black Adonis before him. Jeff was much taller and broader than either Paul or Alex had imagined from brief television glimpses. Sat with his legs open, he clearly had caught Paul's attention who was transfixed now by the very full jeans, presumably the reason why his legs wouldn't close!

The conversation was surprisingly easy among the four, whose commenÙs did not necessarily reveal their thoughts. Each one was imagining one of the group in turn naked and performing ever more outrageous acts together. Casually Andy slotted a video into place and switched on the TV. Alex and Paul focused on the images of male arse-fucking being enacted on the screen, complete with sound effects, groans and flesh slapping against flesh.

"Don't reckon much to the dialogue!" joked Jeff as the two actors parted and went immediately into a 69.

"Don't you know not to speak with your mouth full!" responded Andy. Laughter accompanied the rearrangement of seating. Andy sat next to Jeff, and gestured for the two visitors to leave the dining chairs they rested on to sit on the carpet. Alex moved swiftly to Andy's feet, whilst Paul hesitated a little nervously at the changed circumstances. Jeff raised his left hand and then flicked his fingers indicating to Paul to join Alex on the carpet. He did not need to be asked twice and slipped to the carpet between Jeff's open legs. As Paul settled down, Jeff's warm firm thighs closed slightly in upon him. The smell of denim and the comforting closeness lulled the incredulous teenager into a feeling of total security. He allowed his head to loll backwards onto Jeff's solid crutch as the athlete gently ruffled his hair. No-one at school, in the flats or even the whole estate, would believe that he, Paul, was resting his head on the crutch of the wonderfully charismatic Olympic hopeful, Jeff Manners. How could he expect other people to believe it – he hardly believed it himself.

The images on the screen seduced Paul and he felt a stirring in his groin. Unsure how to react he readjusted his legs to try and disguise the stirring. Conversation had ceased as the athletic activities onscreen fascinated even the most experienced watchers. Paul tilted his head towards Jeff's left thigh and simultaneously felt him move beneath him. Looking upwards, Paul could see that Jeff and Andy were kissing each other with fully opened mouths. Jeff's hands had moved from Paul's head. One was wrapped around Andy and the other explored Andy's inner thigh. Paul sat up and turned to get a better view, astonished by the performance and the participants. His attention was distracted by Alex's wandering hands. He allowed himself to be pulled down fully onto the carpet and he felt Alex tugging at the top of his jeans and belt. Paul assisted the fumbling fingers to release buckle and top stud on the jeans. As he lay there he felt the jeans being tugged open and the zip yielding. Unresisting, he lay on his back as his erect cock was exposed to the eager onlookers. Both Alex and Paul were aware that the activity between Jeff and Andy had ceased. Andy nodded in the direction of Alex who lowered himself and gently licked the firmness of Paul's firm dick. A low moaning soon issued from the writhing Paul as he tried to force himself into the deliberately resistant mouth of Alex. It was Andy who broke the general silence.

"I like it! Would you two be more comfortable in the bedroom?" Before either could answer, they become aware of Jeff hovering above them with a camcorder. The idea of being on video excited Paul and he grabbed Alex's head and as he held him in position he forced his hard cock past lips and teeth to the back of Alex's throat.

"Hope we're getting paid for this!" joked Paul, unaware that the question was music to the ears of Jeff and Andy.

"Sure man, sure!" replied Jeff who kept the cam in position.

Paul astonished the others by exclaiming. "Better get the rest of the kit off then and do it properly." He tapped Alex on his head. Alex released Paul and they both stood up in front of Andy and Jeff who now sat together on the settee. The two teenagers stripped completely and stood awaiting directions from Andy or Jeff.

"Right. Just do what you want and I'll do the rest with this." Jeff held the camcorder in the air and Andy settled himself on the settee. Alex for once was unsure about being videoed and longed for Andy to take part, but he seemed content to be an observer. Paul wrapped his arms around Alex's neck and was clearly going to lead the action. Gripping Alex tightly he kissed him fully on the lips and forced his tongue into Alex. He met a little resistance but Paul was fully charged by the situation and he prevailed. Grasping Alex's cock he furiously wanked him and Alex thought he would come quickly. Suddenly Paul stopped the action and looked Alex in the eye before nodding downwards, clearly indicating what he expected. Keeping his face away from the recorder, Alex duly obliged. Paul stood with his legs apart and guided himself back into Alex's mouth.

"Keep going till you're coming, then pull out and shoot in his face. OK?" suggested Andy, who was now lying on the settee fully absorbed by the performance.

Alex forgot about the video and put all his efforts into pleasuring Paul. The stimulation of the camera gave Paul added impetus. What was happening was not enough for Paul.

"Don't I get a shag then?" he gasped as Alex's teeth gripped him.

"Hold it! Stop!" commanded Jeff. Alex released Paul and Andy threw a condom onto the carpet. It rested there and the two boys hesitated before Paul reached down and picked it up.

"Lube?"

Andy passed a tube to Alex. Carefully taking the condom from the packaging, Paul rolled it down his shaft taking care not to trap any pubes at the base. Alex squeezed the tube of gel onto his fingertips and before lubricating Paul, fingered his own hole, pushing the gel into his now expectant tunnel. Relubricating his fingers, he reached for the latex-covered pole of pleasure, gently ensuring that Paul was fully lubricated and forgetting about the camera, knelt before Andy. He bent over but lifted his head so that his eyes met Andy's. At that moment, Paul moved into position waiting for Jeff to get a good angle before he grasped Alex's arse cheeks. Alex obliged with his left hand as he guided Paul to entry point. Paul thrust forward and Alex gasped as his pleasure began. He liked being entered, he knew that now. Whether it was Paul or Andy it was OK. Slowly at first, Paul thrust into Alex. Andy was excited by the scene and Jeff continued to capture all on camera. Paul enjoyed his position of power and dominance over Alex. Paul's pleasure was heightened as Alex sat up with him still inside. The moment was one of tortuous joy. Paul pushed Alex back down and reached around him to take the throbbing cock in his hand. Paul tightened his grip and Alex gasped as the pressure increased. Paul was now forcefully jerking Alex and at the same time thrusting with increasing violence into his fully stretched hole. Alex's come forced its way past Paul's tight grip. Alex screamed with pleasure as he looked directly at Andy. Jeff moved quickly around the gyrating bodies, determined not to miss anything. Paul began a rhythmic rasping sound that seemed to come from the utter depths of his demanding body. At that moment, Jeff focused the cam on Paul's face as his mouth opened to its widest and from the depths there came a shattering yell as Paul emptied himself over and over again into Alex, before collapsing backwards from the tunnel. Paul hung on to the condom as he exited and fell onto his back. Yet another mind-blowing climax. What a month this had been!

Carefully removing the condom and wrapping it in a tissue, Paul felt that he was on a never-ending voyage of discovery. Alex smiled warmly at his appreciative partner.

"You're good.....very good," commented the aching Alex.

"He certainly is!" glowed the obviously excited Jeff.

"Not wishing to sound like an echo, I must say you're really a talent." added Andy not wanting to be left out of the 'Paul Appreciation Society'.

Alex disappeared in the direction of the bathroom and took a shower. Paul joined him and they liberally soaped each other. The soapy water swirled its way down the drain as teenage tongues entwined. Clear water eventually bathed the touching bodies.

When Alex and Paul returned to the lounge, their naked bodies glowing from the effects of the hot shower, they dressed before two sets of admiring eyes.

"Quite a performance," said Jeff as he smiled his admiration in the direction of the still high Paul. The sheer exhilaration of performing before a live audience plus the constantly probing lens had proved to be the ultimate turn-on for him.

"There's more where that came from!" smiled Paul.

"I sure hope there is. Andy said that Alex had told him how good you were, and they were both right."

"What?" asked a surprised Paul.

"Nothing. He's got his lines crossed!" Alex glared at Jeff.

"You mean you guys talked about me before tonight? Did you tell them Alex about raping me with your donkey-dicked friend? Where is he by the way?"

"Look it's not like that," Alex tried to reassure Paul. He explained to Paul how he had met Andy and shared with him the events of Monday night. How the two of them had talked after sex and that Andy had suggested getting to know Jeff. After letting Alex dig what seemed like a bigger hole for himself, Paul held his arms up and gestured him to be silent.

"I couldn't care a shit what arrangements and plotting you lot got up to. It was great! Now tell me about the money!" Paul laughed in their faces and recalled to himself the comments Alex had made the previous weekend about finding different ways of making money. His body could be his fortune. He knew he had the equipment, all he needed was the opportunity, and he could deliver. After all, there must be a good market for a teenage whore. Shagging to order. The idea thrilled him and his groin ached for satisfaction.

"Who's next?" Paul mocked his devotees.

Alex and Paul left the flat soon after they had dressed. Arrangements were made for a Saturday night adventure. As they were about to leave, Jeff pulled out his wallet and removed two twenty-pound notes. He offered one each to

David Keane

Alex and then to Paul. Alex had been silent since the revelations about Monday night. Paul quickly took the note.

"If I'm as good as you say I deserve more!"

Alex reluctantly took the money, but instead of pocketing it he handed it to Paul, who without thinking took it. Pocketing both notes he looked directly at Jeff.

"Make sure the camcorder is like me on Saturday. Fully loaded!"

Alex was clearly disturbed by events.

"What you gonna do with that tape?"

"Oh don't worry about that boys. Personal use only, I assure you," lied the smiling Jeff.

Alex tried to warn Paul on their return journey that they should be careful about what they got involved in. It could be dangerous advised the now clearly concerned Alex. He was no longer calling the shots and he did not like it. The action with Paul had been good, but the idea of the tape scared him. Andy had shown little interest in him all evening and Monday night seemed a distant memory. He had enjoyed the game, but now he was not making the rules. That tape could destroy them all. Somehow he must regain control, but he had no idea how. Paul was still excited all the way home. Forty pounds safely in his back pocket and the promise of more to come. Sex and cash – a great combination. Paul could not see beyond the next twenty-pound note. He gave Alex a quick peck on the cheek and they agreed to meet at 8pm on Friday, to prepare for Saturday. School would never be the same again!

After the departure of Alex and Paul, Andy and Jeff screwed each other with a vengeance. Both of them imagining a certain teenage boy performing all kinds of degrading acts. Each achieved a massive climax, purely through mental, rather than physical stimulation.

Eleven

Tony had spent most of Wednesday evening fighting a losing battle with the finer points of John Steinbeck's 'Of Mice and Men' for his Literature folder. It was not a happy evening. His parents insisted that he complete whatever schoolwork he had to do before going out. He knew they were right, but that didn't make it any better. Although neither his mother or father were actually watching the television; she was reading a women's magazine, he was drifting in and out of sleep, Tony was not permitted to turn the sound down. On his way through to his room he picked up a couple of bananas from the over-flowing fruit bowl. Eating the smaller of the two he sought to come to terms with the demands of his essay. Gazing at the well-formed fruit, an idea began to form in his mind assisted by his hardening cock. After a quick visit to the bathroom, Tony returned clutching a small jar of Vaseline. Tony's bedroom was his own territory, respected by his parents. They would not enter without asking and usually called to him through the closed door, if they wished to communicate important matters such as his meal being on the table. Tony unbelted his jeans and allowed them to drop to the floor. His eyes were fixed on the banana and as he dropped his shorts he felt a trembling in his thighs. Unscrewing the jar top, he cast it aside and dipped his fingers into the cool gel. Picking up the banana he smeared the under-ripe green and yellow skin. Bending over he held the fruit in his left hand and aimed it towards his arsehole, the tip touching his opening as he gently pushed until the point began to slip easily inside. Gaining in confidence, more was pushed in and his arse muscles began to expand and contract in a welcoming gesture to the yellow passion. The fruit was firmly gripped and as he pushed and pulled, his body reacted to the physical sensations as the invasion went deeper. Tony decided to change his position and with the banana still inserted he lay on his bed, bringing up his knees. His cock was hard and throbbing as the fruit was pushed in further. A searing pain ripped through his body and Tony gasped at the agony. What had he done to his innards? He stopped the banana shag

David Keane

but kept it in position. The pain turned to pleasure and he slowly resumed the shag. The banana adapted its shape to ease its way in and Tony held his cock in his right hand as he continued to fruit-shag himself. Gripping his cock with a ferocious tightness, he wanked rapidly and as his eyes misted over he shot his load in three heavy spasms. As he took his hand away from the banana his body ejected it onto his duvet cover. Tony lay on his bed and wondered for a moment or two whether he was mad. Deciding in favour of sanity, he began to ponder what objects he could ask Chris to shove up him in addition to his cock. Pity bananas don't do spunk.

"Tony love, want a cup of tea?"

"Yes, ta mum. I'll come to the kitchen in a minute," replied Tony as he peeled his love banana. His next problem was what to do with the slime-covered skin. Under the bed for now, get rid of it in the morning. Pulling up his shorts and jeans, a sharp pain tore up his back as he took his first step towards the door, snatching his breath. He shuffled into the kitchen.

"What you been up to?"

"Bit of dead-leg mum."

"Good. Got your work done?" asked his mum absently as she passed him a mug of tea.

"I think I've done enough for tonight."

"Nice."

The pain passed and Tony reminded himself to put the used banana skin in his school bag, and dispose of it in a rubbish bin on his way to school the following morning.

Twelve

Alex and Paul saw little of each other for the rest of the week, the main reason being that as soon as school finished on the Thursday, Alex went immediately to Dale's home. Dale's mother had not left the house since his disappearance. Afraid to be away from the telephone in case he phoned, she also had not been sleeping well. Unfortunately for Alex, although she was close to exhaustion, someone had to suffer for the disappearance of her son. After welcoming him in, she accused him of not telling her or anyone the truth regarding Dale's disappearance. Alex must know something. After all he was Dale's best friend. She asked if Dale had got a girl in trouble. These things happen, she said and after all he was a good-looking boy. A fine catch for anyone. Suddenly she realised that she had used the past tense. She flung herself at an astonished Alex and began to beat him with her fists.

"Tell me! Tell me!" she demanded. Alex was out of his depth and he did not know how to respond. He could not tell her they had, as he now realised, been lovers. It hadn't been a game. Dale cared and he, Alex, had been a selfish fool. Some games could be dangerous he now realised, and he could do nothing to help this woman.

"I promise you I don't know where he is. I'd tell you if I did! He told me nothing. Perhaps we were not as close as I thought." Alex felt guilty as he spoke and he remembered the moment he had shouted Paul's name. He could not escape the thought that that moment and Dale's disappearance were connected. Feeling totally inadequate, he looked at the distraught woman before him. He knew he could do no more to help. After promising he would contact her immediately Dale contacted him, he turned to leave and she made the same promise to him.

"Wait!" she called him back.

"He's in a ditch somewhere you know!"

What she said frightened Alex, but what frightened him more was that she spoke to him now with quiet control. It was as though she really knew.

"Don't be silly! He's....."

"He's what?"

"He'll be fine. He'll be back for the weekend."

Dale's mother looked Alex firmly in the eyes.

"You sound like my husband, and I don't believe him either."

Alex shook his bowed head and left, breathing a sigh of relief at his final escape.

"Come on Dale you bastard. Please....Please....Please phone!" A lost and guilty soul muttered to himself as he drove away.

The horsebox driver experienced no problems as he boarded the ferry at Dover. He was driving an empty vehicle and therefore was of no interest to anyone. He had to wait to board and was advised that in future it would be better to book. Otherwise no problems. On arrival he drove away from Calais along the coast road towards the Belgian border. After a short distance he pulled off into a picnic area with toilet facilities. Parked by a water-filled gravel pit he watched from his cab as cars and lorries pulled in and out of the parking bays. Eventually his was the only vehicle in the park. Night was beginning to fall and he moved back into the living quarters of the van. He rolled back the carpet and removed the storage area lid. A pale corpse with open eyes looked up at him. He lifted the dead weight of Dale from his temporary resting place. He knew the task he must perform after nightfall. The gravel pit could have this one and then he could get on with his journey. Wasted enough time on the girly boy already he told himself.

As dawn broke at the water's edge, a pale corpse lay face down in the mud. The sports bag stuffed with clothes was thrown towards the artificial lake's centre. It took an agonising time to sink, but eventually the waters swallowed the discarded bag and garments.

By sunrise, an English registered horsebox was heading toward Brussels on the motorway ring road, with its driver whistling an unidentifiable tune with a care-free air.

Standing close to the phone, Dale's mother was still startled when it began to ring. She told the caller from the police that her son was still missing and that she was certain he had come to harm. It was out of character for him to run away and would be grateful for any help they could give. Yes, she was aware that it seemed Dale had left home voluntarily, and he was over eighteen. As a mother she knew, she just knew he had come to some harm. Whatever his reason for leaving he would have contacted his mother, or his friend Alex. That was if he was able to.

Alex made it clear to the policeman when he called round on the Thursday evening that he didn't know where Dale had gone. He was surprised by his friend's disappearance and could think of no reason why he should run away. They had not had an argument he told the policeman, but if he remembered anything he would let them know. Leaving the house, the policeman was certain that Alex was holding something back. Presumably there was a girl involved somewhere along the way. These kids today had no control over their hormones. One shag after another. The condom revolution. The lucky devils! But where was he? His mother did seem a nice lady and a caring mum. The kid should know better than to upset his mother like this, just because he can't control his balls.

Friday morning near Calais, a local man was out walking his dog at the water's edge furthest from the area containing the facilities. Off its lead, the dog was enjoying his daily bout of sniffing a variety of smells left by fellow canines and various species of wildlife. Suddenly the dog stopped and began to bark. Its owner called the dog to heel but it would not be deflected from calling the attention of the world to what it was standing over. The owner reluctantly moved towards the still barking dog. As he walked, he noticed that it seemed something had been dragged across the ground to the water,s edge.

Thirteen

Alex picked Paul up from outside the flats at 7.45. Friday evening. By coincidence, or perhaps telepathically, both were wearing tight black trousers and white T-shirts. Alex noticed as Paul walked towards the car, how he filled his trousers. That so-attractive front bulge excited him from his first glance. A care-free Paul leapt into the passenger seat.

"Take me away from all this!" commanded Paul with laughter in his voice. He glanced across at Alex and became filled with inner warmth as he thought about what he fully expected would happen to his body later. Not too much later he hoped. That night Paul looked older than his eighteen years. A certain sophistication had emerged that Alex had not seen before. He wasn't sure whether he had changed his hairstyle slightly or whether it was the clothes. The truth was that over the past month experience had taught him a lot.

"Where we going?"

"I don't know. Surprise me... again!" replied Paul.

"OK!" Still unsure where they were heading, Alex drove for about fifteen minutes away from the estate. Then he spotted a pub with a young crowd lounging about outside. He drove onto the carpark.

"We'll try here for starters."

"Oh yeah! And where for finishers?"

"You're in a funny mood tonight." commented a nervous Alex.

"Just happy. Very happy," Paul beamed in reply.

They entered the pub to be met by a wall of sound from a live rock band. Pushing their way to the bar, Alex ordered two pints of lager. The barman, assuming both boys to be over 18, filled two pint glasses with ice-cold liquid. Taking the money offered he then moved on to the next drinker. Moving away from the bar and around the corner, they were lucky to find a spare table. They sat opposite each other with their knees touching. Paul took a long drink and as he replaced his glass on the table let out a deep breath.

"Needed that!"

"So I see," Alex paused before continuing.

"Enjoy Wednesday?"

"Get real! Fucking great so to speak! What about you?"

"Yeah, fine."

"Only fine? You've got to be joking! It was fucking magnificent. You didn't do too bad either!" Paul laughed out long and loud at his joyous memories and failed to notice the stern expression on Alex's face.

Eventually Alex raised his hand to request Paul stop laughing and listen to him.

"Look, yes it was fun, but we need to be careful. I thought shagging for cash would be fun. Once. Just for the sheer stupid hell of it. For cash, and I do like an audience I must admit, but......"

Paul listened carefully to Alex.

"To be absolutely honest I just don't trust those two. I mean why, what are they really up to? I don't need the cash, that's why I let you have it all. Shagging you should be well er special and personal."

"So I became a charity case did I?"

"Don't be daft. I know that Jeff has a lot to lose if anyone found out. So what's the game?"

Paul thought before answering.

"Why should they be playing a game? It really turned me on when Jeff had the camcorder, and I really liked being watched shagging you. A real turn on and get paid for it too! For the, er, personal bit, well tonight we can be as personal as you like because my mum's out all night again. Anyway I've got a twitchy cock!"

Try as he might, Alex could not stop himself laughing.

"How could I resist such an offer?" and he dismissed any worrying thoughts from his mind.

They stayed just long enough to have a second pint. As Paul took his last drop of lager, he leant towards Alex and whispered in his ear.

"I want to fuck you.... now!"

Alex rocked his head back and laughed.

"Could you wait till we get back to your place?" He was in love with this up

David Keane

front guy. Andy was something else. Perhaps, he thought, he was in love with two guys at once. How would Dale fit in when he eventually returned? Sort all that out when it happened.

Alex had to cope with Paul's antics as he drove along. Paul unzipped Alex and pulled his hardening cock free. He went down on the receptive quivering juice-tube, licking the firm and gorgeous purple head. Alex could cope with the situation until they reached a red traffic light. As they came to a halt another car came alongside. The twentyish female passenger was astonished as a head appeared to rise from the car alongside its drivers lap, before plunging down once more. She could see clearly the blushing driver's face. When the lights changed to green, Alex sped away, leaving the other car for dead. It appeared from the rear that the Fiesta, only contained a driver. In fact Paul had gone completely down on Alex, working furiously trying to gratify his lover. The task was not completed by the time they reached the flats. He didn't want to fulfill Alex in the car, but to tease him close to a climax, then pull back. He did this successfully.

"Bastard!" grinned Alex as he zipped up again with difficulty.

Upon entering the flat, they stripped quickly on their way to the bedroom, casting clothes aside as they went. Alex flung himself on the duvet on his back, with his cock standing proud and his hands tucked behind his head.

"Oh no matey! Get yourself ready for fucking. I'm going right up you and you'll scream like fuck."

Alex listened intently to Paul and felt a surge of anticipation seize his balls.

"Back pocket of my trousers," gasped Alex.

Without hesitation and no fumbling, the fingers that were becoming rapidly experienced completed their task and deftly rolled the latex tube down his expectant shaft.

"Doggy! Doggy! Doggy! Here I come!"

Moments later Paul had pushed inside Alex, his pubes resting upon the trembling arse cheeks of the enraptured youth. Slowly at first, then with sudden intensity, Paul pummelled away at Alex's tunnel. The violence of the intrusion tore away at Alex, and Paul's nails dug deep into his flesh. Paul was encouraged by the gasping moans and then the scream as quivering flesh entombed his exploding cock.

Fourteen

A meeting took place during Friday evening between Jeff and Andy. Jeff was full of ideas and was going to make sure the camcorder batteries were fully charged and back up available for Saturday night. Andy could clearly see the excitement felt by Jeff. As they settled down for the night both were in their minds with someone else.

Across town, two teenage boys lay trying to recover from their exertions on the single duvet. Alex was becoming annoyed with the images that were persistently invading his thoughts, images of Dale. Why was he haunting him, and why didn't he phone, or even better, come home? As Alex wrestled with his thoughts, Paul reached for him once more.

"Give me a moment will you?"

"I want you."

Alex was genuinely tired but Dale was not the only subject occupying his thoughts. Saturday night was a subject he must discuss further with Paul. From being a shy participant of only three weeks ago, Paul was becoming the dominant activist.

"Paul? Be careful with Jeff and Andy."

"Why? What do you mean?"

Alex chose his words carefully.

"I'm worried about the tape. What do they want to tape us for and who's seeing it?"

"Does it matter? We get paid... so?"

"I don't like it. I don't mind them watching but I just wish he didn't use the cam. Agreed, it was quite a buzz, especially as he's quite famous. Another thing I can't understand is why Jeff in particular, doesn't seem to worry about being blackmailed. I think he could be dangerous. Where is he leading us?"

Paul responded quickly.

"Don't know and I don't really care. Look I had a fabulous shag with you and got home forty quid better off. Don't knock it. Come here and let me shag you!"

Alex gave in with as much grace as he could muster, because his cock was beginning to stir once more. Any problems regarding Saturday could wait till Saturday. With that thought in mind, Alex took Paul's cock in his mouth and tenderly sucked. Occasionally stopping to lick the dusky boy's deep-purple head, he tasted Paul's pre-come. Releasing the gently throbbing tool, he licked his way up Paul's body, before forcing his tongue past wet lips to the throat of the panting boy.

"On your back you whore!" demanded the totally roused Paul. Alex responded immediately and with rising excitement watched Paul take a second condom from the back pocket of the discarded trousers. The dark shaft gratefully accepted the protection. Alex stroked his latex covered friend and bent to kiss its tip. Paul's cock twitched and the extension that was awaiting his come, flicked from left to right. Alex did as he had been ordered and lay on his back, with his legs wide open, and he brought his knees up as far as they would go. Paul got off the bed and stood with his legs apart at the foot of the bed. Alex looked along his side at Paul. Alex's arse muscles were flexing in anticipation. The waiting was torture.

"Beg for it you bastard! Beg for it!"

Alex's body writhed with excitement. He wanted this stud to dominate him, to punish him over and over again for living..

"Fuck me please.... Fuck me hard.... Hurt me.... Please.... Please!"

Paul silently grinned as he lowered himself into place, allowing his tip to tease and antagonise Alex's hole. Alex could feel his opening flexing violently, pleading, and then Paul entered him. Slowly at first, but increasing in momentum, Paul took his pleasure. When he had entered Alex fully, he stroked his lips and Alex lifted his head slightly trying to coax fingers into his mouth. Eventually Paul granted him his wish. Paul felt he was in control of everything. He knew he would only come when he wanted to. Make Alex wait he thought. As his body began to surge he held back, staying inside, but waiting while his balls calmed, then resuming his task. He could have Alex whenever he wanted, and get paid sometimes, other times for pleasure. Wonder what Jeff's like? Would Alex object if he shagged Jeff? Anyway, he'd been screwed by Andy so he couldn't complain. I think I'll make a career of fucking. No sooner had he had this thought than his balls began to ache as he came with strong gushes into the condom tip. The throbbing was strong enough for even Alex's battle-weary hole to feel, and he murmured appreciatively.

When they had cleaned up, they slipped under the duvet cover and slept in each other's arms. They were still in deep slumber when Paul's mother's boyfriend stuck his head around the door at 8 am. He had come to the flat, let himself in, and followed the instructions he had been given. They were to check if Paul was all right and to let him know that his mother would be back in the evening. Give him some cash to make sure he gets something to eat, and while he's there pick up some clean knickers for her. She stayed in bed at her latest's flat. He'd shagged her a couple of times but the earth certainly had not moved, but he was a bankroll. Decent-sized cock, but why did he have to grunt so much, and he had bad breath too!

The man could see two naked youths in a bed, that by its state of dishevelment suggested more than sleep had taken place. Their arms still protected each other. Paul woke with a start and the man threw a ten-pound note towards the bed.

"Your mother wants you to feed yourself and she'll be back tonight. Suggest your friend has gone by then. Understand?"

Paul understood all right.

"Don't worry. Your secret's safe with me. Oh yes, it's safe with me. I'm sure you'll understand." Paul looked at the man and then realised that his erect cock was visible as the duvet cover had slipped across to Alex's side of the bed. He hastily pulled the cover back. The man smiled and Alex slept on.

"Nice one that. You weren't at the back of the queue when they were giving weapons out, were you?" Paul could feel himself blushing, but he made no reply. The man left and Paul was left wondering what the price of silence would be.

Paul checked carefully that the flat was empty before waking his lover. He decided not to let Alex know about their morning visitor. After all, what Alex didn't know he couldn't worry about. Paul felt certain that if Alex had heard anything he would mention it. Alex appeared to be unperturbed so Paul relaxed and produced his usual breakfast of burnt toast. Sat closely side by side, the two boys munched their way through the burnt offerings and washed it down with the usual cheap instant coffee.

"Fancy Nottingham?" asked Alex.

"Don't think I know him. But if I did I probably would!"

Relieved that Alex seemed to be unaware of the visit, Paul bounced happily into his easy conversational style that characterised his relationship with Alex.

"The serious response is yes and do you mean today?"

"Why not? Feel like doing a bit of spending, and Nottingham is as deserving of my cash as anywhere else."

Paul took the smile away from Alex's face.

"I've got money to spend as well you know."

Alex quickly regained his composure.

"Yes, well, we better get ready and hit the motorway."

Alex raised his hands and Paul responded to the high five gesture.

The journey along the M42 was uneventful and they called in at the large services for more coffee. Strangely, although neither confided in the other, thoughts of Dale occupied both minds. Neither understood why as they resumed their journey, and after a further hour Alex was driving into the Victoria Centre Car Park. It was Paul's first trip to Nottingham and he revelled in browsing the video and CD stores. Alex wanted a casual jacket and checked out the stock in Next. It was not long before Alex decided upon a beige single-breasted jacket. Paul's eyes came out like organ stops as he caught sight of the price tag.

"Better get my cock working again before I can have a nice new beige jacket!"

Despite his best efforts Alex still laughed at Paul's whispered comment.

"Got the jacket, now for the shirt!" Alex looked through the racks of shirts assisted by the increasingly extrovert Paul. Holding up a violently lime-green item, he then made simulated puking gestures, complete with sound effects. Alex prodded Paul in the ribs and through his laughter motioned for him to calm down. Eventually Alex settled for a bright yellow shirt that evoked only mild puking gestures from Paul. They left the shop and the centre, with Paul twirling the large plastic, store carrier bag. They headed towards the Old Market Square and Alex pointed out the two large stone lions that guarded the

Council House.

"See those lions. Well, they reckon that when a virgin walks by they roar. And guess what? They've never made a sound!"

Momentarily Paul was duped by Alex's mock seriousness.

"Aw, piss off will you! You had me going then!" Paul laughed and they headed up towards the Castle. They sat outside the Castle grounds drinking from two cans of coke and eating two packs of cheese sandwiches purchased from the Castle kiosk. It was a pleasant English summer,s day. The sort of day that most people regard as typically English, but in reality only occasionally occurs. Paul was still quietly chuckling to himself when he surprised Alex.

"Ever had a girl, I mean honestly really done it?"

Alex hesitated before replying and looked directly at Paul, trying to gauge what hidden agenda there may be behind the question.

"Yes," Alex firmly, but quietly answered.

"What's it like? I don't think I fancy it myself. You see I've never done it. I've had my chances, don't get me wrong, but I don't really fancy it." Paul spoke looking out over Nottingham, not at Alex.

"Well that might answer a few things. Just be yourself and be happy. But don't mistake sex for love. They are not the same."

Paul was not sure what Alex was getting at.

"Do you mean we just have sex? We never make love?"

Alex stood up.

"Come on. Ignore my ramblings. Let's find the river."

Alex pinched Paul's cheek and stepped away.

"Why, have they lost it?"

"Come on lover! Let's go!"

The walk to the river was further than they imagined, but eventually they reached Trent Bridge and stood at its centre with the floodlights of Notts County Football Club visible to their left and the modern stadium of Forest on the right. Paul looked in the direction of the Forest stadium.

"They have these big baths there, you know. Wonder what goes on in them after a game. All the players in there together. Bet there's been some great cocks in there, and some great shags if the truth be known. See how they kiss each other when they score so to speak. Tongues I bet!" Alex smiled and thought that Paul just might like to take his chance in the big bath.

They made their way back to the city centre by bus.

"Hey, you've not spent any of your ill-gotten gains after all."

"No, it's difficult. You see I can't spend it on clothes or CD's because my mum would notice sometime and want to know where I got them from. Can't really tell her, 'it's all right mother, I shag this gorgeous guy while this Olympic athlete gets it on his camcorder.' "

"Yes, I see your point! We'll have to think of something."

On the journey back to Birmingham, Paul asked Alex what he thought Jeff might ask them to do that night and how much he would pay. Alex managed to change the subject and avoid giving an answer. The question began a stirring deep in Paul. They stopped on the return once more at the services. In the self-service café, they both helped themselves to the all-day breakfast.

"Should keep me going well into the night", Paul sniggered. The huge platefull was washed down with liberal helpings of iced cola, and as they left the building Paul tapped his tight flat stomach.

"That was brill. Thanks."

When they reached the car, Paul hesitated as Alex unlocked the door.

"Let's park over there."

Paul gestured to the area well away from the main building where few vehicles were parked in the huge open expanse. Alex did not reply, but once they were in the car did exactly as was asked and drove to the furthest private section. As Alex drove, Paul unzipped his own trousers and pulled his cock free of his shorts. Pulling the handbrake firmly on, Alex gazed down at Paul's hardening cock. Paul was tenderly stroking his shaft and head. No words were spoken as Alex went down on Paul, his teeth nipping the tender head. This brought a little gasp from Paul who looked down at Alex. He watched Alex as he tormented his shaft. Occasionally Alex's face bulged as Paul's tip pushed against the inner cheek. Watching Alex work on his cock and holding him in place was fascinating. Paul stroked his own pubes and then pulled his T-shirt up his body. Alex lunged upwards and bit Paul's nipples, alternating rapidly. Fingers probed Paul's hole and he lifted himself up just enough for them to drive up. Moans of ecstasy filled the shaking Fiesta. Alex went down on Paul just in time to receive his pulsating spurt as it shot into his mouth. With his fingers still in place, Alex left Paul's cock and kissed him passionately and with his tongue transfered the hot spunk into Paul's mouth. For the first time he tasted his own spunk and his cock spurted once more, splashing onto the inside of his dropped shorts. Alex broke free.

"Christ! I've come in my pants!" Alex yelled.

"Never mind! Home James and don't spare the horses!"

Fifteen

Jeff arrived at Andy's flat just after 6 o'clock. Once inside he kissed Andy on the cheek before helping himself to a can of lager from the fridge.

"What time are the lover boys arriving?"

Andy took a can. "About 8, I think."

"Good. I think if we're going to get good value in the long run, we should take it slowly with them. Agreed?"

Andy walked through to the living area and Jeff followed.

"You're probably right. You fancy Paul don't you?"

Jeff smiled and sat on the white settee.

"What on earth gives you that idea?" he grinned at Andy.

"You be careful. He could talk. Or get a taste for blackmail."

Jeff took a long pull from his can, and took on a thoughtful look.

"I know you're right, but I do want him. You had Alex didn't you? I am pre-pared to take the risk with Paul. I just know he'll keep schtum. He'd better. But for fuck's sake I think he's totally gorgeous, and so does my cock!"

Andy laughed as he sat next to Jeff..

"Well, put like that, there's not a lot more to be said. But are you having him for yourself, or is it business? He could earn a packet with that packet, so to speak. So make your mind up, but don't mix business with pleasure."

Jeff returned to his thoughtful look in silence.

A brief news item on regional French radio announced that an unidentified body of a youth had been found by a man out walking his dog early in the morning. Foul play was suspected.

Before going to Andy's flat, the boys went to Alex's house for him to change his be-spunked underwear. Alex took the chance to talk to Paul about the situation with Andy and Jeff.

"Promise me when we go to Andy's you don't do anything stupid."

"Such as?"

"Oh, I don't know. It's just that seriously I don't trust Jeff. I can't get it out of my head. If the video stuff is just for them, OK. But what if it isn't?"

Paul looked thoughtfully at Alex. Then slowly and deliberately replied.

"I want the money. So if you don't want to be in the scam that's up to you. But when I'm with you it's special. I know their game. I'm not stupid. If he wants a vid of me cuming, well he can have one. Anything more with anyone else is another matter. If we stick together we'll be OK."

Alex kissed Paul on the forehead and seemed happy with the idea of compromise.

"If that's what you want and that's as far as it goes, well I think I can live with that. If there are any vids to be made can I be there to try and make sure you're not forced to do anything you don't want?"

"I wouldn't have it any other way."

Although not totally convinced, Alex was happier about the arrangement. After all when he went off to university it would all be part of history, and Paul would do it whether he was there or not. At least this way he had some semblance of control. Another kiss but this time on the lips.

"I love you and I don't want you hurt."

"Don't confuse love and sex remember."

There was a slightly mocking tone to Paul's voice which Alex did not like. Would he ever know this sod, he thought as they set off for the city centre flat.

Waiting for the arrival of the boys became a clock-watching exercise for Andy and Jeff. Neither would have admitted to the other that they were waiting with rising expectation.

"I've got the cottage from next weekend for two weeks remember. How about having the lads over for a long weekend?" Jeff questioned Andy to test his reaction.

"By the lads I presume you mean Alex and Paul?" Jeff nodded in assent.

The doorbell rang to disturb their erotic thoughts. Andy operated the automatic system that unlocked the outer door. Within a few moments of expectation there was a light tapping on the flat door. Andy welcomed the two boys.

For the entire evening, Alex and Paul waited for the come-on from Andy or Jeff. The fact that it never came as such confused Alex, but pleased Paul because it showed he believed that there was nothing to be afraid of from the

David Keane

two guys. It was flattering for Paul to think that a famous, well, nearly famous athlete could spend an evening with him. When Jeff mentioned a weekend walking in Derbyshire it seemed wonderful to Paul. They ˜ere to meet at 7 o'clock next Friday. No problem.

The foursome discussed athletics and Jeff explained the difficulties of working up the ladder of success. No drugs; he was clean. Alex, shyly under prompting from Paul, told Jeff he ran the two short sprints. Alex overcame his feelings of embarrassment by prodding Paul in the ribs and telling him to shut up. Paul lay full-length on the carpet, fully aware he was teasing Jeff. His flirting annoyed Alex, but he made no comment, just glared at Paul occasionally. They drank a few cans, with Alex promising to phone Andy later in the week to confirm the arrangements for the weekend. The boys left at about 10.30.

"Well, was it worth taking a night off?" Jeff asked when Alex and Paul had gone home.

"Probably," was the non-committal answer.

"A fucking good investment there! And no, I'm not going to mix business with pleasure. Buy plenty of condoms and gel this week and we'll fuck till it drops off next weekend. Did you see that horny bastard? He wanted it. Boy was he asking for it tonight? A weekends training and we've got a fresh gold-mine. You just keep Alex sweet, and no problem. I'll teach the other tart all I know! Can't wait! Come on, let's go to bed."

Andy grinned his response and led the way. One hour later when exhaustion took over they slept.

"Told you cleverdick, nothing to worry about!"

Paul teased Alex. He had explained to Alex earlier in the day that his mother was expected back for the night, probably with boyfriend, so they could not spend the night together. Alex understood and they made arrangements to meet on Tuesday to sort out any details for the weekend. A quick goodnight kiss and Paul stepped from the car outside the entrance to the flats.

"See ya," and with that Alex was gone. Paul let himself into the flat to be confronted with his mother and her boyfriend laying on the settee.

"Had a nice time luv?"

"Yes thanks mum. Goodnight."

With that he disappeared into the bathroom, and then to bed, for, he hoped, an undisturbed night's sleep. He was knackered.

Paul felt he was experiencing a weird dream. He jolted awake and then quickly realised he was not dreaming. From a source near his face there was the odour of bad breath. Hands were toying with his hard cock. Paul reached for the switch on the bedside lamp, but a hand knocked his arm back down.

"Oh you've decided to wake up have you?"

Paul lay there horrified at what was happening. He was no longer in control. The bad breath came closer as the man kissed Paul's neck and a hand forced its way between his legs and fingers tried to enter him. Instinctively Paul closed his legs and tried to move away from the bad breath.

"Come on Paul!"

Paul tore himself free and got out of the bed.

"Get out you shitbag!"

"Now, now keep calm. You'll wake your mother!"

"Good! Then you can explain to her why you're in here!"

The man got out of bed and without speaking left Paul's room.

According to the French regional radio, police had been unable to identify the body of a young man found near Calais. Their enquiries would be extended to Belgium and England.

Paul was woken by the sound of his mother's voice in the kitchen.

"Go and wake Paul will you love? Tell him breakfast's nearly ready."

The bedroom door opened and in came the man.

"Go away! I heard mum."

'Bad Breath' came up to the bed and leant over Paul with his hand under his pillow.

"Not a word. Now get up!"

"Fuck off. I might just tell on you... you old perve!"

The man did not respond, he just turned and as he left the room, turned once more towards Paul and looked long and hard at him with silent threat. Paul went towards the bathroom and saw just outside his door a small wallet, which he picked up. He returned from the bathroom and dressed fully before going into the kitchen clutching the wallet.

"This yours?"

The man turned to look.

"Why, yes it is. Where did you find it?"

Paul considered his reply.

"Outside my door. You must have dropped it, er, on the way to the bath-room."

The man smiled at him, exposing yellowing teeth.

"Thanks. I'd lose my head if it was loose!"

Paul kissed his mum on the cheek, and reached for the kettle of hot water.

"Oi, you little shit! God he's had twenty-pounds out of here!"

Paul turned, momentarily unsure what was happening. The man lunged at Paul and his mum stepped between them.

"What's this about?"

"Your precious son has had a twenty-pound note out of here!" Paul stood holding the kettle in silence.

"I bet it's in his room. Come on let's take a look shall we?"

"I haven't had any money of yours... ever."

The man marched towards Paul's room and they followed him. Once inside the man pulled the drawers out and turned the contents onto the car-pet.

"Mum, stop him! I haven't done anything!" She remained silent and watched as the man moved to the bed and threw the pillow onto the floor, sending a twenty-pound note floating through the air.

"You thieving bastard!" the man yelled at Paul.

"How could you?" screamed his mother.

Paul was shocked that his mother could even consider believing that man rather than her own son. He knew he must tell her about the night before.

"Mum, I haven't nicked his bloody money! Ask him what he was doing in my bedroom last night? Go on! Ask him!"

"What do you mean?"

Paul took a deep breath and walked out of his room and returned to the kitchen.

"Last night, when I was asleep he came in my room and tried to do things. You know sex stuff."

His mother glared at him and then without warning slapped Paul across the face, first the right cheek, and then with increased ferocity, the left. His head rocked and the pain ripped through his brain.

"Shut up! Don't say such evil things!"

Without a word Paul went to his room, the skin on his face burning, but the pain in his heart the worst he had ever felt. It was completely beyond his understanding that his mother had not believed him, not even listened to what he had to say. Inside his own room he felt protected, safe, even though the room had been tainted.

"Stay there!" screamed his mother, on the verge of hysteria. "Do you hear?"

Paul did not reply as he had nothing to say to her. He looked in the mirror at his reddened cheeks and allowed the tears to flow freely down his boyish face.

An hour passed and his mother returned to the door.

"We're going out now."

No mention of the money, or the abuse. What was this woman all about? She did not believe him. She didn't want to believe him and lose her bankroll with Bad Breath. The hatred he felt tore him apart: total hatred of the woman that had given him life, and was now taking it away. Suddenly his mind was totally clear: he knew exactly what he was to do. Packing a sports bag did not take long when you had little to put in it anyway. He looked around his room and realised he wanted to take very little from this world. Nothing he wanted to remember or treasure. Leaving the flat was not difficult, even though he knew he would never return. Leaving the estate with purpose, he began to work out his route to the motorway and the anonymity of the city. His body disgusted him and he was sure he must have given the man idea he was available. Without seeing anything around him, Paul walked and walked to nowhere.

Dental tests showed the dead youth had probably received treatment from an English dentist. The French authorities had passed on the information to their English counterparts, the radio station reported.

Fortunately for Paul, the weather was kind to him. Dry, and a gentle breeze caressed him as he pondered his future on a park bench. In front of him children from the ages of just toddling through to pension age were chasing balls and various other thrown objects, running in all directions, totally unaware of the loner on the verge of despair. Checking his pockets he found he had the grand sum of £2.52 with which to finance his future. Then he remembered – the side pocket of his sports bag was the hiding place for the money earned at Andy's. Suddenly, things didn't seem so bad. Now he knew exactly what he was going to do, but first he must buy food.

A burger and chips later, Paul was heading towards the city centre. His mind was clearer and he felt completely free. Almost back in control of his own destiny. Recent events had taught him that he was a saleable commodity. Now, whoever wanted his body would pay for it. His dusky colouring would thrill, and he at last realised that in important areas the word 'average' did not apply.

He decided not to call Alex for the time being. Earlier in the day he had needed to talk, but that had now passed. All he wanted now was a roof over his head, a shower, or even better, a long soak in a bath, and to be left to his own thoughts. He realised that eventually he would miss his mother, but at the moment he hated her for not listening, taking sides with Bad Breath. There would be no going back, not to the flat, not school. Suddenly the thought overwhelmed him. Effectively he had left school. Clarity of thought as he planned his future wandering through the quiet city on a summer Sunday. Back in control, he strode purposefully towards an executive block of modern flats. As he got closer there was a slight self-doubt that he quickly put aside. Finding Andy's flat number he pressed the bell, outside the building. A click, then an echoing voice.

"Yeah, who is it?"

"Me, er, Paul. Can I come up?"

Hesitation.

"Er... yes. Push the door when it buzzes."

The buzzer did its job and Paul pushed the door open and went up to Andy's flat. The door was already open and Andy called for him to come in. Andy was wearing just his jeans, his upper body was naked and looked as though it had been smeared with oil. He was taken aback to see the sports bag Paul was carrying.

"I need somewhere to kip for a few days."

As Paul spoke, Jeff appeared in the doorway wearing American Stars and Stripes boxer shorts. Paul looked at the carpet in embarrassment.

"Sorry. I, er, didn't think. I'm sorry."

Jeff interupted him.

"Don't be. Sit down and tell us what's going on."

Paul at length explained the events of the night and the reaction of his mother. Andy and Jeff immediately accepted Paul's version of events and how he had been set up by the man. Andy agreed that he could stay for the time being. Jeff was very keen that Paul move in with Andy. Paul asked if he could phone Alex and he used the mobile number.

"That's right I'm staying at Andy's. If anyone asks, you know nothing. Please don't tell anyone, it's most important. I'm not going home, ever. Come and see me tomorrow. Please."

Andy paused before answering, taking in the full extent of what he was being told.

"OK. I'll come round in the morning. Easy to escape school. I've no lessons until the afternoon. Be good!"

With that Alex was gone. Andy took the phone from him and asked if he was hungry. All he wanted was a drink and a bath. Jeff volunteered to run the bath. When Jeff stood up he was fully aware that his shorts had slipped a little, exposing his tight black pubes. He smoothed his hand over his shaven head and then adjusted his shorts, pulling them up and as he turned them slightly, the outline of a long, yet flaccid cock was apparent to Paul's searching eyes. Jeff headed to the bathroom and Paul noticed his small, tight arse above firmly defined thighs. Paul felt the inevitable hardening between his legs, over which he had no control. Andy brought Paul a mug of filter coffee and sat beside him.

"Look, you can stay here as long as you like, but do think about going home."

"Nothing to think about. No way am I going home." Paul turned to face Andy and he spoke with directness.

"I'll pay my way."

David Keane

Andy knew exactly what was in Paul's mind.

"I know I should send you packing, but I'll show you the second bedroom instead!"

Paul smiled his thanks and kissed Andy on the cheek, then they both went the second bedroom and Paul threw his bag into the corner.

"Thanks a million Andy."

"It's OK. Just don't pay too much."

As Paul tried to think through what Andy was hinting at, Jeff called from the bathroom.

"Bath ready!"

Paul headed to the bathroom and Jeff was still in there. The shorts had slipped again, a little further this time and were resting on the base of his cock. Jeff remained as Paul stripped and his semi-erect cock was revealed. Paul stood naked before Jeff who reached out and tenderly touched his cheek. Rapidly hardening Paul felt himself blushing, not from embarrassment, but from desire.

"You better get that bath."

Without further contact, Jeff left the bathroom and Paul got in the bath and lowered himself into the sandalwood perfumed bubbles. The silky texture of the water smoothed his body and relaxed his muscles. The tensions of the day just floated away and he was ready for the night. Wiping himself dry in the folds of a huge, soft, white bathtowel, he thought about wanking his semi-erect tool, but decided to wait for later pleasures when he would offer himself to Andy and Jeff. Beautiful men of his choice. His mother couldn't attract men as beautiful as these. He tightly wrapped the towel around his body, outlining his maturing frame and the key to his future.

Despite his thoughts and plans, he was still surprised by the scene as he entered the lounge. Andy was astride Jeff and from the expressions on both their faces it was clear that Jeff was fully inside Andy. Lifting himself slightly, Andy then plunged down Jeff's shaft once more and then began to repeat the movement more frequently. Jeff lay on his back, his shaven head glistening and his hands grasping the large cock before him. Glancing upwards, Jeff saw Paul and as he was about to try and speak Paul allowed the towel to drop to the carpet. He knelt beside the two joined bodies who were momentarily stilled. Andy leaned backwards with Jeff still in place. As he did so, Jeff released Andy's cock. Paul did not need further invitation and he went down on Andy. He had never had anything so big in his mouth before and he choked slightly as the head forced its way into his throat. Jeff's fingers grabbed Andy's nipples and then his nails dug deep into his pecs, before ripping at the hard brown nipples. Andy cried out and Paul lifted his head as his fingers sought Jeff's entombed weapon. Sitting up, Paul then dug his teeth into Andy's left nipple and the cry became a scream. Alternating between biting and sucking, the nipple hardened under Paul's assault. In Andy was now not only Jeff's cock but Paul's fingers forced their way into the already over-stretched hole. Andy screamed and Paul plunged down onto his throbbing tool, just in time to receive not only the biggest cock he had ever taken, but spurt after spurt of hot cum. Paul swallowed repeatedly. Andy finally lifted himself clear of Jeff's cock, and revealed to Paul was an even larger pleasure length of ebony. Jeff ripped a tight and fully stretched condom from his tool and obligingly Paul tried to find space in his mouth and throat for his first tool of black beauty. Positioning himself in place for a 69, Jeff took Paul gently in his mouth. Jeff's tongue teased the shaft and then sucked deeply. Paul could feel teeth rubbing his shaft and he began to spurt into the athlete's mouth, quickly followed by further gushing down his throat. The taste and smells were erotically different, the pleasure mind-blowing. They rolled free of each other and watched Andy fuck himself with a 12-inch dildo. Paul was astonished at the size of the toy, and the depth it penetrated, but he knew then he would soon be riding the same toy. Andy did not cum again before exhaustion devoured his body, but both Andy and Jeff were pleased that their Sunday romp had been disrupted.

"Welcome to Paradise Apartments!" Andy welcomed Paul and Jeff stroked his welcome along Paul's still demanding shaft.

Sixteen

Each day grew longer and the nights were never-ending for Dale's mother. Phone calls from double-glazing companies created the most torment. A futile waste of a call, and one that brought hope, then despair. All the family were suffering the torment in their own way. Dale's sister firmly believed that he would walk through the door at any time, smiling some apology, after a week of sex and drugs somewhere. The main problem with that scenario for her was that Alex was still at home, and if he was telling the truth about not knowing where Dale was, then a nagging doubt entered her mind. Dale's father outwardly expressed the view that Dale was doing some 'lad thing' somewhere and would return soon after losing his virginity to some waitress. Inside, his thoughts were different. He thought he knew his son enough, despite the usual parent-teenager differences, and he could not believe that if he could contact them, than he wouldn't. The reality was that he did not know his son at all. He wasn't really into lad things: although his virginity had been lost soon into his teenage years, it had all been a sham. Recently the feelings he had been pushing to the back of his mind had intruded to the forefront. It might just be a teenage thing he had told himself, but he did love Alex, and although it had been unstated, he was sure Alex felt the same. Dale had been preparing himself to talk about love with Alex. Then Alex had done the unforgivable, shouted that name, when his only thoughts should have been of Dale as the love juice spurted and freely flowed. His father hadn't a clue.

Dale's mother knew, she just knew that Dale could not contact them, now or at any other time. She was beginning to despise the attitudes expressed by her husband and daughter. How could they be so unfeeling?

Sunday morning and a group of boys including Tony, Chris, Shamir and Gordon, were enjoying a kickabout in the park. They have moved in their fantasies from Villa Park to the twin towers of Wembley. Just as they and their friends were about to start the Cup Final, Tony noticed Paul walking with his sports bag across the park.

"Hey Paul! Over here!"

Paul just walked on, oblivious to Tony's call.

"Oi! You wanker!"

Still no recognition. Tony turned to the others.

"Not with his Fiesta friend today, but too stuck up for the likes of us! Come on lads match to play!" With that he took a hefty kick at the ball, sending it goalwards and setting off a chase of screaming, yelling players, some trying to kick the ball, others anything that moved.

Shamir and Gordon watched Paul leave the park, not too inclined to get involved with the football melee around them, as youthful exhuberance exploded into a frenzy.

"Don't look too happy does he?" Shamir observed.

"Shall we go after him, to see if he's OK?" asked Gordon.

"No. If he'd wanted us he would have come over when Tone shouted at him." Shamir decided the fate of Paul. If he had been deflected from his wanderings at that point he would never had made the journey to Andy's. By such chance meetings and decisions taken, are lives formed and destinies set. Paul with his head down left the park as the final began.

Alex knew he must contact Dale's mother, although he was uncertain of the reception he would receive this time. He knew she would have contacted him if there had been any news, likewise he would have contacted her if Dale had contacted him. The silence had been deafening. On this occasion Alex could not believe the old saying, no news is good news. Deep down he felt responsible for Dale's disappearance, but he could not tell her that, or anyone. Guilt swept through him as he approached the house, unaware that he had been spotted by Dale's mother. She rushed from the house hoping against hope, that Alex was bringing good news, despite her fears. Obviously he didn't want to use the telephone, he wanted to tell them personally. As soon as she saw the questioning expression on Alex's face she knew that there was no news.

"Hello. Any news?" asked Alex, already knowing the answer.

Dale's mother put her arms around Alex and kissed him with a grieving mother's kiss.

"No, nothing yet, but I'm glad you've come. I'm so sorry about the other day. I know you would tell me if there was anything to tell. Please forgive me. I just had to turn my fears and anger on someone and unfortunately for you, you came along." She continued to hug Alex, and the feeling of guilt rose within him. In return he hugged her and mutual tears flowed. One set of tears for a missing, seemingly lost son, the other; tears of regret at the loss of a first love.

The cup final in the park had just finished as Paul had walked into the living room with a towel tightly wrapped around his dusky, demanding body. Tony had taken charge as team selector, referee and linesman. Not surprisingly his team won, but no-one was sure of the score. Paul was taking further steps along the path of his chosen career. His tongue was working overtime as he serviced two guys at the same time paying the rent with the only currency he had in abundance. Tony took his ball home and when he went to bed he reached under the mattress for a magazine, in which some of the pages had stuck together. A similar process, with a different magazine, took place in the homes of Chris, Shamir and Gordon. Meanwhile Paul discussed a price list for various services that he knew his body could provide.

A typical Sunday in the city. Lights go on everywhere, but some are extinguished totally.

Seventeen

Jeff left the flat about midnight, leaving Andy to sort out the problem of Paul. Andy was feeling more comfortable with the idea of Paul staying. All things considered, he knew he could not throw Paul out on the street. If he did that Jeff would never forgive him, and that would never do. Andy made a final cup of coffee for himself and his unexpected visitor.

"Better get some clothes sorted out for you in the morning."

Paul was reassured and took Andy's remark to mean that he could stay. Before he could remind Andy that he was expecting a visit from Alex in the morning, he was taken aback by Andy.

"A little problem in the afternoon. I'm working from 6, but before then I've a client coming round, if you know what I mean."

Paul knew what was meant.

"You've got a man coming round for... and he pays. You want me to make myself scarce?"

"Well, it might be best. I'll give you some cash for the cinema or something. He'll be here for an hour. That's what he pays for."

Andy drank the last of his coffee. "Are you absolutely certain, that apart from Alex and of course Jeff, no one knows your here?"

"Certain. Don't worry."

Paul had several questions spinning around his head that he wanted to ask. "This geezer that's coming.... what will you do?"

Andy smiled as he replied.

"You don't mess around with your questions do you?

Believe it or not we just chat for a while, then I strip and he wanks me at the same time he wanks himself. Usually he cums first and then he leaves me alone. We have a drink, he pays up and off he goes. That's it really. Then I bugger off to work."

"How much?"

"Why don't you ask what you want to know?" laughed Andy.

"Usually thirty, but sometimes fifty. Extras cost more."

"Such as?"

"Leave it there shall we?"

Paul didn't want to leave it there.

"Get me some men will you? I need the cash. If they want to wank me, no problem."

Paul went quiet for a moment, then with a hard look on his face that Andy had not seen before continued:

"They can fuck me or I'll fuck them. It's all the same to me as long as they pay. Well?"

Andy was taken aback by Paul's directness even though they had indulged each other earlier.

"I think we'll talk about that later... Anyway Jeff wants you. Play your cards right and you will be earning with Jeff and still be able to have your lover Alex. Best of all worlds!"

"Alex isn't my lover!" exclaimed Paul. "Is he?"

Andy smiled but said nothing.

They slept in separate bedrooms. Andy needed the rest and he thought Paul must be tired too. Also he needed space and time to think. What Paul did not know was that he was already sold. Andy knew. Jeff had some, rich weird and demanding friends. Paul was all they wanted. He came from nowhere and could be used like a hired car then discarded when a new model came along. Paul thought he knew it all, yet he knew so little. His education was just beginning, his initiation into the unforgiving world of sex for sale. The countdown to his sell-by date had begun.

Paul slept well. It had been a tiring Sunday, emotionally as well as physically. He woke at the time he normally would have when going to school. This Monday was different, a school day and he had no intention of dragging himself there, ever again. The dawn of a new day and a new life. He stretched like a cat waking from a deep slumber. As always when he awoke, his cock was rigid, waiting to be stroked, caressed and mounted. He flung the duvet free of his naked body, just as Andy knocked on the door and entered simultaneously. Andy's attention was not only taken by the well-endowed dusky body, but the way he lay on his back, demanding unknowingly to be fucked.

Every inch of Paul's body was well-formed without being exaggerated. He lay there in innocence, his arms by his side and then he slowly drew his legs up into the foetal position. Andy wanted him. He wanted to screw him and be screwed in return. Yet he knew he must not touch. Jeff would claim ownership and must not be angered. He may share him, like yesterday, but no more than that. Paul had not an idea regarding his new status. Jeff would use him, screw him and expect to be shafted upon demand. Then there would be days and nights when he would share him with his so-called friends. Watch as old men would fawn over this dusky young stud, who would do as he was told to keep in with a celebrity. Then Jeff may get bored and visit the amusement arcades and find another dusky shag, who would do anything so that he could feed the machines and snort a line. There had been several and Andy had provided the room, the dope, the condom and gel. Jeff liked to video of his conquests and show his friends who would select the boy they wanted to shag. Discretion cost money and Andy and Jeff were paid well for their services and discretion. The shagged youth would return to the arcade with enough to play the machines for a couple of hours, and his despair eased away by a good line of coke.

Paul would be different perhaps. Firstly he didn't do coke and he shagged for pleasure. Also he was living in the flat. Andy knew that for the foreseeable future Jeff would insist he lived with Andy. That is until he grew tired and told Andy to get rid. Then as before, Andy would do as he was told, maybe. Andy's thoughts moved to Alex as Paul slowly rose from the bed.

"What's for breakfast?"

"What do you fancy?"

Paul laughed and suggested toast and coffee. While Paul was showering, Andy's thoughts dwelt on Alex. He was a good shag and sensible. Andy looked forward to seeing him again. The cottage in Derbyshire could be fun, to say the least.

Over breakfast Paul explained that Alex was coming round, and Andy suggested they go shopping. It was going to be a good day all round. Cocks twitched at the prospects.

Paul's mother checked his bedroom. "Not there. Be with one of his pals' expect. Well, he can please himself. Stay in bed love."

Eighteen

As Andy and Paul shared a cafetiere of fresh coffee, the doorbell rang to announce Alex's arrival. Andy operated the 'open' buzzer and Alex made his way warily up to the flat. Paul, wearing a T-shirt of Andy's that covered him like a mini-dress over the mini-briefs he had also borrowed, greeted Alex with a full kiss on the lips that embarrassed Alex momentarily. Andy stepped back and let the welcome continue and Alex responded with a full pressure reply and his tongue pushed its way past Paul's lips.

Paul broke the hold. "Steady on."

"What have you done?"

"Look, if you two want to talk, go into Paul's room. I'll just make myself busy in here. Coffee?"

Alex nodded yes, but Paul declined. "Paul, remember we're going shopping. Say about half an hour?"

"Yes. Fine."

Paul led Alex to his room.

Once the door was closed, Paul explained the events of the previous day and his hopes for the future. Although Alex was unsure about Paul staying in the flat he accepted the situation as he could not come up with a better idea. They lay on the single duvet, and after Paul's explanation, Alex moved down the bed a little as Paul propped himself up against the headboard. Alex lifted the large T shirt and began to lick Paul across the top of his briefs. Paul stirred and did not resist as his cock fought to gain freedom from the tight briefs. Alex's fingers lifted the top of the briefs and out popped the dusky shaft, hard and available.

Neither spoke as Alex's tongue teased the head. Andy entered the room almost unnoticed and he watched as Alex took the cock in his mouth and gently sucked. Paul gestured Andy over.

"Shopping or fucking? What a choice!" said Paul.

Alex continued as Paul and Andy discussed the merits of the two options. "I think shop now, fuck later!"

Paul made the decision and broke free of a surprised Alex. Alex wanted to cum but he would have to wait as Paul leapt around gathering the clothes he had arrived in to wear for hopefully one last time.

"What time you working Andy?"

"4 til 5."

"Plenty of time to recharge batteries. Changed my mind. If you two want to use my bed be my guest."

Paul smiled as he saw the longing in the two sets of eyes. Andy reached out for Alex who obliged by moving forward and kissing Andy's eager lips. Andy swept Alex from his feet and carried him to his own bed. Paul continued to dress and went into the living area to watch morning TV. He curled up on the settee pressing the volume control to high as it was clear Andy had entered Alex. Realising the bedroom door was slightly ajar, Paul regarded this as an invitation to at least watch. He pushed the door open and saw Alex with his head buried face down into the pillow and his hands tightly gripping the pillow sides. Andy was fully into Alex and each thrust brought on agonised cry from the fucked meat. Paul could see the glazed look in Andy's eyes as he increased his momentum. Alex pleaded for the fucking to stop. Andy ignored the cries and increased his thrusts. He looked at Paul and saw his smiling response of encouragement. The cries increased and Alex struggled to free himself but Paul rushed forward to hold him down for Andy to perform to fulfillment. Alex's screams were joined by Andy's yells of orgasm. Then the room was still and Andy withdrew slowly. Paul watched with admiration as the white-latex covered shaft withdrew and its owner turned to fall on his back with his cock still semi erect. As Andy left Alex, there was an agonised cry of release from the seemingly paralyzed youth, who loudly sobbed as pain still seared through his body. Unbeknown to Andy and Paul, the pain had brought Alex to a huge climax and his cum was smeared over the duvet cover and his stomach. He lay on the cum-covered duvet and his legs twitched, although the whole bottom half felt detached from the rest of him.

"You two go shopping. I'll stay here, if that's OK. I feel as though I'll never walk again!"

David Keane

Paul studied the prone figure before him.

"Evens for Skipton! Welcome to the job club!"

Now he had climaxed, Andy was concerned for Alex. When Alex was screaming he wanted to hurt him more and more. Then after climax he felt guilty for the agony he had caused.

"I'm fine. That was great! The pain got my brain and cock. Wonderful!"

Andy looked at Alex in amazement.

"You mean you enjoyed that, and the other night?"

"I sure did!"

The cries of pain were followed now with roars of laughter.

Andy agreed that Alex could stay in the flat while he took Paul shopping. For Andy, the big advantage of city centre living was the fact that all he seemed to need was on his doorstep. Clothes shopping was so easy, just a short walk and boundless opportunities, from the small boutique to the chain store, were there to pick from. Andy took Paul to a small, fashionable, quality boutique where Jeff had an account. Andy had been fortunate in the past to be able to purchase on Jeff's account; this time it was Paul's turn. For Paul it was like an Aladdin's Cave. Sweatshirts, T-shirts, casual jackets, trainers and shoes all came under critical scrutiny. Paul could not believe the amount he was being encouraged to spend. Mike, the boutique manager, was used to such visits, but he along with Andy was astonished at the amount pre-arranged by telephone. The slightly camp Mike was well-known to both Andy and Jeff.

"He must really fancy this one. Mind you he's got good taste." Firstly it was sweatshirts, T-shirts and underwear. All designer labels, even the selection of socks. Paradise! Next to be selected three pairs of jeans. Mike was keen to help in this area, ensuring a perfect fit, the beads of sweat on his forehead testament to his full commitment. Sports shirts by the half-dozen, just sign and take away. Some to be carried, others to be delivered. The new Paul was dressed and ready to do as bid.

Alex showered and felt movement returning to his body. His recovery rate was better than the last time, but he was pleased he hadn't a 200metres to run in the near future. When the shoppers returned they were welcomed by the smell of freshly prepared filter coffee. Toasted cheese and tomato sandwiches were on the lunch menu and the three guys were easy with their relationship.

"I just don't know how I'm going to be able to thank Jeff for all this."

Paul made an expansive gesture across the pile of large carrier bags containing his new wardrobe. More bags were expected mid-afternoon.

"I think I've got a pretty good idea!" spoke an unsmiling Alex, still harbouring uneasy thoughts about his friend's safety.

Alex was concerned that some people might associate Dale's disappearance and Paul's together, and come up with him as a common factor. Both of the missing boys went to Skipton, one, Alex's best friend, the other had shared his tent. Also Paul had been seen in the company of Alex since their return to school. Although he had no idea about the whereabouts of Dale, he knew exactly where Paul was. If asked would people trick him into revealing the secret? What if he was questioned by the police? It was as though Paul had read Alex's mind.

"No need to worry about the police. My mother won't say a word, especially if I phone her and tell her I'm OK. At least if I'm not at home, she doesn't have to feed me etc. Just stick 141 before the number and she can't trace the call. Not that she would bother."

Andy passed the cordless phone to Paul.

"What now?"

"No time like the present, if she's at home."

Paul pressed 141, then his home number.

The call was answered quickly.

"Hello mum. I'm going away for a bit. I'll phone you from London when I get there, and I didn't nick the money. Bye." The call was disconnected before she could reply. Paul didn't want to risk hearing her voice, especially if she got emotional, so just in case he disconnected. He still wanted to get over the point he had not stolen any money from her bank roll. He would let her stew over what he told her had happened during that night in his room.

Across the city, the call did not cause too much of a stir.

"It was him. The bugger's not coming back yet. He reckons he's going to London."

"Let him stew! Serve him right." was Bad Breath's comment.

David Keane

"I hope he's OK."

"He'll be back. You'll see!"

No attempt was made to trace the call.

Andy liked the false information regarding London. He considered Alex's situation and although he thought it might be safer if he did not come with them to the Derbyshire cottage, he needed him there. It was agreed that they would not see Alex for the remainder of the week, but he would drive to the cottage alone on Friday evening. The Tuesday meeting was cancelled. Andy wrote instructions on how to reach the cottage and they bid farewell to Alex.

"See you Friday." said Paul.

"Take care." advised Alex.

When the register in the Sixth Form Block was called, three names, Paul, Alex and Dale were greeted with silence.

Paul and Andy spent a lazy afternoon avoiding discussing Paul's situation. Andy had been a little worried that he might have taken too much out of himself during the morning session. As the afternoon progressed, he knew there would be no problem, as he would fantasize about Alex and Paul pleasuring him, while being groped by his client. He had done similar things before when he didn't fancy the client. They always wanted him to cum, so he would close his eyes and imagine some youth, or Jeff doing the business. Always worked and he could cum to order, then count the cash. There had been occasions when Andy was embarrassed by his large cock. He always filled his jeans, and when walking down the street he was amazed at the number of men and women who were clearly attracted by the bulge, their eyes fixed on him as he approached. One day as he walked through the Bull Ring Centre, he saw a man in his early twenties coming towards him with his eyes firmly fixed on his groin. Andy deliberately bumped into him as they passed, apologised, got chatting and took him into the nearby pub cottage lock-up and let him suck him off. Then they went their separate ways, no names no phone numbers.

Paul knew the time was approaching when he would have to make himself scarce so that Andy could perform and earn. Andy, by his body language of fussing around picking up odd pieces of errant fluff, and pumping up cushions, gave a clear message to Paul.

"I'll make myself scarce, shall I?"

Andy offered Paul a spare key for the flat and outer door. This felt like a significant moment for Paul. His own, his very own key. Surely this meant the present arrangements would stay in place for the foreseeable future?

"Punter will have gone by 5.15 OK? You don't mind do you?"

Paul was pleased by the apparent concern. Something he was not usually familiar with.

"Course I don't mind you divvy. You've got to earn a living." Paul paused, then added with deliberation,

"So have I."

There was no spoken response from Andy, just a knowing thin smile.

Paul thought he might just walk around for a time but was a little concerned that he may be unfortunate and meet someone he knew. One thing he intended to do though was to hang about outside and cast an eye over Andy's mysterious punter. From a conveniently concealing doorway, Paul waited. The punter was due shortly, and on cue an MG sportscar pulled into the front parking area. From the car, stepped a tall blond man in his thirties, wearing a blue business suit, elegant in style, clutching dark shades and walking with purpose. Very nice thought Paul, but he was to be disappointed as from the entrance to the flats walked an equally blond female, wearing very little, but with style. They both got in the MG and as they left the parking bay, a dark Mercedes parked in their vacated spot. From the car emerged a short, overweight, sweaty man whose bald head glistened in the afternoon sun. Wearing a slightly crumpled blue business suit, he looked carefully around as he locked the car. He moved to the flat doorbells and to Paul's disappointment he pressed the one belonging to Andy. Seconds later he pushed the door open and disappeared from sight. Paul promised himself he would be more selective in his client list, mistakenly believing he actually had a choice.

Paul stayed in the doorway for about fifteen minutes, watching the various comings and goings. Only two more men went in the flats, both young and dressed in designer gear. One elegant woman exited, and Paul imagined her as a model. The guys had looked good and Paul imagined them stripping for him and then taking him. These thoughts prompted him to gaze up at the

David Keane

building in the general area of Andy's flat and he imagined a huge lump of lard stroking and then pulling Andy's cock. Well when at work he thought you had to take the rough with smooth. Clearly today was a rough day for Andy. Paul was brought back to reality as a policeman strolled into view. Quickly Paul withdrew into the shadows and the policeman continued unhurriedly on his way. Was it always going to be like this he wondered. Perhaps that was the price to pay. Leaving the protection of the doorway, he walked in the direction of the city centre, past the boutique and into an amusement arcade.

A brawny bouncer stepped aside and Paul entered. When his eyes had adjusted to the overly bright light, he noticed that the punters were young, underage, or in several cases, pensioners. His attention was drawn to a guy around his age with unkempt mousy hair and well-worn jeans and jacket. He was playing a machine trying, seemingly unsuccessfully, to win the jackpot. Coin after coin was being fed in to the hungry machine and at the same time the boy's buttocks were being stroked by one of the pensioners. No-else noticed, or if they did, no-one cared.

Returning to the flat just after 5.30, he found Andy reclining on the leather settee, wearing black shorts and no top. His body glistened and this sharply defined his hairless pecs. His short dark locks were tousled, suggesting fingers had run through them and perhaps hair had been grabbed by the handful, as the attached head performed some task.

"Been anywhere interesting?" asked Andy.

"Just around. Has your bloke been?"

"Yeah. Just a wank on me. He tossed himself, and that's fifty quid."

Andy nodded in the direction of a wallet lying on the coffee table.

"Put kettle on will you. I'm just going to clean my teeth."

"OK."

Why can't you tell me the whole truth thought Paul. Mind you, perhaps he wouldn't tell the world he'd sucked a lump of lard's cock for fifty quid.

Andy returned from the bathroom and his breath smelt of antiseptic mouthwash.

"Jeff will be round later, while I'm at work. Don't forget to thank him for the clothes will you?"

Paul was annoyed at the unnecessary reminder.

"Course I won't forget !"

"OK...OK...Didn't mean to annoy you. Tomorrow afternoon I've got a visitor and then Thursday I'm booked for a full night session. Not here, but in the Rotunda Hotel. London businessman who likes my cock for some reason! You'll be OK on your own won't you? Then I'm clear for the weekend. That will be great. Promise."

Paul digested the information and of course he would be OK. Why the hell shouldn't he be? He'd looked after himself for years really.

Andy went off to work in the bar. Paul raided the freezer and had to choose from a selection of complete meals. Eventually the lasagne won on two accounts. Firstly it was two servings and secondly, it was just one container to put in the microwave. Not having a microwave at home, Paul thought there might be problems, but a search of the nearest kitchen drawer produced the required instruction manual. Five minutes' reading, twenty seconds of button pushing, then five minutes whirling in the microwave, the meal was ready. Paul decided to save on washing up and ate the double portion from its microwaveable dish. Curling up on the white settee, he waited for Jeff to arrive, his mind full of ways he could thank him for the clothes.

When Jeff turned up he took a dozing Paul by surprise. At the sound of the buzzer, Paul was shaken awake and fumbled to press the correct button to open the outer door. Together they sat on the settee, after Jeff had helped himself to a shot of brandy. He offered the same to Paul and he unhesitatingly accepted. Taking his first sip, Paul grimaced, as the unfamiliar spirit burnt his throat. Paul assumed it was an acquired taste, one that Jeff clearly had aquired as Paul watched him refill his glass.

"Jeff thanks a bundle for the clothes. Hope we didn't spend too much."

"You're welcome and no, you didn't spend too much." As he replied Jeff stroked Paul's hair, rousing immediately both groins. The remaining clothes had been delivered just after Andy had left for work and the carriers were still lying with their cargo on the carpet. Jeff dropped down onto the carpet and pulled a very brief pair of red and black underpants from the nearest bag. He held them in the air and looked at Paul.

"Try these on for me, now."

Paul took them from Jeff and flung the tiny garment onto his shoulder.

Departing in the direction of his room he turned his head to Jeff.

"Don't go away!"

When Paul returned a couple of minutes later he was wearing only the tight briefs. Standing motionless in front of Jeff, the viewer was able to observe not only his dark skin tones, but slightly hairy inner thighs plus that enticing line of navel hair. Slowly Paul lifted his arms to reveal two black bushes. Holding his hands above his head, Paul began to thrust rhythmically in Jeff's face.

"You are a quick learner."

"Had some good teachers lately."

Jeff leaned forward and took the thrusting brief between his teeth and sank his teeth not only into the warm material but through to a hard shaft. His hands explored the back of the red and blue briefs. Instead of thrusting forward, Paul now moved his hips from side to side, still in the grip of Jeff's teeth. The rear of the briefs were pulled down clear of the smooth dark arse cheeks. Paul instinctively opened his legs and Jeff's fingers sought to gain entry. Momentarily, Jeff released the briefs from his teeth just long enough for the hard cock to be freed. Gently and with great tenderness Jeff took Paul in his mouth. A caressing and teasing suck began, tortuously slowly, that in contrast to the biting sent surges of pleasure through the young available body. Jeff's hands slid down firm legs and then rose slowly upto the slightly trembling inner thighs. Nearing Paul's solid balls, the exploring hands came to a halt. Paul looked down at the shaven head that had taken his cock. Resting his hands on it, he caressed and stroked the gently moving man. As he looked down, Paul had difficulty comprehending that this pleasuring mouth belonged to a nearly famous athlete, one who could and probably did shag any girl that crossed his path. Jeff stood up, still fully clothed and gestured in the direction of Andy's bedroom. Silently Paul followed and watched as Jeff stripped very slowly. When totally naked Jeff lay on the bed and gestured for Paul to join him. Their mouths immediately sought each other and hands explored with ferocious desire. Paul grabbed hold of the huge black twitching cock that was pleading to be pummeled inside a tunnel of joy, Paul's tunnel. Once again Jeff broke free and in his hand had a condom ready for fitting. Stretching and tugging the latex down the deeply black shaft Jeff could sense Paul's fears.

"Don't worry if you can't take it tonight, with practice eventually you will. There's all the time in the world. I'll get something to help you."

Paul looked around as Jeff left the bed and crossed to a wardrobe. Sitting up Paul could see on the shelves an array of toy cocks from the average through to the grotesque. Some were pink, some were black. Some were vibrators others manual. All mind-blowing possibilities. Jeff selected a larger than average black tool and began to smear it with large quantities of gel. Jeff's cock had remained firm with its stretched latex covering. Paul was transfixed by the real thing but he was about to receive a toy. Jeff handed the gel-covered weapon to Paul.

"Fuck yourself with it while I watch."

From the wardrobe shelf Jeff picked up a camcorder. The sight of the camera excited Paul as he positioned himself on his side and began to probe his own hole with the dildo. Jeff assisted by pushing his gel-covered fingers into the gasping Paul. Then with Jeff's help, the dildo entered him. Paul took over and writhed on the bed as the pain of self-shagging seared through his body. Jeff moved around the bed to get the best shots of Paul's agonised face, around to close-ups of the shafting plastic. Jeff put down the camera and Paul's mouth received strawberry-flavoured latex. The dildo now moved easily within Paul, a fact that Jeff was fully aware of. Taking Paul's hand away from the dildo, Jeff pushed it hard into the fully stretched tunnel. Paul screamed at the height of pain he had never experienced before, but was soon to be surpassed. The dildo was pulled from Paul and his body went into involuntary spasms that Jeff ignored as he manoevered into position to take his pleasure. Almost before Paul realised what was happening the strawberry latex was thrusting inside him and as the pain level moved to new heights, he momentarily mercifully passed out. Searing pain jerked him back to consciousness but he was powerless to speak. Just when he felt he could stand no more, there was a final jerking thrust from Jeff and his cum tried to explode the latex barrier. Realising the pain he had caused, Jeff withdrew quickly and leaned over the still spasm-ridden body. Through his tears, Paul tried to put on a brave face, but was unable to control either his tears or his convulsions. Jeff left him on the bed and went to the bathroom. Paul slowly lay on his back. To do so was painful. Just for a moment Paul wondered if the clothes were

David Keane

worth it, as Jeff came back and vigorously took Paul's erect cock in his mouth. Quickly Paul filled Jeff's mouth with hot spunk. Suddenly it was all worthwhile and the clothes were brilliant. The pain had gone and Jeff assured Paul it would be easier from now on. He did not have to wait long to find out.

It was a fairly slack evening in the bar, giving Andy plenty of time to imagine what was happening back at the flat. Obviously Jeff would want to try Paul's body for size. Andy was sure that Jeff's curiosity would get the better of him and he would want Paul despite their decision to take things slowly. He just hoped that Jeff didn't push his luck too much and cause problems. Paul was certainly keen, but in reality very inexperienced. If they were going to get their money's worth out of him it had to be a long-term project. Although Jeff obviously fancied Paul, characteristically he would want to share him with friends and then put him on the market. Before Paul could realise he was regarded as saleable meat it would be too late. He would have no-one else to turn to, and although Jeff may by then have fresh interests, Paul, like others before him, would be blindly allowing himself to be shagged by anyone who cared to for the price of a meal. Andy knew he would do nothing to stop it as he was in the same trap himself. Jeff and his friends paid for the flat. He liked Continental holidays and smart clothes and restaurant meals, but he had started on the game when he was twenty. Poor Paul was only eighteen and he could be an old tart by twenty. Andy knew that he could trade on his body, especially the size of his cock, from the moment some stranger wanked him off in the cinema. It was a pleasant experience that the darkness gave a frisson of excitement, and one that he repeated whenever he had the chance. Then he asked for a little present, then real notes. The meeting with Jeff in the bar had been a natural extention to his career. He hated Jeff for what he would probably do to this over-sexed, well-endowed youth. Andy had no intention of biting the hand that fed him. Sadly Paul would have to find his own salvation. As Andy thought through the issue, Paul was paying one of the installments. His cries of pain were muffled by the thick sound-proof walls and door. Jeff was taking his pleasure causing pain with his usual thoroughness, but this one spiked on his cock seemed challengingly different, which made his climax all the more explosive and satisfying. He enjoyed the taste of this guy who was neither black nor white. This one was different and he would share him proudly with his friends. At a price, a good price.

Andy hurried back from the bar after closing, ignoring the possibility of a couple of good fucks that were on offer. When he entered the flat, the first person he saw was a naked sleeping Jeff on the settee. He moved carefully to Paul's room and found it deserted. He found Paul naked on his double bed asleep curled up tightly as though trying to protect himself. He knew that Paul was beginning to pay back. Andy looked at Paul and saw a certain innocence that needed protection. Paul began to stir and as he uncurled, Andy was reminded of Paul's attraction, not only to Jeff, but also to himself.

Andy ignored Jeff in the living room and gently pulled the duvet from beneath Paul. Then he covered the murmuring body. Andy stripped down to his shorts and joined the whimpering youth in the double bed. Tenderly, almost apologetically, Andy kissed the hot boy's sweaty forehead. He would have loved to have taken him in his arms and taken away his pain. He knew that pain. He had been along the same path.

Accompanying his whimpers, Paul made occasional involuntary leg jerks, that struck Andy and made sure he also had a fitful night's sleep. As dawn began to break Paul began to sleep more restfully and his spasms subsided with the arrival of the early morning sun. Andy carefully wrapped his arms around the wounded youth, once more kissing him, this time on the cheek. Paul snuggled up to the blond Adonis, who was surprised to find that he and Paul were both erect. Paul's dusky frame pressed against his well-oiled body. Andy felt pangs of shame as his body craved the damaged youth. Sleep enveloped both until the bedroom door burst open and Jeff's naked frame filled the doorway. The two bodies in the bed were violently dragged from their slumbers. Andy's arms still enveloped Paul, as though protecting him from the outside world.

"Oh! Very cosy! Who's been shagging my whore then?"

Andy barely managed to control his anger.

"Don't be fucking stupid. You left Paul in my bed I assume when you'd finished with him. Look at him, you pillock! You don't care a toss do you, how much damage you do? You literally shagged him till he could take no more, then ditched him where he lay. You bastard."

"Finished have we?"

Paul remained silent as he witnessed the exchange of angry words. Jeff left the doorway and returned to the living room.

"You OK?"

Paul nodded a silent yes. The pain had gone to be replaced with a dull ache. His lovehole felt as though it had been stretched and remained like a cave. At least next time would be easier. He hoped that Jeff would understand that he had not had sex with Andy. It was beyond his understanding that Andy was so angry. Jeff was teaching him the ropes, he had to learn. Surely the pain would never be the same again. Deep down he hoped Jeff would not want to shag him again that day. He became aware that as they sat up against the headboard, Andy was stroking his hair. Jeff reappeared in the doorway, dressed this time. He stepped forward and threw two twenty-pound notes at the bed.

"There, twenty for the whore and twenty for his shagging pimp! I'll leave you to it! Oh yes Paul, make sure he uses a rubber when he pumps you up. You never know, you can't be too careful considering what he shags!"

Paul lay there in stunned silence, and Andy only just managed not to reply, fearing he would have exploded into violence. What Paul did not know was that this display by Jeff was typical. Recently Jeff and Andy had engaged in a violent argument as, Jeff, angry that Andy breaking a date with him, had chosen to entertain two Japanese tourists he had met in the bar. For discreet hotel sex they were prepared to pay very well. Andy performed according to the fee agreed. The Japanese paid very well, so were exhausted by the Englishman who fulfilled their fantasies of a Viking, an ancient Greek god, or a Roman Gladiator. Totally satisfied, he was rebooked the following night. Although Jeff and Andy tried to believe their relationship was purely business, Jeff still had a jealous streak. On that night he had attacked Andy, first with his fists, then with a knife. Andy overpowered Jeff and they then screwed violently till both were spent.

Paul looked at Andy through anxious eyes.

"Don't worry. He'll be back."

Nineteen

School hardly noticed the Paul's absence. When he truanted earlier in his academic life, the school authorities, usually House Tutor Jack Price, would phone Paul's mother. She would either lie and say he was unwell, or promise to make sure he was in school the following day. Paul knew the score, so when his mother told him that Mr. Price had phoned, he would promise to be back in school the next day. It was easy, he gained a few days' freedom and without too much fuss he would blend back into the old routine. This time it would be different. Jack Price phoned Wednesday morning but Paul was not around to return the following day. Price explained that Paul was in danger of failing his GNVQ course, not because of a lack of ability, but by not reaching the required attendance level. On returning the phone to the cradle, she immediately began to experience feelings of panic. Strangely, for the first time that week she seriously became concerned as to where her only child was, because despite his eighteen years he was still her child. Bad Breath was not around to deflect her concerns. Now her imagination began to move into overdrive. What if he really had run away? What if he had come to harm? What if he was telling the truth about the other night? Sitting alone in the kitchen with a cold cup of tea, she willed Paul to come home.

Paul slept alone Tuesday and Wednesday night. Andy would have liked to have spent the nights with Paul, just to hold and protect him but he resisted the temptation. He did not want to confuse Paul by creating a situation that he may misinterpret. After all he did have work to do as well.

Andy performed Wednesday afternoon and Paul went to the arcade once more. The strains of the heavy session with Jeff had passed and having sampled the delights of an athlete, he wanted more and quickly. Looking around the punters in the arcade, there were few that he felt likely to excite him as much as Jeff. The arse-stroker was there, this time with a very young-looking guy with blond streaks in his brown hair. Wearing a denim jacket and tight

David Keane

blue jeans, he allowed the stroker's hands to wander front as well as rear, as he tried to save the universe on a machine. Paul wondered if the boy would let the old guy have more. With these thoughts in mind, he watched as both disappeared in the direction of the bog. Paul waited for several minutes before following. The bog appeared deserted when he entered, except the lock-up door was showing the engaged sign. The noises from within suggested the boy was earning his next video game money. As he returned to the main area of the arcade, Paul pondered if the old dude would swallow the boy's juice. That thought set Paul's imagination racing, and he guessed that over the years the old guy must have swallowed litre after litre of juice. What a waste he thought. While he teased himself with lurid images, the boy came out of the bog. Quickly glancing around, he went to the cash desk and offered a note for changing. He picked up the coins and headed for a row of video game machines. Once he was in place, Paul made his move. Moving alongside the boy, Paul leaned close to whisper in the boy's ear.

"Lets take a walk."

Paul's approach startled the boy.

"What?"

"You heard. Follow me if you know what's good for you."

Paul left the arcade and the boy followed, intrigued and nervous. Once clear of the arcade, Paul stopped and allowed the boy to catch up with him.

"How much did he pay you?"

"Pay? Who?"

"Cut the shit. The old guy in there." said Paul.

"Nothing."

"Look I know he gave you a blow job. I heard you in there as you told him you were nearly coming. So, once more, what did he pay you?"

"Oh, so you want a go too? Why should I tell you? If you want me it'll cost you a tenner, OK."

"No, I don't want sex with you. I just thought you needed to be careful. I heard you. I could have been the manager, then what?"

"I charge him a tenner as well! He likes to lick my arse first then I..."

Paul interupted the youth."OK, OK. That's enough. Where do you live?"

"Nowhere. What's it to you? Are you buying or not? If not fuck off and leave me alone."

The youth looked directly at Paul and when there was no response he turned and headed back to the arcade. Paul glanced at his watch and was sure that Andy would have completed his business and returned to the flat. Sitting with Andy drinking coffee, Paul described what he had seen and the conversation with the youth.

"Don't get involved there," advised Andy. "Well known for pick-ups, but it's not for you. I know I worry about you and Jeff, and yes he will be back, but he's much better and safer than any quick blow job you're going to come across from there. Promise me you won't lower yourself by working there. Promise!"

Paul had no intention of working there, as Andy put it, but he was astonished that it really was that easy. At that moment Paul promised himself he would only work the top of the meat market. After all, he was quality. Jeff made him feel that he was the best. Neither mentioned the business that Andy had completed that afternoon.

Thursday night and Andy set out for his shift in the bar and then later he would be performing to order. Literally to order. The client loved to feel power and if past experience was anything to go by Andy would earn his cash, twice over at least.

Jeff had phoned Thursday afternoon and chatted to both Andy and Paul as though nothing untoward had occurred this side of the turn of the century. He made arrangements with Paul to come around early evening and planned to stay the night so they could have an early start for Derbyshire Friday morning. Could Paul contact Alex and see if he could be ready for a Friday morning departure. All so simple, no problems.

Paul looked in the back pocket of his jeans where he had kept Alex's mobile number. He stared for a while at the scrap of paper. It was a strange moment for Paul as he felt a tenderness towards Alex, just by looking at a number on a scrap of paper. He wanted Alex as his lover, yet he needed Jeff. Perhaps neither of them would force him to decide. He knew that Jeff could clothe, feed and give him a roof over his head, yet perhaps because Alex had been his first real fuck, that was complicating his decisions. Then there was Andy. Paul knew he wanted him and if Andy tried something on he would get

David Keane

exactly what he wanted. Paul rang Alex's mobile number at the end of the school day. He was rewarded with an immediate response.

"Hi! It's Paul. Can you talk?"

"Oh hello. Yes."

"I'll be quick. Can you be here in the morning to travel to Derbyshire? Please be here, say ten o'clock. Fuck school, they'll not worry about you. By the way, any news about Dale?"

Alex had answered so swiftly because he hoped it would be Dale trying to contact him. Mild disappointment followed when he heard Paul's voice.

"No news and yes I'll be there. Must return Sunday though. OK?"

"Fine see you then. Love you." Paul rang off before Alex could reply.

Paul thought the trip into Derbyshire might give him the opportunity to sort things out. He just wanted Jeff to get him working. Now fucking for cash was a really exciting thought. The thought of total strangers playing with him, screwing, paying then disappearing into the night was a real-turn on. Surely Jeff would not make arrangements with somethone gross! If Andy was right, Jeff would make his move soon and offer him work. He liked Andy's lifestyle, even working relatively part-time he lived well. Yes, this was a far better alternative to school and the estate.

Jeff arrived carrying a bottle of red wine. He went immediately into the kitchen to open the bottle.

"It needs to breathe." Paul nodded in agreement, even though the mysteries of wine-drinking were still a secret to him. Jeff moved across to Paul and kissed him on the lips. "How you been gorgeous?" Jeff asked.

"Fine."

"Missed me?"

No mention from Jeff about his actions and attitude the last time they saw each other.

"I haven't had it with Andy you know."

Unthinking, Paul told the truth. Jeff laughed as he replied.

"I know that. Just don't want him to think he can. You're mine, and don't you forget that either. Especially if you know what's best for you."

Jeff delivered the most frightening form of a threat, the one delivered with a smiling face.

They sat side by side on the white settee drinking red wine. Jeff's tight white trousers left little to the imagination and as the wine brought a glow to his inner self, Paul longed for those long black fingers to invade him. Another glassfull and the French wine invaded his cock, bringing a hardness that wanted release. Jeff sensed the moment and once more kissed the unresisting youth full on his moist lips. Paul's tongue frantically pushed its way into the open mouth of a pimp.

"Hey, hold on! We got all night!" Jeff broke free.

"Are you looking forward to the weekend? You haven't mentioned it."

"Course I am. It's just that I haven't been there and don't know what you want me to ask."

Jeff stroked Paul's inner thigh.

"OK. Fair comment. Well, it's a cottage, two bedrooms, near Bakewell. We'll do some walking, eating ,drinking and talking. I'll go for a couple of steady fitness runs and when I return you'll be waiting for me." As he spoke, Jeff began to unzip Paul's jeans and slipped his hand inside the briefs he had bought. Paul relaxed and allowed the strong black fingers to roam his crutch. Jeff's free hand undid the belt buckle and Paul instinctively waited for Jeff to make his demands upon him. What happened next slightly surprised Paul.

"I want to video you. OK?"

"Yes but doing what?"

"Strip and I'll talk you through it."

Without protest, Paul began to undress and Jeff went into Andy's room and returned with the video camera.

"I want you to stand there and wank yourself off. Catch your spunk in your hand and then lick it and swallow it. OK?" The tones Jeff used were the same he used to ask Paul if he wanted sugar in his coffe. Perfectly reasonable, but that was the way he worked. Standing totally naked, Paul began to oblige. He stood with his legs apart and began to wank, slowly, gently at first. Jeff moved around him, videoing at close range each hand movement. A close focus on Paul's cock was replaced by a shot of his face that revealed his closed eyes and slightly parted lips. Without direction from Jeff, he began to finger himself and stopped wanking to stroke his pubic hair. Leaving his pubes, he lifted his hand up his body, with the other hand pushing fingers deep inside himself, the

David Keane

free hand's nails digging deep into his hard nipples in turn. Fingers were released from his arse and he grabbed his throbbing shaft and began to wank at a determined pace. He wanted to please Jeff. He was successful in his achievements, as spunk shot from his purple head, his hand missing the first spray. Then he cupped his hand just ahead of his twitching tool to receive three large pumpings of juice. As the third finished its issue, he tilted back his head and brought his sticky full palm up to his face and furiously licked his hand clean. He had never tasted his spunk like this, and there was a look of pleasure on his face as the juices of his still hard cock found their way down his gulping throat.

"You're something else!" gasped an excited Jeff. He tapped the camcorder, knowing his "friends"would be delighted with this new addition to the meat market. Jeff's imagination was running riot as he thought of the money to be made.

"I'll have a shower." With that Paul was away to the bathroom, leaving behind a huge bulge in tight white trousers.

Paul showered, with no interruption from Jeff. Although he had only brought himself off, he had found the prescence of the audience and camcorder particularly stimulating. The water and exotic shower cream had the required effect. Skin cleansed and revitalised, delicate to his touch and perfumed to entice, Paul was better prepared to face the demands that were likely to follow. Events did not take their anticipated course when he returned to the living area, wearing black boxer shorts and a multi-coloured towelling robe he had removed from Andy's wardrobe. Curling up alongside Jeff, he confidently expected black hands to roam, but all Jeff was interested in at this time was to order a takeaway Indian meal.

"Not too hot," Paul requested, causing laughter at the unintended innuendo. Chicken Tikka Masala and Chicken Korma with pillau rice, plus poppadoms, pickles and naan bread completed the order. While they waited for the meal to arrive no memtion was made of the wank or the video. Paul thought about asking about the video, remembering Alex's doubts about the game, as they called it. One day Jeff would explain, although perhaps he really did want the video for himself. Paul persuaded himself that when Jeff lay alone in bed at night, he would watch the videos and bring himself off imagining the two boys performing. On special occasions he would watch Paul working himself. These thoughts teased Paul's imagination, as he convinced himself of their accuracy. The meal duly arrived and Jeff paid the young smiling Indian delivery guy, pushing an additional note into the youth's palm as a tip. As he put the meal onto warmed plates, Jeff smiled at Paul.

"Fancy shagging an Indian boy?"

"Dunno. Why?"

"Just wondered. He was rather nice wasn't he?"

Paul burst out in free and easy laughter.

"You're a cunt you are. And yes he was nice."

"I may be a tart, whore and a bitch. But please, not a cunt. Chutney or lime pickle?"

Loud carefree laughter filled the apartment. Paul was enjoying his new life.

Meal completed and dirty plates consigned to the built-in dishwasher, the evening was flitted away drinking beer, having finished the wine earlier. Talking of Derbyshire hills, pubs, walks, moors and sheep, Jeff cracked the inevitable jokes featuring sheep, wellingtons and shepherds. Paul asked increduously if shepherds really did fuck sheep. Jeff's laughter, and non committal reply, failed to provide a satisfactory answer. The evening faded into cosy comfort. Jeff's more tender side began to emerge. He entranced Paul with stories about his rapid rise through the ranks of Britain's junior athletes, to that of an Olympic hopeful and ad-man's dream. His perfectly developed body, was now on hold. His finely chisselled features could have made him a living as a photographic model. Instead he had become a symbol for the young, especially young blacks and his image was being carefully crafted. A muscle strain meant everything was in limbo. Jeff knew that one day he would be forced from the closet. When that day came would he become a gay icon, or the ad-mans nightmare? For now he would relish the delights of a working-class boy from Birmingham and forget the rest of the world. His business of finding friends for clients was extremely dangerous, but it gave him a kick. He did not see himself as a pimp. Jeff always had difficulty facing up to the truth, even when it smacked him between the eyes. As Paul began to find his eye-lids becoming heavy, Jeff led him to Andy's room. They undressed in silence and slipped under the duvet. Jeff's hands sought their target and stroked the semi slumbering Paul to erection. Both lost the battle of consciousness as sleep conquered and every desire had to wait for Derbyshire.

Twenty

Paul woke feeling smothered. When he had fully come round from a deep sleep, he was aware of being encased in strong dark arms. The warmth of Jeff's body transferred a glow to Paul. This morning there was no ache in his body, just contentment. Jeff was still asleep and as he lay in Jeff's arms, Paul's thoughts drifted to unknown Derbyshire. Thoughts of happy moments away from the city. Suddenly Paul realised he was not in his own bed, but with Jeff in Andy's. What Paul did not know was that Andy had returned just half an hour before he had woken. Andy looked in and saw the sleeping lovers and decided to grab a few hours' sleep in Paul's bed. Andy had been surprised that despite being tired from his work, his body was excited by the smell of Paul's flesh. Hard but tired, Andy drifted into sleep, his dreams teasing at his shaft.

Paul was drifting back to sleep when Jeff awoke.

"Morning gorgeous."

That greeting enhanced the glow of contentment felt by Paul. No-one had really spoken to him before within such endearing terms. Jeff kissed Paul's cheek, then his lips. As he did so, he tightened his grip around the quivering, dark teenage body. Tongues clashed like sabres, hands roamed with determination. Paul lay on his back as Jeff tried to mount him and he brought up his legs as he almost by instinct opened them wide.

"Any life in there? Are you two coming or not?" Enquired Andy from the other side of the door. Jeff's cock was teasing Paul's tunnel entrance when Andy called. The sudden urge to take Paul with little foreplay disrupted beyond recall, replaced by laughter.

"We were!"

"Well, get your butts out here. It's nine o'clock. Things to do, places to go!"

Each showered alone and a breakfast of toast was consumed on the run. Paul packed a selection of items from the recently purchased goodies, ensur-

David Keane

ing that nothing of his past would travel with him. Even the sports bag used was one belonging to Andy, the side pockets containing a selection of fruit-flavoured condoms, and what looked like heavy-duty ones. Paul wondered what they were for. They looked thick and surely would be insensitive. He was to find out that night, his first in Derbyshire. Tubes of lubricant completed the pocket contents. Paul assumed Andy had packed them for him but did not refer to the items. He assumed men didn't.

Alex arrived ten minutes early and was greeted by a kiss from Andy. Paul would have liked to do the same but just muttered.

"Good to see you."

"You too."

It was decided that as Alex needed to return on Sunday, and perhaps Andy also, two cars would be taken. Andy knew the way so he would travel with Alex, Jeff and Paul in Jeff's BMW. Alex explained that he had told his folks he needed a break and that he was going hosteling in Derbyshire but he didn't know where. It would depend on where he could get in. He would phone them on his mobile sometime during the weekend. That way he could not be traced and could make contact when he wanted. The family thought the break would do him good, but what were they to do if Dale called? Alex told them he didn't think he would. His reply had been so matter-of-fact that it sent a shudder down his spine. He was astonished by his own certainty.

Paul was thrilled to be travelling in the BMW. Never in his wildest dreams did he think that this could happen to him. His only regret was that he could not share the moment with old school friends, apart from Alex. His mother never entered these thoughts of regret. The journey took them out of the city and via Litchfield and Ashbourne the open spaces of Derbyshire welcomed them. Although they avoided motorways, they soon lost Alex and Andy, the Fiesta making no attempt to try and keep up with the BMW. Jeff and Paul arrived around midday. Just before the town of Bakewell, Jeff turned along what appeared to be an old farm lane. The limestone cottage came suddenly into view about a quarter of a mile from the main road. The two-storey building was approached appropriately from the rear; the front overlooking a valley that took Paul's breath away. The rear was where the cars would park, next to an old wooden barn that served as a store and home to a cockerel and his harem of hens. The front had a tidy English cottage garden, much sought-after by visitors, especially Americans, but rarely found. The valley view stretched for miles and was composed of grazing land with sheep and cattle, small wooded areas and distant heather-topped hills.

"Like it?" asked a smiling Jeff.

"Wow! It's....It's....."

"Thought you would! Come on, let's get the car unloaded while we wait for those dead-beats!"

The inside of the cottage was surprisingly modern but with furnishings reminiscent of a Victorian age of chintz and lace. Large settees that swallowed up anyone resting on them contrasted with a modern television and video. A large Swedish chrome music centre took up a whole swathe of space along one wall. The view of the valley through leaded windows was equally imposing from the cosy comfort of the lounge. The kitchen area consisted of two rooms made into one and was full of state-of-the art gadgetry.

Stairs came down into the lounge and Paul rushed up them. He went into the front bedroom and immediately noticed the king-size double bed that dominated the room. The furnishings were in keeping with the rest of the cottage: soft pastel colours with a subtle light pink the basis of all with flower patterns everywhere. With that feeling of comfy cosiness once more, Paul leapt onto the bed as Jeff entered the room.

"Is the room to your liking, sir?"

Lying on the bed, Paul lifted his head to take in the valley view through the window once more. Although each view outside, groundfloor and bedroom were basically the same, each had subtle differences brought about by perspective. As Paul gazed, his attention was distracted by Jeff slowly unzipping his grey slacks. Jeff pulled his cock free and it visibly grew before Paul's eyes. Jeff stepped up to the bedside and Paul moved across to lick the dark mysterious tip. A hand gripped the back of his head as the tip sought to push past his lips. Paul opened his mouth wide to receive the huge magnificence. At that moment a car could be heard coming to a halt at the rear. A horn sounded and loud, laughing voices could be heard as Jeff struggled to put his equipment away and rezip. Andy and Alex entered the kitchen.

"Anyone home?" Andy shouted upstairs.

"Have you been taking lessons on perfect timing?" Jeff shouted from the top of the stairs with a grinning Paul behind him.

After the newcomers had brought their luggage in, Jeff inspected the contents of the fridge.

"Looks good in here. Enough to feed an army and all good stuff."

Plenty of bacon – smoked and unsmoked, eggs, cheese, milk, steaks, quiche, plus frozen ready meals supported Jeff's claims.

"Folks from the farm look after the place and stock up. They are down the lane about another quarter of a mile. They are discreet and won't bother us. The chickens are their's of course but the eggs are ours while we are here. Two brothers work the farm, one about your age Alex, the other same as me. They run things now as their parents were killed in a car crash last year. I was here when it happened. Awful it was. They don't talk about it. A subject best avoided. Nice guys aren't they Andy?"

Andy's reply comprised only of a grinning nodding head.

Lunch consisted of a Spanish omelette, cooked to perfection by Andy. He accepted the praise and assured his companions he was not just a pretty face. Paul, who had never been particularly sure what the trip was going to be like, truly adored the cottage. Although he had only been there a couple of hours, the feeling was one of calm among friends. It was generally agreed that a walk would be taken during the afternoon. As they left the cottage Paul filled his lungs with the fresh Derbyshire air. He turned to Alex.

"Beats Skipton and it definitely beats Brum!"

"Agreed. Pity there isn't a shower block," was the cryptic reply. It had been decided to work through the pots and pans, so the dishwasher received its first load before they left on their walk.

Keeping to paths, they walked the hills around Bakewell and were never more than a couple of miles from the cottage at any time. The views brought silence from the walkers. Paul seemed mesmerised by all before him. He noticed sounds and smells that passed the others by. From the edge of a path he picked up a perfectly formed and undamaged small bird's skull. Despite the entreaties of his companions, Paul determined to keep his souvenir. Carefully he slid it into his jacket pocket, after wrapping it in a tissue provided by Jeff. He had been fascinated by the tiny bones that made up the bird's jaw. No, there was nothing like this in Birmingham, at least not his Birmingham. They took a breather overlooking the small market town. The church spire dominated the landscape. No-one spoke for some time as they sat on the short, coarse grass. Jeff put an arm around Paul's shoulders. Andy did likewise and the two younger guys accepted the gesture of more than friendship. It was Paul who broke the silence.

"Just listen. You'd think there was silence, but no, listen to those birds and there's at least one lamb that will not shut up. He sounds as though he's laughing. Hear him?"

Smiling companions nodded their agreement. Jeff ran his fingers through Paul's hair.

"Come on gorgeous. Let's make tracks."

From within Andy's arms, Alex felt the pangs of jealousy within the pit of his stomach. He was not alone. Andy gazed unspeaking into the distance. Jeff stood up and thrust his crutch in Paul's face. Paul pretended to bite the thrusting crutch which then moved quickly away as Jeff jogged along the path. The others caught up with Jeff and the foursome made their way back to the cottage. A few cans of beer and a steak dinner later, with the chef being Jeff, the foursome settled down to watch a straight porno movie. Various comments were made regarding the inadequacies of the male performers and Jeff thought his companions could do much better. All four were quite tired and as they relaxed on the floor and on the settees, at least two sets of eyes were struggling to stay open. Alex suddenly sat upright and pointed to the window.

"There's someone out there! I saw a torch!"

Jeff moved to the window and looked out, then pulled the flower patterned curtains shut.

"No, it must have been a car headlight on the bottom road."

"There was and it was no headlight," said a determined Alex. Paul sat on the deep-pile carpet with his arms wrapped around his hunched-up knees. He looked up at Jeff and was immediately reassured by him. Shortly after, it was decided that it was time for bed. Nothing had been discussed regarding sleeping arrangements but it seemed to have been assumed that Jeff and Paul would take the front bedroom, with Andy and Alex occupying the smaller rear bedroom.

David Keane

Paul and Alex went up first and spontaneously Paul kissed Alex on the forehead.

"Be good." said Paul as he touched Alex on his cheek.

Alex said nothing, but turned into the bedroom, leaving Paul at the top of the stairs. Although the cottage was small, both bedrooms were en suite and all occupants once behind those flimsy-looking doors need bother no-one else.

Paul went into the front bedroom, while downstairs Jeff and Andy looked out of the window once more.

"Shall we lock the doors?" asked a smiling Andy.

"No way!" responded a grinning Jeff.

Twenty One

Friday was treated with the usual clock-watching enthusiasm by Paul's peers. Tony and Chris couldn't wait because Barry, the video shop manager, had finally agreed to supply a video that was going to blow their minds. Giant cocks stuffing gaping, well-used holes guaranteed. The vid was to be collected in a carrier bag by Tony after school. He had invited Chris, plus his new friends Shamir and Gordon. It would have been good to have had Paul along but no-one seemed to know where he was. Same went for Dale. It would have been fun to have had a Skipton reunion, but that was simply not possible. Alex was a very cool dude. Bet he knows something about Dale and Paul. Alex was a mystery and the girls still fancied him like mad. Tony's parents were going to a club in Coventry with some boozy mates from the car factory. They would not be back until the very early hours, so a good vid, plenty of cans, some fun and send Shamir and Gordon home, then to bed with Chris. All nice and neat for his mother to find him sleeping soundly with his friend.

The end of school bell went and groups of babbling youngsters hurried on their way towards the escape exit. Some to watch television and videos all weekend, others to play sport, others to watch, some to shop, others out with parents and some to do their best to increase the population levels of Birmingham. The carefree, it-will-be-all-right-just-once attitude, defying all the sex education lessons school could provide. Absent pupils would, in one case, be performing unaware that the label prostitute had become an accurate description. Another would be laying anonymously in a French mortuary, waiting to be found.

Tony picked up the video without any problems. Soon after Tony's parents had left for Coventry Chris arrived, to be followed by Shamir and Gordon. Chris and Gordon arrived with two six packs of lager each. Laughing and giggling at nothing in particular the boys settled down to watch the video with enthusiasm. Shamir declined the offer of lager from Gordon. As Tony slid the

David Keane

video into the machine, an expectant silence fell across the group, disturbed only by a belch, courtesy of Chris. Cigarettes lit, cans in hand, they peered at the slightly foggy image before them. The video, being a poor copy of the original, immediately opened with an erect cock being orally devoured by a blond girl, genuine peroxide, complete with bright red lips. The scratchy musical accompaniment competing with sucking and breathy sounds.

"Look at that cock!" was the amazed reaction from Chris.

"Not bad for an old guy," said Tony.

"He's not that old, he's about twenty-five."observed Chris.

Gordon and Shamir watched in open mouthed silence as the camera zoomed in close to show spunk issuing from the side of the girl's mouth. She pulled away to be hit just above her mouth by a full gushing spurt. The camera panned back to show a smiling blond wiping her lips with her fingertips.

"Is it real?" asked an incredulous Shamir.

"Every inch and drop!" exclaimed Tony.

"Cor!" replied Shamir.

The video moved on, more sucking, then onto the shagging. This aspect really grabbed the attention of the boggle-eyed youths. Without exception, each observer had one hand in his pocket. Inevitably it was Tony who drew attention to the fact. He was sitting on the carpet, when he leaned backwards to lie flat. His erection was apparent to all. No-one spoke as Tony began to unzip his jeans. Inevitably eyes switched from screen to crutch and back again. Tony slid his hand inside his briefs obviously toying with a very stiff shaft. He looked in the direction of Gordon, who averted his eyes to the TV screen. Getting no reaction there, he transfered his attention to Shamir, who did not avert his eyes. Holding Shamir's gaze, Tony flicked his hard cock from the restraints of his underwear. Gordon and Chris, their attention firmly held by writhing bodies on the screen, did not immediately notice that Shamir had moved alongside Tony and was staring down at the erection Tony was waving from side to side. Despite his hopes, Tony was still taken by surprise, as Shamir plunged down on his shaft, enclosing all in his mouth. It may have been the video, the lager, the audience or Shamir's deep sucking action as his tongue teased the head of Tony's cock, but rapidly spunk flowed into Shamir's mouth and down his throat. Once the cock was away from his mouth, Shamir shocked his compatriots and himself by announcing to all

"Who's next? I'll take you all, one by one!"

There was a moment's hesitation before Chris opened his jeans, then pulled out a thick cock. Shamir kept his promise, and as he did so, Gordon produced his superb length. Tony watched the action and kept his erection. Shamir moved from one spear to another, his tongue and neck muscles working overtime. Tony reached for Shamir's zip and caressed his hardness before releasing into the room a dusky, perfectly formed shaft. Shamir fulfilled Gordon and Chris's desires before filling Tony's mouth with his own hot love-juice. The video played on to unseeing eyes.

Twenty Two

In the protective shadows of the farmyard, two young males loitered. They waited until all the lights inside the cottage were extinguished. They waited a further five minutes before moving towards the unlocked cottage door. The older of the two was tall with crew-cut fair hair and broad, work-developed shoulders. The younger was shorter but stocky in build and had similar crew-cut fair hair. They hesitated once more before pressing the old-fashioned door catch and entering the dark cottage. They walked slowly to the stairs without tripping or falling. Creeping silently up the stairs, they separated when they reached the top. The older guy crossed to stand outside the door that concealed Andy and Alex locked in a tongue-entwined embrace. The younger stood outside the door concealing Jeff and Paul enjoying the delights of a 69. No sooner had the cottage occupants slipped beneath the duvet covers, that they had begun to pleasure themselves. Neither Alex or Paul were aware of the visitors stealthily getting closer. Their entry would not have the same effect upon Jeff or Andy. The cottage inhabitants were about to meet the farmers.

Simultaneously the invaders opened the doors and slipped into bedrooms. The reactions of Alex and Paul were the same. Terror! Both were reassured by their partners as the intruders slowly undressed before them. The darkness added to the mystery, whilst the reassurance given brought about an acceptance. Before the stripping could be completed, Jeff switched on a bedside lamp.

"Hold it. Let's all go next door."

Not another word was spoken as the three moved to the adjacent bedroom. Once in there, the invader finally removed his jeans. Alex looked at Paul with undisguised amazement, Paul just shrugged his shoulders and slipped into bed alongside Alex. Andy slipped out of the bed and moved to stand with Jeff. Paul and Alex watched as their two visitors completed their stripping and stood totally naked before them. Two firm virtually hairless bodies that strutted hard pale shafts of pleasure looked to Jeff for direction.

"Nice to see you again boys! Do join our friends!"

Alex shifted nervously but Paul moved across to welcome the younger brother. The older slipped under the duvet on Alex's side of the bed. Jeff used the dimmer switch to lower the light. Under the duvet hands explored. After his nervous start Alex did not flinch as rough hands seized his shaft. Jeff stepped forward and pulled the duvet from the bed to reveal four bodies beginning to entangle with each other.

"Allow me to introduce you guys! Alex and Paul meet Dan and Steve." Jeff was clearly excited by the situation he had planned over the phone earlier in the week. Both farmer boys were well-known to him. He had fucked the younger, Steve, in the barn on an earlier visit while being watched by Dan. Then the rugged Dan had taken Jeff, violently in the cattle stall. Jeff had screamed as the pale monstrous tool had been forced inside him. The brothers gratefully accepted the cash reward and promised him any future assistance they could give they would be delighted to do so. This was the third time the bedroom fantasy would be enacted.

Andy and Jeff watched and waited for the action to begin. They were not disappointed. The excitement of the occasion worked wonders on Paul who began to lick Steve's chest, finding erect nipples en route to a quivering stomach. Steve's muscles were tense and his body sought release as Paul licked his demanding shaft. Steve began to moan as his brother sought to open Alex's legs. Resistance was strong as Alex saw the size he was expected to accommodate.

"Here put this on," Jeff threw a condom to Dan. Dan obliged. Jeff threw a tube of lube to Alex.

"Use this. It'll make it easier for you," Jeff's tone was quietly persuasive and Alex followed the instruction, believing that resistance would be futile, probably dangerous. Once prepared, Alex raised his legs in the air, arched his back and prepared to receive Dan. Alongside the preparations had been repeated, with Paul slipping on the rubber as Steve used generous amounts of lube on himself.As though choreographed, Dan and Paul began to enter their targets. Alex grimaced but gripping the bedsheet held on as Dan brutal-

David Keane

ly forced his way into him. Meanwhile, Paul was getting a warm response from Steve as he gently pushed his way home. Paul began to move in rhythm with Steve and their movements captivated the watching Jeff. Alex decided not to resist Dan, he just prayed for it to end soon. Jeff was annoyed with Alex's performance, but Dan was accepting what little was being offered. He was so wrapped up in his own satisfaction he was blissfully unaware that Alex was not enjoying the session. The pain was strong, the end blissfully quick. Dan soon throbbed in the tunnel and filled the condom teat. He withdrew and along with Jeff and Andy watched fascinated as Steve and Paul performed with grace and passion. The two youngsters had only met minutes before but their bodies convulsed in unison oblivious to those around them. Only Alex ignored the performance, staring at the ceiling as he gradually straightened his legs. Andy and Jeff retreated from the bedroom to go next-door where they screwed each other in turn. For Jeff it had been a wonderful night and he knew that Paul would not disappoint his financial aspirations. He had found a star! Pity about that Alex, but you can't win them all. During the night as Dan and Steve slept Paul reached out for Alex. The rebuff was clear as Alex silently moved away as far as the restrictions of the bed would allow. Paul turned to Steve and was not spurned. A glow of raw sex seared through their bodies as they pleasured each other without an audience. Paul's climax was still intense as his cock gushed its appreciation. Likewise next door, as Jeff was being screwed to the mattress by Andy; his thoughts of Paul increasing his moment of ecstasy. Just before dawn the intruders returned to the farm.

As dawn broke, the placid normality of the hills and valley remained seemingly undisturbed. The cockerel crowed in triumph as his harem scuttled around the farmyard. Jeff smiled in dreamy sleep.

Alex slept fitfully through the remainder of the night. His inner anger suppressed the physical pain within him. Despite his disturbed night, Alex was unaware the invaders had departed. He now knew the reality of being raped. The difference from the norm being that his assailant was totally unaware he was a rapist. No words had passed between them as Dan had plunged deep inside him. Alex's moans and gasps had been interpreted by Dan as a testament to his prowess and general ability to give pleasure. Dan was not regarded as being very bright by the villagers. Just a beefy hunk who could perform with whatever he was confronted with. Living on a farm had opened up the possibilities for varied gratification. Alex had unintentionally given him satisfaction by the tightness offered. Some of his farm experiences were unknown to the world with one exception – Jeff. He had refused Jeff's overly generous offer to be the sole human star in a video. Jeff was not a person to take no for an answer and would probably be back with an improved offer. Dan could not understand why Jeff did not realise that he did not want his face shown to a video audience. Dan did not realise that his face would never be featured. After all, it certainly was not his best feature!

Paul had fond dreams of Steve. His body had surprised him in quickly responding to the questions asked by a stranger. Paul knew that Steve was boyishly better-looking than brother Dan, but even so, how quickly they were in tune with each other's desires still shocked him. The big disappointment during the night was the rebuttal from Alex. After pleasing Steve, Paul longed to enjoy Alex. Sadly this was not to be; perhaps the morning would bring a change. Like Alex, Paul was unaware of Dan and Steve's departure. It was pleasant for Paul when he awoke to find Alex by his side. Alex began to moan and turn on his side as Paul watched his every move, his every intake of breath. Paul leant over to kiss Alex's bare shoulder. The tender touch brought a reaction from Alex of a jolting groan, and suddenly Alex moved onto his back with his eyes wide open.

"Oh it's you!"

"Sorry, who did you expect?"

Alex's action had taken Paul by surprise.

"That was awful last night. Having that rural thug up me was more than I could cope with. You know, I could feel his sweaty body and smell his bloody pigs or cows on him. Then I had this horrible thought that the rubber would split and his spunk would be inside me. I felt his cock shoot over and over again, and all I could smell was animals. The bastard! You realise we had no choice last night don't you? We were set up for those two queens to watch, to be bloody ogled at while they played with their deformed oversized tools! Anyway it's over! We're back to Brum today. Right?"

Paul lay on his back, looking at the ceiling and not Alex. He paused choosing his words carefully.

"I'm not going. Sorry."

"Are you mad? You do realise what you're getting into? They want you to make money. To be in videos, to shag to order with whoever Jeff wants you to. Even when he is with you alone it's not love. It's ....?"

"Finished? Yes your probably right."

Paul flung the duvet from the bed revealing their naked bodies. Alex in a foetal curl, Paul stretched out on his back showing his ever erect cock.

"Look at that."

Paul gripped his shaft firmly.

"That is my future. Yes, fuck to order for cash. Great isn't it? Look, I've got what it takes, so why not? You've had your share of it haven't you!"

Alex lost control and hit Paul across the face, hard and savagely. The beautiful relationship was torn and crushed in one swift moment of jealousy. Paul gently touched the wounded spot with his finger tips. Only with a supreme effort did Paul manage to hold back the tears. He had lost his first love and that's what really hurt.

"I'll pack."

Alex's feeble response brought no outward reaction from Paul. Alex left the bed and gathered his few items into his sports bag. Within five minutes he'd left the cottage, unknown to his hosts. Only then did the tears burst from Paul's eyes. The deep wailing from a broken spirit woke Jeff and Andy. They both rushed into the bedroom to discover the traumatised Paul. Jeff took him in his arms.

"What's happened?" asked Jeff.

"He's gone. Gone home! Why? Why?"

Jeff nodded towards the door. Andy left the room to make coffee. Jeff held Paul tightly and his tears turned to sobs and then faded. Jeff could not resist what he saw and gently but deliberately stroked Paul's firm cock. At that moment the tears began again.

Eating breakfast soon enabled Paul to regain his composure. Jeff was agitated and concerned that Alex would tell the world about their activities.

"He's dead if he blabs. Dead," uttered Jeff through clenched teeth.

"He won't say a word. He's not a snitch. He'll just go home," reassured

Paul.

Jeff reached across the breakfast table and gripped Paul's jaw in his hand.

"He'd better, or you'll join him somewhere pretty nasty. Get it?"

Paul nodded his clear understanding.

"That's enough!" protested Andy.

Jeff got up and walked briskly to the back door and exited, slamming the door for effect.

"Don't worry. It's the usual temper-tantrum. Leaves me a bit in the shit your mate deserting us. I'll have to go back today by train from Sheffield. God knows how many changes, but I daren't risk Sunday travel."

"Aren't we all going back tomorrow?"

Andy looked questioningly at Paul.

"No, hasn't superstud told you? He wants you here with him for a few days, or more. That's OK isn't it?"

Paul stood up and walked across the room to gaze through the window across the valley.

"Suppose so. I think he did say something."

"Cheer up. You'll be OK. He really does like you."

"He's a funny way of showing it." Paul continued gazing through the window, thinking how he had hoped for something more than being liked.

Jeff returned one hour later. He breezed in and demanded coffee.

"Good walk that. What you two dicks been up to?"

Andy was the first to reply.

"Nothing to worry you. I'll have to go back today now. Can you run me to Sheffield for the train?"

"No need. You can go from Derby direct tomorrow, and yes, we'll run you to the station."

As Jeff spoke, Paul glanced at Andy and a look of relief crossed his face. He was happy that Andy was staying and felt more secure. Jeff pulled a small notebook from his pocket and picked up a pen from a jar on a kitchen shelf. Both Andy and Paul watched as he wrote.

"Just writing down your earnings my gorgeous little spunkbag. Call it fifty quid so far shall we."

Silence had been bought and Paul's career move finalised.

Alex did not return home. He drove through Bakewell and headed out on the Buxton road. Unsure of a destination, he just wanted to keep moving. Buxton seemed as good as anywhere. He would stay for the weekend. It would mean fewer questions.

Back in Birmingham, Tony's mother decided that despite her late return from Coventry, that at 10 o'clock it was time for the two boys to wake up. They had been awake for over an hour. It was a good thing she had slept in until 09.30 and not visited her son's room earlier. The shock may have caused injury. The boys were getting careless. A near-miss!

Two mothers sat waiting for the phone to ring. One had a chance receiving of a call. The other began the day by resorting to prayer. A prayer to know her son's fate. Prayer had become her only comfort as her husband chose to ignore questions regarding their son's fate. A father suspects he knows, a mother always does.

Walking the streets of Buxton past the spa and around St. Ann's Crescent, Alex eventually spent much of the day on a bench in Pavilion Gardens. Just watching the world pass by helped clear his mind. He would find a guest-house for the night, then return to Birmingham late Sunday afternoon. His thoughts turned to home and he could not get Dale out of his mind. Looking across the gardens, every young man reminded him of Dale. At first he thought he was going mad, then he realised how tired and hungry he was. Leaving his bench, he walked across to the main Pavilion building and entered the tropical conservatory. Well-maintained, the whole building communicated its Victorian ancestry. Lots of glass supported by ornate frames and pillars, the place gave comfort to a wounded soul. Alex went up the modern staircase to the verandah café and helped himself to a selection of sandwiches from the self service buffet. Restored to a reasonable condition, Alex returned to his car and set off for Tideswell, for no other reason than he liked the name he spotted on the map. On arrival he soon found a guest house that had a small single room available for one night, bathroom along the corridor. It was only 5 o'clock in the afternoon when he lay on the tidy single bed and before he could take in the Victorian chintz furnishings of yet another Derbyshire cottage, he fell under the spell of deep sleep. His grateful body did not stir until 9 o'clock that evening. A quick shower down the corridor and away to the village chip shop, just in time before early closing. Now fortified, he briefly considered a return to Bakewell to rescue that stupid little tart, but soon abandoned the idea. Before returning to the guesthouse, he phoned home on the mobile. He explained he was near Buxton and having a wonderful time. He was saddened at the not entirely unexpected news that there was no news. Guesthouse and sleep. All was nearly well again. Just Dale and Paul to worry about. His weary body did not allow him to worry for very long. Sleep the protector and comforter did its job well.

Paul found it difficult to cope with Jeff's mood changes but he did his best. Although inexperienced in years, he was a quick learner.

"How about a ride around and see what we can find to amuse us?"

Andy and Paul readily agreed, both openly relieved at Jeff's bright turn of mood. They set off in the BMW fully-equipped for a day's walking. They parked the car in the village of Cressbrook and started to walk in the direction of Litton, the neighbouring village to Tideswell. Jeff decided they would return to the car, ride to Litton and start their walk there. They did not take the direct route but followed a walk that Jeff was familiar with. The weather was kind. Not cold and not too warm either, a gentle refreshing breeze. Walking along the main street of Tideswell mid-afternoon, they passed the chip shop and the large parish church before finding a small café where they joined fellow walkers for cream teas. A final stroll back in the direction of the church and up the hill in the direction of Litton and the car. It was just before 5 o'clock and a Ford Fiesta entered the village behind the walkers.

By the time they returned to the cottage, Paul was back to his bright and bubbly self. Jeff was carefree and Andy worried, concerned they would be confronted by another Jeff mood change. He decided to go along with whatever was suggested: the safe option. Once more they showered separately, a fact that surprised Paul as sex in the shower for him was one of life's delights. Each dressed in the clothes they liked, designer jeans and T-shirts.

Jeff cooked a tasty chicken dish, loads of breast, spicy sauce and vegetables, all washed down with a couple of bottles of white wine. Paul felt he was treated as an equal. Not patronised, not used. How could Alex have made those stupid remarks? As Paul and Andy loaded the dishwasher, Jeff paraded about the kitchen waving the camcorder.

"Let's earn some dosh shall we guys? It's payback time." grinned Jeff. Andy looked across at Paul who grinned back at Jeff.

"Now you'll find out what you've really let yourself in for. Hope you've got fully-charged balls.... You'll need them. I've seen that look before!" Andy said as the grin began to slip from Paul's face, but not Jeff's.

"Think we'll start in there," said Jeff, looking in the direction of the living room.

"Get your kit off my gorgeous spunkbag and I'll make you a star. Trust me.... just do as I say and you'll do good."

Jeff waved the cam in the air and left the unspoken threat of what could happen if Paul didn't do as he was told. Paul missed the inference, but Andy was fully aware. He had seen Jeff's previous efforts when he was making stars. It was going to be a late night.

Paul did exactly as he was told, and moved into the living area. He peeled his T-shirt up his body and arms slowly. He had learnt quickly the effect the slow removal that tightened muscles, and showed his dusky skin to good effect. Fully aware that the boss was watching, he equally slowly loosened the designer belt that held his designer jeans in place, allowing the denim to slide sensually to the deep-pile carpet. Stepping from his jeans, having earlier removed his designer trainers with equal attention he peeled off his socks. He stood before Jeff naked apart from the designer boxer shorts. Jeff was still fully dressed, and, unnoticed for a moment by Paul, a naked Andy came into the room. He was flaccid but still very impressive and Paul felt a little self-conscious.

"It's easy folks! Just do what you want when you want and all will be fine. I'll video everything, I can edit later. I want you to include arse-licking, really get the tongue in, 69, nipple-biting and sucking each in turn before shagging. By the way Andy, I want you right up his gorgeous arse. OK? No holding back!"

Jeff did not ask Paul whether any of the scenario was against his wishes. He knew it was going to be painful, but work was work. He was unsure about the arse-licking, but there was a first time for everything.

"OK my lovelies, lets do it."

Andy moved to Paul and began to stroke his stomach, before slipping his hand inside his boxers, his free hand pulling them down. They fell to the carpet and Paul stepped from them. Andy knelt before him and took Paul's blooming manhood in his mouth. Paul glanced at Jeff who was moving the cam up and down the youth's body, taking in every movement. Paul knew it was too soon to cum, so he tapped Andy on the head. Andy got the message and moved up Paul's body to kiss him hard on the lips. Stepping back, Andy gestured for Paul to lie on the carpet. Carefully Andy arranged Paul's body how he wanted it. Arse pointing to the sky. Andy knelt behind Paul and his tongue sought Paul's lovehole. When it came in contact and then licked the entrance, Paul shook with a new pleasure that flooded his brain with desire. He was having to consciously fight the desire to shoot, so he imagined his mother with Bad Breath. This did the trick as Andy pulled the arse cheeks before his face wide open and then thrust his tongue into Paul's tunnel of love. Andy left Paul slapping his arse as he withdrew. Paul found himself facing Andy's arse, and dutifully pulled the cheeks wide, and then began his exploration by tongue. New sensations, all of them good. Both actors were now unaware of Jeff's presence as he moved around them changing angles for maximum effect. Andy once again took the lead and they lay side by side so that Jeff could seize the moment to photograph their rock-hard erections. Paul's eyes took in the shining magnificence of Andy. Its tight skin, cut and waiting. Paul knew the agony and thrill would begin soon. He prayed that Andy would take care and consider him, not just Jeff and his camera. Andy moved into position for a 69 and gently took Paul, as he pushed his cock to Paul's lips. Once again, oblivious to Jeff's presence, they enjoyed each other. Andy was careful to interpret the little twitches his mouth felt, as he wanted Paul to enjoy the session but no shooting just yet. Andy pushed to the back of Paul's throat, then withdrew feeling he was about to cum. His experience allowed him to remain in control. Paul licked Andy wherever he could. Tasting his sweat, needing him to take him. Dismissing thoughts of his mother and Bad Breath, he saw Andy rolling a condom, that had mysteriously appeared alongside them, into place. Paul took in a deep breath, and mentally prepared for the pain. Andy commanded Paul to crouch before him and smothered his hand in lube before using his fingers to ensure that the lube was in Paul and at his entrance. Andy deliberately chose this position from experience. It

David Keane

enabled Jeff to video both their faces as they shagged: one in pain, the other calm. Paul began to cry out as Andy pushed deep into him. Andy responded to the cry by plunging in even further. Paul gasped for breath. Blood pumped in his head and Andy continued to plunge in and out, not fully withdrawing before plunging to the hilt. Then Andy began to yell.

"Yes! Yes! Yes!" and Paul could feel the massive throbbing inside him as Andy took his final pleasure with a violent thrusting vengeance. As Andy withdrew, Paul could see Jeff stripping with a fury. When naked, Jeff took hold of the camcorder once more and videoed Andy peeling off the condom and revealing his glistening shaft. Andy turned the condom inside out and offered the contents to the still crouching Paul who realised what he had to do. Obediently he licked the condom free of its hot contents. As he did so Jeff was rolling another condom down his shaft. Paul hoped it was for Andy. He was exhausted. Jeff moved around Paul.

"No. Please. No. Later. Please later," the pleading in his voice excited Jeff. Just what he wanted. His reply to Paul was to thrust forcefully against him and enter him without any hesitation.

"Now you shit. Now open your fucking legs wider. I said wider, you shit."

Without a thought for Paul, Jeff plunged with even more fury than Andy had into him. Andy, aware of Paul's agony stood close to the locked bodies. One dusky-brown, not responding, just crouched there taking the deep black muscular form on its back.

"Hey take care." feebly suggested Andy.

"Piss off shit!"

Then Jeff gasped and shouted out loud and increased his thrusts.

"Fuck! Oh Fuck! Jeff screamed as he pumped inside the barely conscious body beneath him. Jeff withdrew quickly and removed the condom, throwing it at Andy's face, just missing its target.

"Thanks lads. That was great! Great video! Get dressed! Better lock the door tonight!" Jeff laughed loudly at his own attempt at a joke. Paul thought it not a joke but a very good idea. No more tonight, he desperately hoped as he slowly came to his feet. Andy surprised him with a kiss on the cheek.

"Hope it wasn't too bad." Andy spoke quietly, almost guiltily.

"No, it was fine," Paul lied.

"Good. He likes you, you know."

Jeff had departed to the bathroom.

"Really?"

"Oh yes. Ignore the verbals. I'm sure you've earned a ton tonight."

"Really. Great. It was fine OK." Paul was not lying this time. The thought of having one hundred pounds for sex with Andy was very appealing and his body was recovering quickly. Perhaps the thought of the money helped. He knew it did and there was the other fifty. One hundred and fifty pounds. He had never known such wealth before. Good thing his powers of recovery were excellent.

The rest of the evening took on a bizarre aspect as the trio drank lager and played cards, and Monopoly. No talk of sex, not even dirty jokes. Occasionally Jeff stroked Paul's hair and then his leg as he considered his next move at cards or Monopoly. Late that evening Jeff imparted a piece of information.

"Got visitors tomorrow night. Pity you can't stay Andy. "

Andy glanced towards Paul then back to Jeff.

"Anyone I know?"

"No. Big spenders, if you know what I mean."

Andy knew exactly what he meant. Paul was too tired to care. Jeff locked the cottage door. Two farmers returned home later after trying, but failing to open the door of the darkened cottage.

A late full English breakfast was just what Alex needed. As he awoke, the taste bud-exploding smell of frying bacon had seeped under the bedroom door. Suddenly, in the comfortably furnished bedroom the world seemed a better place. Away from men wanting to use any body that crossed their path. The smell of sexually-created sweat, the cries of pain, lust and satiation seemed a million miles away and all the better for that. Today was going to be for Alex and no-one else. He was determined to walk and walk until the fresh country air had cleansed his inner soul. A good start to the day would be to let the shower water wash away any traces of that cottage somewhere near Bakewell. 'Things must be getting better' he smiled to himself with a little joke as the shower water did its job. He joked that Bakewell with its tart was the ideal place for the Jeffs of this world. Refreshed and feeling fully cleansed, at least on the outside, he patted himself dry with a thick, fluffy, white towel. Dressed and hair combed, down to breakfast at the large oak table that filled the cottage breakfast room. Two other guests were already in place, to Alex's surprise who was unaware of any other guests. A few awkward moments and the usual guesthouse breakfast chat among visitors began. They were from Doncaster and were enjoying a weekend walking, something they did several times a year, always coming to the same guesthouse because it was nice. They thought that it was nice that Alex was having a walking weekend and he had to take care as he was alone and it was a shame he did not have a friend to walk with. Tentative offers were made for him to join them on their walk, but these were politely refused much to the relief of the couple, who found this youth a little distracted and odd that he did not share their interest in the mineral deposits of the Peak District.

Breakfast was a hurried affair at the Bakewell cottage. It had been decided that Andy would catch an earlier train from Derby so that Jeff and Paul could make full use of the day in any way they wished. The three guys left in the BMW, watched silently by two sets of eyes. Paul caught sight of Steve from the car window and each stared with a holding glance that seemed to make an unspoken promise. The journey to Derby was a short and uneventful one. The conversation had little substance and any eavesdropper would have learnt nothing of the weekend's events. Paul felt that Andy would have liked to have said something but his fear of Jeff influenced all his decisions, whether they be major or minor. Jeff still amazed Paul. The Jeff in the car today was the kind, friendly, 'you can trust me with your life' one. The generous one who had bought him a full wardrobe of designer clothes. Paul knew what was expected of him and it was not that that he worried about. His fear came from the violent uncaring way his body was used by anyone who Jeff wanted. The fact money was involved was not a problem, in fact that was a real bonus. It was simply the violence. He knew that there would be a price to pay for a roof over his head, but he prayed Jeff would be gentler in future, as the car sped to Derby's railway station. A quiet Sunday in a quiet Midlands town. Once the farewells had been spoken there was little to delay the remaining pair's journey back to Bakewell.

"Take care of him," Andy instructed Jeff.

"But of course. He'll be well-looked after. You can be very sure of that."

A repeated conversation and a repeated caring and at the same time warning look in the direction of Paul from Andy. The concern genuine but the will to actually do anything to protect Paul too much to ask. He must take his chance along with everyone else. That was the price to pay.

Andy was swiftly into the booking hall and away out of sight. No need to pay for parking, Jeff wanted to be on his own with Paul as quickly as possible. He had plans for the day, before guests would arrive during the evening. They did not stop on the return journey, Paul lazing in the luxuriant white leather seat, thinking one day he would have a BMW just like Jeff's. With these thoughts in mind, they arrived back at the cottage. Straight upstairs, the two changed to their walking attire. Jeff slowly stripped completely and walked across the room fully aware of Paul's attention. As he reached into the wardrobe for a fresh pair of jeans, his well-defined muscular development glinted in the mid morning sun pouring through the uncurtained window. His black skin glistened as he walked from sun to shadow and pulled the jeans up his taut body to cover his underwear-free crutch. Paul decided to mimic this style of dress and likewise chose to wear no underwear. He was unsure why but firmly believed it must be the latest fashion trend. Paul slipped on his favourite white Lacoste T-shirt and followed the similar clad Jeff downstairs. Already his cock seemed to be chafing against the rough denim and for him it was not a pleasant feeling. The fullness of the two pairs of jeans was apparent to any observer. Two sets of eyes were firmly fixed on the front door of the cottage. Waiting, wanting and not to be distracted. Dangerous.

Twenty Three

Strolling through Tideswell, Alex watched as locals and visitors entered the Cathedral of the Peak; Tideswell Parish Church. The previous day, the magnificence of the parish church had not registered with him, but today his perceptions were totally different. The short path from the main road led to the welcoming doorway. Alex felt compelled to follow the worshippers into the church. Almost apologetically, Alex placed himself at the back of the large main body of the church. The handful of worshippers had been devoured by the huge rows of pews. Alex stayed for about ten minutes and joined in the opening hymn. Sitting alone, he offered up a private prayer for Dale. He implored God to persuade Dale to return home and to keep him safe wherever he was. Alex just hoped he was not too late. He begged God's forgiveness for referring to Dale as the stupid sod, but he couldn't help it. Finally he asked God's protection for Paul, who he was convinced was getting involved with something that was beyond his control. Quietly he slipped out of the church into the bright, sunny tiny market place. He had already checked-out of the guest house, so when he returned to the Fiesta it was to drive out of the village. After checking his map, he decided to travel to Matlock Bath. The riverside village took Alex by surprise. It was reminiscent of a Rhineland village, or maybe a little Switzerland. It was Sunday and that meant that the village was taken over by hundreds of bikers, as it had been for many years. Bikers of all kinds and ages. Hells Angels in their leathers, strolling side by side with family groups. Just people doing their own thing in their own way. The steep-sided valley, its Victorian villas clinging to the cliffside defying all the rules of gravity as they had done for around one hundred years, overlooked disdainfully the crowded waterfront. Alex wandered unhurriedly along the waterfront and into the park. Families were picnicking or hiring rowing boats as Alex just wandered. Back onto the main street, he drifted into an amusement arcade that incongruously filled a prime position. Groups of youngsters fought battles in castles or on race tracks. No-one took any notice of him and he liked that. He tried his luck on a couple of machines, but it seemed his luck was out. From there he went and joined the queue at a fish and chip shop. Momentarily he had forgotten his enormous breakfast and the sight of the huge portion of chips, along with a large battered haddock he thought he had taken on a challenge too great. No worries, perched on the small wall separating the park from the road he consumed the bagful without much difficulty; the fresh air must have sharpened his appetite.

Too soon it was time to return to his car and begin the journey back to Birmingham. For Alex the weekend had been a remarkable success, in that he had experienced the clearing of his troubled mind. At the moment he could do nothing to help Dale, but on his return to school he would start the process as he saw it, to save Paul. He just hoped his resolve would hold, aware that if he told the truth he would be implicating himself in the web of abuse and cheap sexual gratification. A few miles out of Matlock, Alex's resolve began to waver just a little when he fully considered the contribution he had made to Paul's disappearance. And then there was Dale. Perhaps he would just play the situation by ear. Not a good idea to destroy his career before it had started. After all, they had both made their choices. It was just that neither Dale or Paul had shown good judgment. But it was their choice.

As he drove away from the cottage, Jeff had decided to head for Matlock Bath. The thought did cross his mind that as it was a Sunday the place would be crowded out with bikers. All very well if leather was the mood for the day, but today it wasn't. He had neglected his medically-imposed training programme, and would have to lie to his personal trainer on his return. The roadwork to rebuild tired muscles had been neglected, even though as a sprinter the road work did not figure strongly in his recuperation plan, it had its place. Weighttraining, vital to his recovery, had been neglected over the weekend. He would work doubly hard upon his return he promised himself. He needed a break, and Paul was just the distraction required. Anyway, there were clients to keep happy, so must get Paul sorted during the day. Forget Matlock. Without discussion Jeff changed his plans and headed for Hathersage.

Paul was totally besotted by the BMW. Like many males before him, the car was almost capable of bringing him to orgasm. They sped along. Paul

David Keane

never questioned their destination, all that mattered was being in the car with Jeff. He knew he would have to perform sometime during the day. As they approached Grindleford it was Jeff that raised the issue.

"Expecting visitors tonight."

"Yes I know."

"You know what I mean when I say visitors?"

"You mean work for me don't you?" was the attempt at a confident reply from Paul.

Jeff laughed."You could say that!"

"What's he like?"

"There's two of them, you don't have to like them when it's work. Nervous?"

Paul hesitated before replying with some honesty.

"A bit. Do I have to do for two?"

"Yep! But there's nothing to it. Just do as they ask. Take your lead from them. It's that simple. When you've had enough just shoot your load. But not too quickly mind! They want their money's worth! They're businessmen. Not rough stuff like our farmer friends. Good practice for you they were. I mean, sex with total strangers that you don't know really. Just remember – it's only a job."

Jeff glanced at Paul before adding, "The real stuff's with me remember. Never forget that!"

Again the implied threat.

"You'll be there won't you, tonight? I'll be OK if you're there. It's just that, well you know..."

Behind the mask of a sickly smile Jeff replied,

"Oh yes, I'll be there."

Paul relaxed. "How much will I earn, and when will I get paid?"

"Don't be in such a rush! You'll get your share."

Again the sickly flashing smile that owed nothing to sincerity.

On arrival Jeff parked at the outdoor activities shop. Strolling through the store Paul was amazed at the price of the clothing. Brightly-coloured water-proofs, reds, yellows and blues. Paul tried a red and yellow hooded water-proof jacket that nearly buried him. Finding the correct size, he put it on and proceeded to twirl and parade. His eyes nearly popped out of his head as he checked the price tag, £265.

"Like it?" asked a smiling Jeff.

"It's brill."

Jeff turned to the loitering assistant.

"We'll have this one," said Jeff producing a Platinum credit card. Paul just looked in open-mouthed amazement, then removed the coat for wrapping.

"Thanks Jeff. It's totally brill!"

Before they could leave the shop, Jeff was asked to sign several autographs as he was recognised. Accepting the best wishes offered regarding his recovery from injury, they left the shop to put the large carrier containing the coat in the car. Paul felt a warm glow of importance as he walked alongside this guy who people recognised. He smiled inwardly as he thought they haven't a clue as to what they did together. Paul's big moment came when a youngster asked him for his autograph. Jeff nodded for Paul to sign as he explained to the small crowd that Paul was his protégée and they were to remember his name as he would be famous one day. After signing five more pieces of paper Paul thought to himself that he could get used to the idea of being famous.

Alex arrived home just before 9 o'clock in the evening. Late enough to avoid having to discuss at length the trip, tired through walking and driving, plus not too late to cause concern as to safety. He had worked his timing perfectly. Needed an early night and had an essay to finish for the morning. His mother briefly told him there was no news regarding Dale. Alex thinly smiled his thanks at the non-news. His family fully understood, and off he went to his room, reality neatly avoided for the time being. Later as he lay in bed gently stroking his erect cock, his thoughts dwelt on Paul. Alex felt fearful: fearful for the safety of an over-developed, naive, beautiful boy. An eighteen-year-old boy with whom he was in love, no matter how he tried to avoid the issue. Alex achieved a climax; not explosive but soothing to his weary body. Before he lost consciousness, Alex decided he must do something to help Paul, even if the boy did not know he needed help.

Jeff and Paul walked for miles on a round trip from Hathersage that took them up into the hills and on to the bleak, purple heather moors. Although within a stone's throw from the city of Sheffield, the air felt crisp and clean. This weekend was no different from any other. A large proportion of Sheffield's population had headed for the hills, but Jeff and Paul walked into a world they felt was theirs alone. For Paul, these moments were bliss, however transient.

They sat for nearly an hour on a huge boulder that gave them a panoramic view across the valley. To Paul, Birmingham seemed a million miles away and it could stay there. Jeff's fingertips gently stroked Paul's thigh and reminded him of the reason he was there.

After arriving at the cottage late in the afternoon they once again removed their outdoor clothes. When they were both naked, Jeff reached out for Paul. No words were spoken as he led Paul into the bathroom and then the shower. The hot water eased both sets of aching muscles and strong arms reassured Paul as they wrapped around him. Jeff's tongue licked Paul's neck as the embrace tightened. Both were aroused and needed relief. Their lips met and their tongues entwined. Paul's fingers stroked the hugeness of Jeff, whose hands forced Paul's head down the black firm flesh. Paul paused on his journey to tease the black navel with his tongue and one set of fingers toyed with the short, black, coarse pubic hair, whilst the other caressed the taut inner thighs that were spread to receive them. Hot shower water coursed its way between writhing flesh and Paul's lips sought the tip of Jeff's dark weapon. Jeff's hands held Paul firmly in place and with a tenderness that took Paul by surprise, Jeff gently pushed his textured black tool to the back of Paul's eager throat. Water gushed over Paul's head, some finding his nostrils, causing him to leave Jeff as he spluttered his mouth and nose clear of water. Jeff quickly pulled his head back into place and the thrusting of Jeff's hips encouraged the fully aroused Paul to complete his task. Jeff screamed his pleasure as he shot his full load down the receptive throat, time and time again. Paul's whimpers of joy quickly changed to gagging sounds as strong hands refused to give him space to breath. Once released, Paul swallowed repeatedly to clear his throat. He stood up and tried to take Jeff's hand to his hardness.

"Hey, not now. You'll need that fully-charged tonight for work."

Jeff stepped from the shower and began to towel down. Paul felt the pangs of rejection and his hardness began to sag. Once Jeff was clear of the bathroom, Paul dried himself and returned to the bedroom to dress. Jeff was already dressed.

"Don't take it to heart. You're a great suck! Work must come first. Just look after that cock of yours. You gorgeous load of spunk!"

Paul dressed in silence taking care despite his rejection not to upset Jeff. Perhaps after work Jeff would fulfill his desires. Paul knew in his heart he would do exactly what Jeff asked or demanded.

Jeff, as usual, found the way to Paul's heart was definitely via his stomach. The combination of hill-walking, fresh air and sex made the presentation of a huge mixed grill very satisfying. Paul under Jeff's watchful gaze, attacked the meal with gusto, following a bowlful of ice cream. Paul's expression of thanks was to lean back, pat his stomach and belch.

"Oh! Sorry about that, but it was a great meal. Thanks very much."

Jeff nodded his appreciation of Paul's remark.

"When are they arriving then?"

"Soon. Soon. Relax, you'll be fine. You know you're good. You've a fortune between your legs and don't forget that. When we're together that's just for us. When you're selling it's nothing more than that. Come for cash! Fair enough. You've enough for all. Just look after that hole of yours!"

A nervous laugh came from Paul. He took a deep breath and prepared for action. He didn't have to wait for long.

Fifteen minutes later, there was a knock on the door. Neither Paul nor Jeff heard a car arrive, the reason being that their visitors had parked down the lane and walked the final 200 metres. Their arrival did not go unnoticed. Jeff let the visitors in. The first one was a short portly man of about fifty, with an almost completely bald head, apart from a few light brown wisps. Both were wearing grey suits that seemed completely out of keeping with the surroundings. The second man was a clone of the first, except he was heavier; tall as he was wide. Jeff introduced Paul to the men. He shyly stood before them looking down at the carpet. This was going to be very hard work he thought. What if he couldn't get a hard-on!

"Very nice Jeff. Look at me lad!" Paul obliged.

"Oh yes, very nice."

David Keane

The fatter man grunted his approval.

Jeff poured gin and tonics for his clients, while they prepared a line of cocaine. Jeff and Paul declined their offer to share. As the clients snorted their brains away, Jeff started a video. On it Paul was surprised to see two boys, about his age, playing with each other's small but well-defined cocks. They wanked each other then licked up each other's cum self-consciously in front of the camera. These two stars clearly wished they were somewhere else. Fatman sat beside Paul and they were joined by the portly man on the other side. Jeff moved to the chair furthest away, indicating the two men they could get on with whatever they wanted. Each man began stroking Paul's thighs under Jeff's approving gaze. The video was now showing a group of athletes in a changing room performing a multitude of mind and body-bending acts. Paul watched the screen fascinated, longing to try some of the action with Jeff. His mind was brought back to reality as Fatman fumbled to open Paul's zip.

"Get your gear off," demanded the portly one. Paul obliged and sat naked between them with his flaccid cock hanging between his open legs. A look of concern crossed Jeff face. He needn't have worried. The portly one went down on Paul, who as he gazed at the ceiling, hardened-up on cue. Jeff smiled his appreciation and then moved around in his chair, indicating to Paul that he should move around to heighten the men's pleasure. Paul remained static trying to work out what Jeff wanted him to do. Jeff mouthed to him:

"Fucking act. Move!"

Paul did exactly as he was told adding appropriate sound effects that stimulated the blob sucking his cock. Abruptly the sucking stopped and Jeff produced a suitcase revealing an assortment of condoms and dildos of varying sizes from big to tear-jerkingly enormous. Paul's immediate reaction was to think 'no way' until he remembered it was work and that meant food, clothes and a roof over his head.

To Paul's horror, the cottage door opened and in walked Steve and Dan. No-one else was concerned and everyone seemed to know each other.

"Glad you could drop in lads," was the smiling welcome from Jeff and the two clients nodded their agreement.

"Glad to be of service," said Dan as he and his brother began to strip. Paul sat between the Blobs and Dan stepped towards him offering his firm cock. Without any hesitation, Paul accepted the offered shaft, much to the joy of Fatman. Steve likewise offered himself to Portly Man. Paul was astonished by what happened next, as the two brothers began to kiss each other fervently, tongues splashing in and out of each other's mouths. Steve and Dan pulled away from the others and fell to the carpet. Tongues continued their battle as nails clawed each other's flesh.

"Brotherly love!" exclaimed a joyful Jeff. Paul's eyes were firmly focused on the eager brotherly lovers before him. The two visitors huffed and puffed as they divested themselves of their clothes. The only clothed person in the room was Jeff, who switched the video off as being superfluous to requirements. Dan and Steve manoevered themselves into a 69 and Fatman went down on Paul, who suddenly found a small dick being offered to his lips. He managed not to laugh and took the offered mini gift. Jeff smiled his approval and gave Paul a thumbs up. Paul, despite rolls of fat obscuring his vision, watched as Dan entered his younger brother. Screams from Steve stimulated Paul and helping increase Paul's efforts on the small tool, much to the evident delight of Portly Man. Jeff was lost to Paul's vision momentarily. He had retreated to the bedroom, returning naked except for a leather hood, with small slits for his eyes and one narrow one for his mouth. On his feet he wore a heavy pair of black leather ankle boots. In his hand Jeff clutched a whip, made up of several strips of black leather, fed into a handle of hard-woven leather. The two clients broke free from Paul, but the brothers continued to shag each other on the carpet, Dan thrusting deeply into his screaming brother. Dan slowed his actions and waited while Jeff went to the bathroom and returned with a small towel. Jeff grabbed Steve's hair and pulled his head upwards and pushed the small yellow hand towel into his mouth. Dan continued the fearsome shagging of his brother.

"Time for initiation I think," yelled Jeff, lashing Dan's back with a flick of the wrist, that brought the leather strips cracking onto pale flesh that immediately turned pink at the point of impact. Dan smiled his thanks and withdrew from his grateful brother. Steve remained on the carpet and Paul on the leather settee, as the two blobs stood silently by Jeff.

"Take him!" comanded Jeff, and before Paul could react, he was grabbed

David Keane

by each arm and pulled to a standing position. Steve stood up with difficulty and moved past the group to open the cottage door. The two men held onto Paul, and Dan picked up the yellow towel and forced it into Paul's mouth, his terrified eyes telling all that he expected death.

"Walk him," ordered Jeff, and Paul was frog-marched through the door into the now cool night air. Terror struck at Paul's heart as he was at the head of an obscene procession of naked male flesh, brought up at the rear by the masked Jeff. They entered the dilapidated barn and Dan switched on the bright lights that now floodled the scene. Ahead of him, Paul could see two straps hanging from a beam and he was marched to a point beneath them. His arms were thrust upwards. He gave Steve a pleading look, but he averted his eyes and shrugged his shoulders.

"Let initiation begin," announced Jeff.

Dan removed the towel from Paul's mouth and he gratefully gasped in gulps of farmyard air. From behind a bale of hay, Steve produced a black cloth hood which hung limply from his hand. Paul was lifted from the ground and stood on a bale of hay by the two men. Standing alongside Paul, Dan pulled down the straps and fully stretched them. Each wrist was attached in turn, leaving Paul standing but with his arms fully stretched above his head.

"Steve!" shouted Jeff, and at his command he stepped forward with the cloth hood which he handed to his older brother.

Many thoughts flashed through Paul's wounded mind. What a place to die, and for what reason? Suddenly he was plunged into darkness as the hood was placed over his head. Dan tied a cord around the base of the hood around Paul's neck. Paul's terror was there for all to see as his short sharp breaths pulled in and out the black cloth covering his petrified face.

"Let's do it!" yelled the fully-aroused masked Jeff.

Dan and Steve stepped forward and pulled the bale away. Paul swung grotesquely by his wrists and his legs swung wildly in the air.

"Don't, please, don't," was the agonised cry from beneath the mask. The pleading was music to the ears of the clients as they stepped aside for Jeff to step forward. His leather-masked head kissed the arse cheeks of the hanging masked beautiful youth. He had lost his identity hanging there like a carcass. All Paul's strength went into trying to support his hanging torso. The leather-masked head moved to the front the body and rubbed his leather-coated face against the ferociously erect cock. Jeff stepped back and gestured Steve forward.

"It's me," whispered Steve trying to comfort Paul. He then lightly placed his lips around Paul's shaft and gently sucked as he ran his hands up and down the hanging body. Paul was in agony from his aching stretched arms. He thought that if he came, then it would all be over, but although fully erect, the pain he was experiencing overcame his need to orgasm. Bizarrely, he thought that just being masked, and not strung up, would be sexually stimulating, not knowing who was actually sucking. He gave Steve credit for doing his best. In his darkness, Paul felt as though his arms were leaving his body. Suddenly there was a crack of the whip that was being lashed across Steve's back and forced his teeth to dig deep into Paul's now wounded cock. Paul's scream seared through the night air. No-one stood close to Paul's hanging torso. Jeff's breathing came in rapid bursts as he stepped forward raising the whip high above his masked head.

"Prepare yourself. Now is the time for you to join us. Be brave."

Before Paul could reply, the whip lashed across his naked back, cutting the flesh on impact. The nerve-shattering scream that exploded from the pained body was terrifying. Ordinary people would've been shocked, but these spectators were thrilled by it. Dan pushed his brother to the ground and Steve gratefully allowed him to mount him once more. Dan's thrusts were deep and brutal, his load gushing forth quickly. Dan's best climaxes had always been in his brother and this matched or exceeded any of the previous ones.

Jeff moved around Paul, kicking up the barn dust with his booted feet and raised his whip arm. Once again, with all his strength the whip came down, this time searing across Paul's chest. This time it was a piercing yell that reverberated off the barn's sides. Jeff rushed to Paul's rear and thrashed him again across his back. There was no cry from the trussed bleeding body. What Jeff did not know was that when he was lashed across his chest the pain was so severe that Paul's mind mercifully shut down his brain and he lapsed into unconsciousness. The clients held his legs as Dan removed the hood and Paul's head lolled back. Dan and Steve untied his wrists and held his limp bleeding body. Steve was overcome by the horror of what he had been involved in. It had never been like this before. He gave Jeff the benefit of any doubt, deciding he was only mad.

"Get some water and revive him. I've not finished with him yet," demanded Jeff.

Fatman grinned with pleasure, the other client less sure as he looked at the youth's torn flesh and his closed eyes, in a seemingly dead face.

Dan protested,"Cut it out. He can't take any more!"

"He can and he will!" proclaimed Jeff to the exultant support of Fatman.

Paul was carried outside the barn by Dan and Steve. Now that he had screwed his brother, he was seeing the world through clearer eyes. Jeff strode across the farmyard and returned with a bucket of water, which he threw over Paul. The shock of the cold water did its job, bringing Paul back to pain-racked consciousness. He struggled in the grip of Steve and Dan.

"Take him back to barn," ordered Jeff.

"No way. He's going into the house and you're not going to touch him," objected Dan.

"How dare you! Do as I say!" yelled the enraged Jeff.

Fatman foolishly joined in the discussion.

"We've not had what we paid for yet. We've only just started. You promised us we could fuck him when you've done with the slut, and that's exactly what we're going to do."

Dan passed Paul to the strong arms of his brother and crossed to face Fatman.

"Look, you get your clothes and get dressed, then get your fat arses out of here!"

Fatman looked as though he was going to protest but thought better of it and went into the barn, along with his stunned silent friend. Jeff was not so clever and lunged angrily at Dan. A deft sidestep and a swipe across the shaved head of his attacker saw Jeff lying in the farmyard dirt.

"You bastard!" yelled the wounded Jeff as an unbooted foot crunched into his genitals. The cry from Jeff was loud and long, as the foot crunched into its target once more. Jeff curled up in the farmyard dirt trying desperately to protect himself. He was crying. Pleading.

"No more. I beg you no more!" he gasped painfully. He cut a hideous figure lying there clutching his crushed equipment whilst still wearing the mask and boots. Steve and Dan carried Paul into the cottage and locked the door. They carried Paul to the bathroom and Steve began to run the bath. Dan went downstairs and returned with two large containers of coarse seasalt from the kitchen. He emptied both into the bath water, then they lowered the quietly sobbing body. The piercing scream that issued must have echoed down the valley below.

Twenty Four

Moving across to the coffee machine, Alex was unaware that three members of the Sixth Form had spoken to him. Other things were on his mind: Paul. He decided that he must do something, but was unsure what. He deliberated on the merits of driving to Derbyshire and fetching him back. Problem with that was, what if he refused to get in the car? The other problem was that Paul did not know Alex was in love with him. Alex at last understood that there was a big difference between sex and love. Dale and the others provided the physical need and the necessary relief. Paul was different. Without knowing it, he provided so much more. Now because of weakness and lack of courage, Alex felt he had left Paul to his fate, whatever that may be. He was angry with himself for not dragging Paul into the car. He must do something and soon. An opportunity was soon to present itself.

Alex was surprised by the light tap on his shoulder.

"Oh! Hello Mr. Price. What can I do for you?"

Jack Price guided Alex out of the Common Room and into the corridor.

"Can I ask you about Paul, Paul Montgomery?"

"Sure." Alex could feel his face warming. He turned away from Jack Price to look aimlessly down the corridor.

"It's just that he's gone missing and I wondered if you had heard anything. You know grapevine information and all that."

Still looking down the corridor Alex replied.

"No, not heard a thing. I'll tell you if I do."

"I would appreciate it."

Jack Price left Alex and headed down the corridor. He was a little puzzled. Alex, not usually a shy boy, did not look him in the eye.

When Mr. Price disappeared round the distant corner, Alex deliberately banged the back of his head against the wall. Repeated bangs of head on wall until the bell rang for the start of first lesson.

"Hey, anybody seen Paul this morning?" asked Tony. The only response he got was a group shaking of heads.

Twenty Five

The two clients did not hang about. Once dressed they were down the drive to their car and away into the night.

Jeff, his balls swollen and aching, tried to sleep in the BMW. It was a fitful night. The pain between his legs decreased as his balls seemed to get bigger. He made three attempts to gain entry to the cottage, without success. After removing the leather mask he found a travel rug in the boot. After taking off his boots he wrapped himself in the rug and accepted a night in the car. The rug irritated his skin and the cloudless sky made it a cold night in the BMW. A full moon gazed down on the troubled scene. Just after dawn, Dan approached the BMW, wearing just a pair of jeans and shoes. He tapped loudly on the window. Jeff stirred immediately.

"How are you?" asked Dan in a just-passing-the-time-of-day tone.

"Could be better," was the plaintive response.

Dan looked at the crumpled, curled-up heap in the car. Didn't look much like a medal winner.

"If you can behave yourself you can come into the cottage."

No sound of protest, no angry scene. Just submission.

"No problem. Where's Paul?"

"Asleep and if you try anything with him, I'll have your balls. OK?"

"No problem."

Dan stepped back from the door and with difficulty Jeff stepped from the car and shuffled towards the cottage. Once inside they were greeted with Steve wearing a tiny pair of shorts and sweatshirt, enjoying an early breakfast of bacon, egg and sausage. Steve grinned as a clearly pained Jeff had difficulty sitting on a chair. Dan went upstairs and returned with a toweling dressing gown which he threw at Jeff.

"You could have killed him you know!" said Dan. Jeff nodded.

"You went too far."

Once again the nodded response. Then Jeff looked up at Dan.

"I was so turned-on. It was fabulous. Seeing him hanging there. You know, when I hit him the third time I shot my load, but you didn't notice. You were too busy being a hero! Although I came I wanted more and more. My whole body wanted him humiliated. If you hadn't stopped me I would have killed him. The really frightening thing is I would have loved it and had the world's greatest orgasm doing it."

Dan and Steve exchanged looks.

"What exactly do you mean?"

There was a long silence.

"I can't stop it happening."

"You're kidding," said an astonished Dan.

No verbal response from Jeff. The heavy silence consumed the trio, each with their own thoughts. Dan made the first move.

"Come brother, we've got work to do."

Dan and Steve hurriedly left and made their way to the farmhouse. Neither spoke until there was distance between themselves and Jeff.

"He frightens me!" volunteered Steve.

"Seriously weird," was the only comment from a seriously concerned Dan.

Once inside the farmhouse, the door was locked, and a shared shower was undertaken. The warm water rid their minds of thoughts of Jeff. Brotherly love reached its ultimate state.

Physically, Jeff recovered quite quickly. Pain gave way to a soreness and aching. Ponderously Jeff left the cottage and unnoticed made his way to the barn. Many problems were now plunging Jeff into the depths of depression. The interruption of his career, perhaps he would never race again. The possibility haunted him. Then what would life be? No star status and then maybe the guys would be less likely to perform for him. Teenagers were his specialty, especially virgins. Shag them for a while, then rent them out when a new one came along. Suddenly Jeff despised himself. A deep loathing swept through his mind that made him cry out in a gut-rending yell. There had to be a way out. Then entering the barn he had the answer. Lying coiled on the floor was a strong hemp rope. It almost spoke to him as he picked it up. It would be his friend. Facing him, below a beam was a small pile of hay bales. His mind was made up. Alongside the rope was a rough old sack. He carried the rope and sack, then clambered onto the top of the bales. A feeling of peace overcame him. He was sure now what he had to do. Choice did not come into it. Execution. Execution for his crimes. Self-inflicted execution. Suicide. Suicide by hanging. Confidently he flung one end of the rope over the beam and then tied the free end to a barn upright. The dangling end of the rope beckoned him, enticed him, seduced him. His fingers fumbled as he tied a noose that due to the rope's thickness did slip easily. Once he had satisfied himself that the noose would hold, he placed the musty-smelling sack over his head. A conscious thought of consideration towards whoever may find his body. Hanging may well distort his features and he did not wish to haunt any-one. With both hands he placed the noose over his head and allowed it to rest caressingly around his neck. With difficulty he tightened the knot. With his left foot he reached out for the edge of the bale and then brought his right leg alongside. One step away from oblivion. Before taking that step, one final prayer begging forgiveness for his life. As he tried to form the never-to-be spoken prayer in his mind, the bale that supported his last moments on Earth rocked, slowly at first, then fell away, allowing Jeff a final thought of not feel-ing ready yet. The noose tightened as Jeff dropped just a few centimetres but his feet were clear of obstruction. There was no mercy at the end as his neck resolutely refused to break or dislocate. Only slow strangulation remained.

Dan left the farmhouse heading towards the barn at the precise moment the bale gave way. He needed to collect a can of agricultural paraffin for the lawnmower. A small patch of lawn in front of the living room window needed trimming. Dan loved farming but resolutely avoided gardening until evasion could be tolerated no longer. As he entered the barn, a grotesque sight greet-ed him. A toweling-clad body capped with a mouldy sack twitched and legs and arms flailed in the air. Dan immediately recognised the robe. He rushed forward to grab the still kicking legs, brought them together and with all the strength he could muster, pulled the legs and body downwards. His grunts of exertion drowned out the sound as Jeff's neck relented to the pressure, and all was still.

Releasing the now swaying corpse, Dan stepped back.

"Hope you're happy now."

Dan left the barn without the paraffin. The lawn would have to wait for another day.

Paul slept safely in his bed.

Dan returned to the cottage and the second bedroom where he found Steve in bed and wide awake. Dan stripped and slipped under the duvet. Taking Steve in his arms he sighed.

"It's over."

Steve dreamily muttered his reply, "Good," but was totally unaware what was over.

Dan comforted Steve for the next hour in the only way he knew.

After his act of comforting, Dan knew there was no other way but to tell Steve the truth about Jeff's disappearance. Steve listened intently in silence to Dan's full and graphic description of events and his involvement. When his confession was complete he waited nervously for Steve's reaction. When it came it was short and reassuring.

"Fine, bro'. Must keep a certain person clear of the barn and get rid of the garbage."

With tenderness Steve took Dan in his arms and lightly kissed his thoughtful brother on his furrowed forehead.

Twenty Six

Paul woke. His body was sore and ached. The silence of the cottage was unnerving, then he was jolted awake as the memories of the previous night came flooding back. No Jeff. Where was everyone? The bedroom door began to slowly open. Oh no. No more, Paul's body and brain pleaded. The door slowly opened to reveal Steve.

"He's awake!" "Morning."

"Morning. What time is it? Where's Jeff?"

Steve moved alongside the bed.

"How you feeling.?"

"Could be better. Where's Jeff?"

Steve looked away as he replied.

"He's gone away and so have those guys."

Paul sat up quickly and a grimace creased his tender looks.

"What you mean, gone? What am I supposed to do?"

Dan entered the bedroom carrying a mug of steaming coffee. Paul looked down at the slash marks across his chest and the pain surged once more. Dan put the coffee down on the bedside table.

"Jeff won't bother you anymore. Stay in bed and I'll go into town to get more salt for a bath. That will prevent infection and help healing. Look, for what it's worth we're both sorry. We should never have let things go so far. Forgive us .Please."

Paul could see the genuine pleading in Dan's eyes. He could forgive, although he may never forget.

"Consider it done. Now, what's for breakfast?"

A warm flow of laughter filled the room as Paul stretched out and touched Steve's arm.

"Stay with me."

Steve looked at Dan.

"That's OK. I'll rustle up some breakfast, then go for the salt," said Dan as he left the bedroom. Steve lay on top of the duvet, alongside Paul.

"You know I can't remember much about last night and that frightens me," volunteered Paul.

Steve answered rather sheepishly. "No that's good. Don't try to remember. You don't want to remember. You just don't," his voice trailed away.

Dan returned with a pile of toast and honey on a tray. More coffee. More regrets.

"Don't go in the barn Paul." Steve looked nervous.

"No chance. I don't think I'm going anywhere today." Paul paused.

"I've nowhere to go anyway," he added plaintively. Steve and Dan lowered their heads a fraction.

"When you do get up, stay clear of the barn. Eat up and I'll go and get the salt. Steve will look after you."

Steve smiled warmly at the face of the boy looking at him who needed someone to care.

Apart from not wishing Paul to go into the barn and awaken a nightmare there were two other reasons. Soon after Jeff had departed this world, Dan had driven the BMW into the barn and then padlocked the door. Jeff's toes were resting on the front edge of the bonnet, his body still hanging from the beam.

Paul made short work of the toast and honey. Feeling brighter now he indicated that he would like Steve to get in the bed with him. Steve began to slip under the duvet but Paul stopped him.

"Do you always go to bed with your clothes on?"

Steve stood beside the bed and peeled his T-shirt from his body. He dropped his jeans. Someone else who could not afford underwear! Steve was flaccid and well-hung. His body was naturally lightly-tanned by working the land. The tell-tale lines where his shorts had been showed a pale soft skin. Obediently he slipped beneath the duvet alongside Paul.

"Steve. Please hold me."

Steve was pleased to oblige and they gently stroked each other's growing manhoods. Carefully, Steve pulled the duvet from their bodies, careful not to irritate Paul's damaged flesh. Slowly, but deliberately, Steve took Paul in his mouth, and slowly and tenderly sucked his bitten cock. Paul murmured his appreciation and as Steve's fingers ran lightly through his pubes, Paul filled his new friend's mouth with his hot juice.

"Thanks Steve."

"No, thank you Paul."

Paul laying in Steve's protective arms soon drifted back to a sleep free of nightmares.

Dan returned from buying the salt and found Steve holding the sleeping Paul. He slipped from the bed and got dressed. Dan just smiled his acknowledgment of the situation.

"What we gonna do about Jeff?" asked Steve.

"He's allright where he is at the moment. I'll think of something. Just make sure Sleeping Beauty doesn't go anywhere near that barn."

"No problem. What are we going to do about Paul?"

Dan led Steve down the stairs.

"Paul can stay here a few days, that's no problem. After that, who knows? No-one in particular is looking for him as far as we know. He's just a runaway. Perhaps Andy can help. Somehow we've got to explain to him about Jeff and unlike Paul, someone will miss Jeff, and pretty soon."

A worried Âxpression momentarily crossed Dan's face but he quickly regained an external composure for the benefit of Steve. There was a lot of problem-solving to be done and soon.

Paul woke again about midday. He looked down his chest and was relieved to see that his wounds although red, were thankfully not as bad as he feared. There were a few cuts, but nothing that wouldn't heal quickly. He hoped his back was OK too. He thought it must be reasonably OK as he was lying on it and the pain was acceptable. Wearing a dressing gown he came downstairs to the kitchen.

"Welcome!"

"What's for lunch?"

Once more, relaxed laughter filled the cottage. Dan's thoughts were still wrestling with an ever-increasing list of problems. He watched as Steve burst into gales of laughter as Paul discovered he was ticklish. Dan allowed them their fun. No need for them to worry about how to dispose of a body. Paul was lucky despite his wounds, for he didn't know there was a body. What a difference a day makes!

Lunch was a huge fry-up. A total calorie explosion. Bliss, utter bliss, as they attacked a plateful each of locally produced eggs, bacon and sausages, topped with baked beans, fried farmhouse bread and for good measure, grilled tomatoes. All washed down with tea from a large brown teapot, that seemed incapable of being emptied. Once again the world seemed a better place to Paul.

After lunch, Steve took Paul for a walk around the farm, away from the barn. At no time did Paul mention the barn. It was some time before he asked about Jeff again.

"Has Jeff gone back to Birmingham?"

"Yeah. I expect so, although he didn't say."

"Right.... Come on, let's walk and walk." Paul unwittingly did a passable impression of Julie Andrews in the 'Sound of Music', by running across the field with his arms outstetched. He only came to a halt when he had forgotten the field was used for grazing, and he trod in the results.

Sometime later, Steve decided it was time to return to the farm

"Look, you take your time and we'll see you later. OK?"

Reluctantly Paul agreed but he did not relish being alone. Steve waved his farewell and Paul went to sit atop a five-barred gate and gazed across a peaceful world.

Steve returned to the farm to be questioned by Dan as to Paul's whereabouts. Dan suggested that while he got on with general farmwork, Steve should tidy the yard and make sure that when Paul returned he kept away from the barn. Steve stared at the barn and shuddered at the thought of the contents. What next? This was the pressing question occupying Steve's mind.

Paul stayed on the gate for some time taking in every detail of the panorama. Once again, Birmingham was a million miles away. His back began to ache and his wounds felt sore. He returned, under the watchful eye of Steve, to the cottage. Steve followed him in as Paul went upstairs.

"I'm going to have a bath. Where's the salt?"

Steve followed him to the bathroom clutching a large packet of coarse sea salt.

"I'm going to have a good long soak!"

"Good idea," encouraged Steve. "See you after." Steve then left him to it and returned to his farmyard-tidying under the lengthening shadow of the barn.

Dan had difficulty getting on with his work for the day. Wherever he looked the barn dominated his view. The contents forever impressed upon his mind. While Steve was out across the fields with Paul he took advantage of the deserted yard to check the padlock once more. That was firmly in place, but as this was virtually an unused barn, apart from storing old and broken equipment, that was not surprising. Walking along the outer wall, through a gap in the old wooden side Dan could see into the barn interior. Little light penetrated the building, but there was sufficient to see Jeff hanging. Horrendously, Jeff still swayed eerily in the half-light. His naked body; finely defined, lacking life, the neck bent so that the head was almost parallel to the shoulders, the shell of a former tortured soul. Dan was relieved that he could only see the back of Jeff's head. The face would have been too much. Faceless, he could cope with it.

Dan looked around for wood to cover the gap. On closer inspection the gesture would have been futile as the only way to cover all the gaps would be to have rebuilt the whole barn. He trudged away deep in thought. What to do about Jeff, the car and Paul. There was one way he could solve all these problems at once but he would need Steve's help. If he could not persuade him, then Steve would become part of the problem.

Twenty Seven

Dan explained to the surprised visitors what he claimed had happened to Jeff, and he was surprised that Andy had not seen or heard from him. This didn't surprise Andy as Jeff could have taken himself off anywhere. Dan was careful to mention the whipping Paul had received and how he had rescued him from the clutches of the mad sadist and his deranged friends. Andy, and Alex in particular, were both very grateful to Dan for his actions and said they did not know how to repay him. Steve was by far the happiest person in the room at the arrival of the 'Birmingham Two'. Coffee was consumed mugful after mugful and the chatter was relaxed. Dan knew his plan was dead. The problems remained. After the coffee came the whiskey, then the trail upstairs. Alex wanted to get Paul on his own to love and hold him all night before taking him away from this cottage of nightmares. He was not to get his way, at least not for sometime. It was Paul who set the pattern for the night.

"Let's have fun! You're all my friends and let's party. Please play a game with me. I'll want you one after the other, you screw. It would really turn me on! I'll go to bed, you draw lots and come to me in turns. Use a condom and stay to watch the next one and so on."

Alex was horrified at what Paul had become; Andy smiled silently. Steve was shocked but already his crutch was reacting to the idea, and Dan was grinning from ear to ear with unrestrained anticipation. Paul leapt up and was quickly away upstairs screaming, "Come and get me!"

In the bedroom, Paul stripped quickly and picked up a tube of lube and fingered generous amounts up his tunnel of love. Lying on the bed he turned off the bedside light and waited for his first shagger to arrive. The draw had been made by drawing high cards. Although he protested, Alex took his card. He was to be the last.

As he waited, Paul gently stroked his tool to its full magnificence. It was to be a wonderful night, with him calling the shots. The door opened and in came

Andy. 'A real big one to start with', was Paul's immediate thought. Andy switched on the bedside lamp. Standing over Paul he undressed slowly, just gazing down at the erect youth who was fingering his own arse.

"No messing about. Just fuck me," demanded Paul.

Andy moved immediately into position as he stretched a condom over his eager weapon. Paul lay with his legs wide open in the air and Andy stooped over the welcoming arsehole. Andy lay onto Paul and Paul's hand took the searching cock and guided it to his entrance. Andy pushed to penetrate and the gasps of pleasure from Paul were heard downstairs. Andy decided he was going to be rough and treat Paul like the whore he had become. Plunging violently into Paul, who was becoming fully stretched but coping with the intruder, Andy simulated a false orgasm in the still-pleasured youth.

"Next!" called out Paul, as Andy slid from him. Next was Steve. Already naked, except for a condom, like Andy he moved immediately into position. This time, Paul bent over standing on the bedroom carpet. Steve slipped into place easily. The hole was taking allcomers well. Steve put his hands on Paul's cock and thrust deeply inside him. Once again the cry of pleasure were prolonged as Steve slid in deeper and deeper. Andy stood in front of Paul with his condom-less dick, took hold of Paul's head and shoved his tool past unresisting lips to the back of his throat, and further. Steve pummeled into the arse and added to Paul's wounds by digging in his nails and then drawing them across quivering flesh.

"Aaaaah, I'm shooting!" gasped Steve as he reached the neck of Paul whose head was gyrating on Andy. Steve's orgasm was full and swift. It was Steve's turn to shout, "Next!", as Paul's mouth was fully occupied. Steve had fully withdrawn by the time Dan entered the room. Another one ready for action; naked apart from the rubber, his shaved head glinting with sweat. He took the position vacated by his brother and despite his size plunged deeply into the relaxed hole. Pain there was and pain was the joy. Andy was still in front of Paul and his professionalism allowed him to control his moment of orgasm. Still in control, Andy leaned forward to kiss the hard-working Dan. Tongues tasting each other, Paul jerked rapidly along Andy's shaft as Dan plunged in deeper than those before him. Dan's moment came swiftly and violently. He broke from Andy and slapped Paul across his head with one hand, whilst the other twisted Andy's left nipple. Andy grinned as Paul was pulled from him by the convulsing Dan.

"Next!" called Andy.

Alex stood in the doorway. Prepared but unsure. He was confronted with the scene of Paul now lying on the bed, legs open and still wanting more. Andy was standing there with the low light emphasising his god-like figure. Dan lay on the floor regaining his natural breathing rhythm. Steve stepped forward and led Alex to his mission. Steve slid his finger around Alex's hole. Alex shook himself free and looked around the room.

"Come on chicken, let's fuck!" yelled the rampant Paul.

Alex, with his eyes closed, mounted Paul. Again the moan of pleasure, again the thrusting, again the orgasm. For Alex it was not pleasant to cum with teeth gritted but he had done his duty. Meanwhile, Andy's cock was just flooding Paul's face with thick luscious cum. The grateful youth wiped his face with his fingers and once more licked them clean. Andy reached over and as Alex had moved away, wanked Paul to an immediate orgasm, the youth shooting high in the air as they all watched his spunk arc through the air to splat repeatedly on his stomach.

"Thank you everybody! I deserved that! I must have let Jeff down for him to dump me here. By the way he owes me at least £200. Good job I got the clothes, eh? Expect I'll get paid when I get back to the flat."

Paul's questioning look was answered by guilty eyes that looked anywhere but at him.

Twenty Eight

Sleeping arrangements were made for the night. Dan and Steve returned to the farmhouse. Andy paraded naked before taking a shower. His superbly-hung body adorned by his blond hair aroused the two teenagers who saw it. Andy invited the boys to join him in the shower, an invitation quickly taken up. The lack of space, the tightness of movement and the soothing warm water, stimulated the teenagers. Andy, fully aware of the effect his powerful frame was having, took the boys, one in each hand. Their heads flopped onto his shoulders as he slowly and carefully stimulated their growing manhoods. Paul freed himself to slip down wet skin, to take Andy's glory in his mouth. A few plunging lunges down the well-used shaft and back up to tongue the firm but sensitive purple head, before he transferred his attention to Alex's equally wanting length. The water-sodden black pubes caught his lips as Alex with his hands forced Paul's head to stay and work. Alex turned his head to the know-ing, smiling face of Andy. Their lips met and a power packed his with fully stretched mouths gripping their heads together. Alex's hand sought Andy's cock and as he pulled it he gripped it tightly. Andy's tongue responded and plunged down the throat of a gurgling, wanting Alex. Paul continued to toy with Alex who opened his legs wide to receive the plunging fingers of Paul. Alex did not want Paul to release him and he was not disappointed. Alex came in sharp, rapid spurts that slipped so easily down Paul's eager throat. Once Alex was spent, Paul stood up and saw that Andy and Alex were still licking each other's tongues. Momentarily jealous, Paul stepped from the shower and was followed immediately by Andy and then Alex. They toweled each other dry, the action bringing a tingling to Paul's damaged but still sen-sitive skin. Andy, naked, flaccid and magnificent, walked to the second bed-room, pointedly announcing that he was going to sleep alone. Was it because he just wanted his own space, or was it because he wanted the boys to be together, or was he simply too tired to make any such considered judgments?: Paul's imagination was working overtime.

Paul and Alex went together into the main bedroom. Both were totally naked and despite their actions there was an understated innocence as they faced each other. Alex slipped past Paul and under the duvet. Paul joined him and was received by outstretched arms.

"Paul, what was all that about tonight?"

There was no answer.

"Paul?"

"What?"

"Well, what was it all about?"

Paul turned to face Alex who was staring at the ceiling.

"I'll tell you if you really want to know. If it's so important to you! One day you'll be off to your university and take up your great career, whatever that's going to be. Me? Well I'll still be in Brum, following my career. And what will that be? Well, listen matey and I'll tell you. I can't go back home and I don't want to either. Tonight I was just practicing. I've got the body, the cock, the arse. Get it? For as long as I can, I'm going to sell my cock and hole. Don't need anybody. Jeff owes me and when he pays up I'll be quids-in. I'll keep living at Andy's and work for Jeff. They'll look after me and I'll have earned a fortune while you're sat with your bloody books, trying to make-out with girls. Face up to it, you're queer, remember, a fucking queer. Well, I'm going to make my fucking fortune out of queens like you, who have their careers, wife and kids but want arse and cock."

Alex removed his arm from around Paul and was shocked by the response he had received. Why didn't the sod realise that he loved him? Well he loved the old Paul, not this hard, old-before-his-time whore. Perhaps it was not too late. Yet how well Paul knew him, better than he knew himself. Like many before him he would do what was expected of him. His mother would make sure of that. As he lay there, images of Dale passed before him. Fuzzy and fading images, not the crystal-clear images of former memories. What was happening to him? It had all been so simple on the drive up from Birmingham. Bring that stupid but lovely fool back, so that their lives could continue. Turn the clock back and have their fun together. Don't need or involve anybody else. He had it all planned; the Paul he looked for was not at the cottage. Paul's learning curve had passed Alex by.

"You don't pull your punches, do you?" said Alex.

"If you didn't want to know, you shouldn't have asked."

"OK. Point taken. But you're better than all that garbage you've come out with. Look I can get hold of some cash and if you really don't want to go home I'll get us a flat and we can have a life together. You don't have to go back to school. We could live in Birmingham and you could get a job eventually and we would be fine..."

Paul also gazed at the ceiling.

"Get real. What would we really live on? What happens when you go to university? You'll tire of me, then what? Out on the street and you go back to your supposed normality. Jeff will look after me and the pay is good. Don't worry, I won't charge you!"

The slap across the face was immediate, the silence that followed deafening.

They lay in silence, both still staring at their chosen spot on the ceiling. It was Paul who broke the spell. He folded back the duvet to reveal his erection.

"That's my future. That's what I've got and I can take the biggest. So tell me I'm wrong if you like, but I don't believe in that love crap. I fuck and get fucked and I love it! How many people can say they love their work? I mean, really love it, when a cock shoots up you or you can feel it throbbing in your mouth before it gives you that hot sticky juice. The more the better. Feeling a man's cock, his pubes and tasting his mouth, feeling his sweat against you, the warmth of his flesh and knowing he wants you. All that and get paid....well? What you offering me? Love? Well you can keep it. I've learnt a lot since Skipton and I can thank you for that, and I do, honestly."

There were tears in his eyes as his bravado slipped.

"I'm sorry about what I said about you and all that. Forgive me please, it's important to me, but I know what I have to do."

Alex looked at Paul. Alex then bent over Paul and took him in his mouth. Paul had never experienced such tenderness before an orgasm before. The tongue-induced climax was full, satisfying, gentle, soft and tender. Paul was surprised by the new experience. A flat with Alex might not be such a bad idea. He could still work for Jeff, surely.

Twenty Nine

Jack Price couldn't decide what to do for the best. There was still no sign of Paul returning to school and this was unusual. Perhaps it would be best to wait one more day. Couldn't really do any harm. Paul's mother did her best. Sure, he should be at school but he's probably got himself a nice little job for the summer. God knows Paul and his Mum could do with the money. Leave it for now.

Tony had heard from a very reliable source that Paul was in London and got a job in a hotel kitchen. When he was telling the others, he told them that he suspected that Paul had probably given the Head Chef a blow to get the job. As it was a live-in post he thought Paul was probably sharing with the Head Chef and performing tricks to order. Shamir was pleased to hear that Paul had been heard of, but he thought Tony was wrong about the Head Chef. Paul would never do anything like that.

Paul and Alex were woken by Andy standing over them with a mug of coffee in each hand. Wearing just a pair of skimpy shorts, he knew that he was arousing the young cock before him. It was all a tease, as he had received a visitor in the night. Dan had fully serviced the Greek god as they lived out their fantasies. Young cock was nice, but there was no substitute for experience, leather, handcuffs and a severe whipping. Not a mark on Andy, but Steve would have to take on some of Dan's jobs for the day. Fortunately Dan had bought two extra packets of coarse seasalt.

Andy found enough items to prepare a full English breakfast for all of them. Dan had returned to the farmhouse during the night. Steve had the doubtful privilege of being up for early milking. From the milking shed in the early morning light the barn dominated the yard. Its contents dominated even more.

As the boys ate their toast, Andy decided it was time to approach the subject of the return to Birmingham.

"We had better go home today. Paul, you can stay with me till something is sorted out with Jeff. He'll get over his sulks and want you again. Just don't let him work you to death so to speak. Don't worry about the money, Jeff always pays his debts."

Paul crunched into his slice of toast before replying.

"That'll be fine. Can't wait to get back to work."

Alex looked up to the heavens.

"Soon I'm going to get a flat and Paul will be able to move in with me," said Alex.

Paul made no comment but Andy did.

"I don't think for one minute that Jeff will allow that."

"What's it do with him where Paul lives?" said an angry Alex.

"Whoever pays the piper calls the tune."

Alex grunted his reply and Paul crunched his toast.

Soon after breakfast and washing up was completed, Dan called in.

"Leaving today?" asked Dan.

"Yes, we'll be getting off as soon as we can," said Andy.

"Make sure you leave nothing behind. Best if it looks as though you've never been here," said Dan with a firmness that caused Andy to wonder exactly what he meant.

"OK," agreed a suspicious Andy.

Packing up didn't take long. Andy was determined that everything would be clean, neat and tidy. Paul looked out across the valley and wished that a return to Birmingham was not necessary. If only Jeff had stayed all this packing would not have been taking place, at least not for a day or two. Paul wondered where Jeff had disappeared to. He could at least have phoned and what about the money? It hadn't been pleasant the other night but the wounds would soon heal.

Their small amount of luggage was soon packed into the Fiesta and Steve joined Dan for the farewells. Generous hugs all round and loose promises to return. The kind of promises that are made to people met on holiday, an exchange of Christmas cards once, then forgotten, although there were aspects that Paul would never forget. Once in the car, Paul didn't look back as Alex drove away. Andy had a few problems on his mind, and they all concerned Paul.

The French Police informed Interpol of the details regarding the body of a Caucasian youth found near Calais. Their investigations so far had drawn a complete blank as to his identity.

Once back at the Birmingham flat, the car was unloaded and the three sat around drinking coffee. Andy immediately checked his phone for messages. There was one from the bar owner suggesting that his patience with Andy was getting a little stretched and could he contact him as soon as possible. A second message from a punter suggested by its content that barwork would not be on his mind that night. Andy was surprised that Jeff had still not made contact. Perhaps he would turn up that night, like he usually did, bright breezy, demanding and friendly, with not a care in the world. This time though, Andy had his doubts. Something just did not seem right.

Dan watched the Fiesta disappear down the farm lane with a heavy heart. Slowly he turned back to face the barn. A lot of work to be done today, and little of it to do with farming.

Steve had returned to the fields to be alone with his thoughts and regrets. He regretted that he had never told Paul that he more than fancied him. He thought he might be in love and there was no-one to talk to, to find out what love was. Was what he did with Dan love? Brotherly love. Surely love did not involve so much pain? He often felt brutalised, especially when Dan ignored his pleas for mercy and pushed his manhood even deeper into him. Paul was different; he made love, he had taken him in such a short time to a new understanding and consideration. Now he was gone, probably never to return, like all the rest. Tonight Dan would be cruelly demanding, he always was when visitors had gone. Steve sighed inwardly and put more distance between himself and the farmyard.

Dan looked around guiltily as he removed the padlock. Entering the barn, he was soon aware of a pungent odour that had been trapped within. Before him he could not ignore the hanging form, that his mind wanted so desperately to be part of a past that had disappeared down the lane in a Fiesta. No such luck, reality was never that easy. Carefully avoiding any contact with the now ridiculous corpse, he moved to the far distant corner where there were stored four large jerrycans, containing agricultural paraffin. He had always known they would be useful one day. Dan checked each can for it's contents. Each was between half and threequarters-full. More than enough for his requirements. Four bales of hay were broken and Dan forked the hay around the BMW. Two of the cans were emptied around the car. The destruction of the BMW distressed Dan more than the fate of Jeff. A third can was emptied from the car to the doorway of the barn. The final can's contents were distributed around the doorway and partially up the wooden walls. Dan stood and looked at his handiwork. He did not understand why, but he found himself reciting the words of the Christian funeral service, "Ashes to Ashes," followed bizarrely by the words of the old, formal death sentence: "May the Lord have mercy upon your soul." Through the doorway he stared at the hanging corpse. Sweat had dried upon the cold flesh. The skin resembled a torso from Madame Tussauds that had somehow found its way into the barn. Still looking at the body, Dan took a small box of matches from his pocket. Leaving the doorway he stepped back from the barn. Checking his feet were clear of straw and paraffin, he struck the first match and threw it towards the soaked straw. The match flared and feebly died before reaching its target. Dan crouched down and gathered a handful of straw, and striking another match ignited it. He reached forward to drop the burning material onto the paraffin soaked ground. A gentle 'whoosh' and the straw was burning, the flames at first gently meandering towards the barn and up the brittle wooden walls. The stench of burning paraffin filled his nostrils and he stepped back and clear of the blaze. Suddenly the inner area of the barn was engulfed. Through the flames and white smoke Dan could see the light playing on the seemingly twitching corpse before the rope yielded and broke releasing the corpse to the blazing earth. Black smoke now engulfed Dan and he had to retire quickly towards the cottage. To his horror he realized that the smoke and burning straw were being drawn to the cottage. Before him, his whole life and that of his dependent brother were apparently about to be consumed by fire. Dan, for once in his life, knew exactly what he had to do. Steve would surely get some insurance money. He'd be fine.

Steve gazed disbelievingly in the direction of the farm as plumes of white, grey and then black smoke stretched skywards. Momentarily he just stood and looked transfixed. With a sudden realisation, he rushed back towards the farm; his steps wide, athletic, strong taking him to who knew what. The stench of the smoke was familiar, but not of burning wood. Paraffin. Through the billowing smoke he could see Dan standing facing the now blazing barn.

"Dan! Dan! Get clear! Get clear! I'll ring the Fire Brigade," yelled Steve with a choking voice.

Although an old, dry, wooden building, the barn remained defiantly intact. Suddenly Dan was overwhelmed by the thought that in saving the cottage the world would discover the awful truth of the farm. He knew then he could not face the future: the questions and their damning answers. Steve came rushing back from making the emergency call. He saw Dan turn towards him, smile, then turn away. Dan made the sign of the cross across his body, hesitate, glance towards Steve and scream out. "Bye!" Without further hesitation he walked to the blazing barn doorway and before Steve could react, to be engulfed by the eager flames. As Dan disappeared within the barn, the fuel tank of the BMW exploded as if mercifully on purpose bringing Dan's agony to an end, as his lungs were seared to burnt fragments within his body.

Steve was still transfixed as the sound of the approaching fire engines got ever nearer. The paintwork on the cottage door and window frames was being licked by hungry flames. Despite the narrowness of the lane, two fire engines screamed into the yard.

"My brother's in there!" yelled the now hysterical Steve. As though on cue, the barn roof crashed downwards as the barn walls imploded with a deafening roar accompanied by swirling smoke, burning debris and red flames tinged with black. Two firemen held onto Steve and no-one else made a move towards the barn.

Apart from smoke damage, the cottage escaped relatively unscathed. It was several hours before the authorities decided the destroyed barn was safe to leave. The police informed Steve that the remains of two people had been discovered in the ruins, plus a burnt-out car, possibly a BMW.

Thirty

The police explained to the still disbelieving Steve that there were definitely two bodies in the barn. They questioned Steve about the BMW and about who he thought it belonged to. The only person he knew with a car like that was Jeff Manners who had visited the farm cottage over the weekend but had returned to Birmingham. A slight disbelieving sigh came from the investigating officer. Steve, in his confused state, failed to make the connection. The officer didn't as he contacted the West Midlands police to check the whereabouts of Jeff Manners. The media were informed that a press conference would be held later in the day.

The officers from the West Midlands force received no reply when they called at Jeff Manners' flat. They returned later; still no reply. They spoke to neighbours. No-one had seen him for nearly a week. They gained entry to the flat. One officer commented that Mr. Manners had a large video collection. The general feeling was that they would be athletic training videos. An officer informed Derbyshire Police of the empty flat and garage.

Andy, Alex and Paul were at Andy's flat. Alex was drinking yet one more final cup of coffee as they watched the late news on the television. All three were stunned by the second lead story, following the story of the U.S. President's visit to London. The newscaster calmly informed the nation, Andy, Alex and Paul in particular, that two bodies had been discovered in a burnt-out barn near Bakewell, Derbyshire. Early unconfirmed reports that one of the bodies was that of Olympic hopeful Jeff Manners had not been confirmed by the Police. Mr. Manners has not been seen at his Birmingham flat for nearly one week. The other body is believed to be that of a local farmer. Police have indicated that the cause of the fire was suspicious and their investigations were continuing.

Paul grabbed Alex's hand.

"It can't be right! He's here in Brum! They're wrong! Oh please God make them be wrong!" Paul was devastated. Andy, though shocked, knew that the three of them faced problems. Alex was bemused but he was frightened by his inner reaction, that he shared with no-one. He was pleased and relieved by the possible death of Jeff.

Andy was the first to respond to Paul's outburst.

"Hotel for you tonight young man." He looked directly at Paul.

"Why? What do you mean? What for?"

Andy began to become agitated.

"You heard them. Suspicious death. They'll be here soon, tonight, tomorrow, who knows! Then what? How do we explain? Steve or Dan will tell them everything, depending who's alive!"

The true horror began to dawn on Paul and Alex.

"Oh my God! Not Steve, please not Steve." Lamented a weeping Paul as he collapsed into Alex's lap.

The trio were silent for several minutes, as each considered their options. For Andy a fear was welling up inside him. Not only fear for Paul and where he was to go, but fear for his own freedom. He had a past, a past that involved youths and enjoying their bodies, not only for his gratification, but dangerously for the gratification of a horny camcorder-wielding maniac. He knew exactly what he had been getting into and now the consequences would have to be faced. It would be possible to stay on in the flat, work in the bar and maintain his client list. Could be good as all the cash earned would be his, and then there was Paul. What to do with the boy? It was tempting to keep him around and work him. Paul's attraction was easy to understand. A well-endowed man's cock attached to the skin and body of a youth. The appeal for Andy was irresistible, not just the earning potential, but he found him stunningly beautiful. Despite his recent experiences, Paul still had innocence, and that made him a wonderful lay. The other side of the situation was that Paul was dangerous. A danger not only to him, but to Alex and the brothers, or at least whoever survived. Unknown clients would be fearful of being denounced. Andy realised he couldn't just throw Paul out. That wouldn't be fair and anyway he could end up working for someone else, or tell the world, especially the police, or school, of his recent history. That must be avoided at all costs.

Paul looked at the situation in a much less complicated way. Jeff had gone. He had to face that, but he would get over it. He needed to work and he could do that from the safety of Andy's flat. He really hoped with all his heart that Steve was OK.

Alex just wanted to be somewhere else and soon.

It was Paul who broke the silence.

"I don't want to go to a hotel. The cops don't know me and why should they? No reason for them to come here."

"Don't be stupid! Of course they'll find out about you, us and much more. Jeff had an address book and listings on his computer. He regarded himself as untouchable and that information would be in his flat. You would be his latest addition. They'll find out about us all being at the cottage. He's well-known and the papers will have a field-day soon. Don't any of you care what really happened to Jeff? One of those brothers killed him, or both. Then I reckon one got jittery and the other sorted him out. Why they killed him in the first place I haven't worked out yet. Perhaps it was one of his weird games that went wrong, I don't know, perhaps we'll never know the truth."

Andy's words hung in the air and Alex and Paul continued to try and make sense of the situation.

"Couldn't we go and get the address book from his flat? You've got a key haven't you? We could destroy the book and his disks, plus wipe his computer files clean. Eh?" Paul suggested, his tone of voice appearing to believe this was the simple easy option.

"Paul, use your brain! This is a suspicious death of a well-known person. The police will have or will be now going over the flat with as fine-toothed comb. There will be a guard on the flat and probably the Press outside. Once the cops get a look at the videos the shit will hit the fan! Apart from that you've just had a fucking brilliant idea!"

A hurt look came across Paul's face. Suddenly he felt lonely, unprotected and vulnerable.

Alex had listened to the others before intervening.

"Look, I'm sure you're right Andy, and if you are, the law could be round here anytime. They may even be on their way now. We better get a move on, but are you sure a hotel is a good idea? Even a small one is very public and it'll look strange a lad Paul's age being on his own. He didn't really ought to be on his own either. I was thinking that....." Andy interrupted Alex as he grabbed a coat and picked up Paul's bag.

"You're right! Come on, I've got a friend whose address is not written down here or at Jeff's. He lives in Solihull and he'll help." Andy looked at Paul's frightened face.

"He's a nice guy too," he added trying to reassure Paul.

It was quickly agreed that Paul should go to Solihull and Alex drove them to the new hideout.

The ride out of the city helped Paul to come to terms with the situation. Andy promised him that once the situation quietened down he would come and collect him. Alex promised he would visit regularly. Andy had no intention of keeping his promise if there was any way he could avoid it. Alex was unsure. He had his career to think of.

They arrived at their destination which was a large house on the outskirts of the suburb. A clearly wealthy area that would be ideal for Paul's needs. After all, no-one would believe a male prostitute would live in such an area. The house was at the end of a short drive and concealed from the main road by a conifer hedge, that stretched all around the property. A tidy mature garden surrounded the 1930's solidly-built house. They were greeted by a man in a short-sleeved multi-coloured shirt, grey flannels and sandals. His cheery face put them all at ease. He had been surprised by the request that Andy had made on the mobile phone, but a teenage lodger was too good to miss. He didn't want to know details and he hadn't been told any. What he didn't know he couldn't worry about.

Paul's new landlord was Jasper Caunt, a successful entrepreneur in his early thirties. He had recently split from his teenage skinhead boyfriend in unhappy circumstances. After a two-year relationship, the break when it came was violent and sudden. Jasper had returned home from a business meeting unexpectedly early, to discover his lover sharing his bed with a youth and his girlfriend. The boyfriend was performing on top of the skinhead girl with considerable athleticism, being encouraged

David Keane

by the youth who was flying high on a drug cocktail. When Jasper entered the room, the boyfriend mocked him before resuming exaggerated pelvic thrusts into the grateful girl. Whether her climax was real or not, it sent a shudder of jealousy through Jasper, who then had to endure the sound and vision of the clearly real moment of the youth's climax. This was a knife thrust to his heart. Jasper screamed for the trio to get out. Their response was to laugh at him and for his boyfriend to peel back the duvet and go down on the shaven hole of the girl. Jasper ran from the room and threw up just as he reached the toilet bowl in the adjacent bathroom. The mocking laughter filled the house. He returned to the bedroom and walked up to his boyfriend who was now dressing. Without a word he looked the youth in the eye before hitting him with all the strength that two years of betrayal could summon. The blow rocked the mocking head of the youth backwards and as he hit the floor, the two visitors left the room and the house hurriedly. They were not interested in the fate of their friend who had serviced both of them on and off for the last two years during his relationship with Jasper. The former boyfriend slowly stood up, completed dressing then turned to face the shaking Jasper and then emitted with great power a large blob of phlegm directly into the face of his humiliated former Master. When he reached the front door the skinhead shouted: "Go and toss yourself you fucking queer load of shit!" and left. Despite the hurt he would not learn from the experience. Within days he was bringing a rentboy home to perform on him. The boy was not satisfied with his agreed fee. He took a sterling silver tray from the dining room and told Jasper exactly what would happen to him if he objected. Jasper did not stop him. It wasn't worth it. He wouldn't hire him again anyway, as he did not do a lot for him. Not the size he liked. Then, as though a present from heaven, Paul arrived.

Paul looked at his new landlord. About thirtyish he thought, a little over-weight and wealthy. He had a friendly smile and made his visitors welcome. He knew he would have to accept that he would be staying there for a few days but the situation was only temporary he believed. Paul relaxed, sitting next to Alex. All would be all right. He was sure.

Alex was quietly pleased as Jasper seemed kind and caring. Paul would be safe from the world there.

Andy was pleased to be able to unload the burden Paul had become.

Alex and Andy returned to town. Andy worried once more in case there was a reception committee waiting for him. He needed to rid himself of a few incriminating items. All was quiet at Andy's flat when they arrived.

Thirty One

The first Coroner's Inquest was brief and to the point. Evidence of identification was given from dental records, and the names of the victims of the farm fire in Bakewell were announced to the media. Local Farmer Dan Osbourne and athlete Jeffrey Manners. Police investigations were continuing and both deaths were being regarded as suspicious.

Andy had removed from the flat a black plastic rubbish bagfull of letters, one address book, photographs and videos. Firmly tied up and all the air squeezed out, he carried the rubbish bag in the early hours to the nearby canal. After checking there was no one about, Andy hurtled the bag high in the air and watched it fall back to the canal's surface. Hitting with a loud impact, the bag rested for a seeming eternity before slowly being swallowed by the dark waters. Bubbles played at the surface, before silence returned and Andy made his worried walk home.

Paul liked his room at Jasper's. It was light, airy and spotlessly clean. The bed was a double with a soft mattress. There were several paintings and sketches hanging from the pale yellow walls. All were of the same theme, naked or semi-naked youths in various poses. The only photograph in the room was hanging above the bed. It was of a skinhead youth wearing just biking boots sitting astride a Harley Davidson motorbike. The big black and white print dominated the room. Lying on the goosedown stuffed black and white duvet, Paul faced the large bay window. The heavy velvet curtains hung down from the high ceiling. The room was warm without being hot, and Paul felt safe and relaxed. He realised he had not felt this way for some time. The bedroom door swung open and in walked Jasper wearing a patterned silk dressing gown. Without a word he lay beside Paul who quickly realised that once again it was probably time to pay the rent. He was learning quickly. Although Jasper was hoping for favours from Paul, he was astonished by the new lodger's directness.

"What's it to be then? Wank, 69, full shag or what? Haven't learnt massage yet."

Jasper sat up and his surprise at the bluntness shocked him, but his outward response was a little nervous laugh.

"Well, I don't exactly know now you ask."

The unspeaking Paul untied Jasper's dressing gown cord, the silky smoothness of whichallowed the gown to fall aside to reveal Jasper's semi-erect, cut, shaved cock. Without a word Paul took the hardening tool in his mouth. For no reason he could think of, Paul's mind drifted to the moment in Yorkshire when Tony allowed himself to be taken in the field. His mind was full of confused images and the thought of school entered his mind, a memory of being a boy. Jasper's hands held Paul's head in place and the thrusts in his mouth soon ended as his mouth filled with Jasper's hot stickiness. Once Paul's head was released he lifted himself free and spat the mess from his mouth onto a convenient paper tissue.

"I need to sleep now, if you don't mind."

Paul's directness again. Jasper meekly stood up in an embarrassed manner, tied his dressing gown and left the bedroom.

'Could have said thanks', thought Paul as he undressed before slipping beneath the soft down duvet as sleep blotted out all images.

Jasper left the house early the following morning. He left a message propped against the coffee jar, unmissable for Paul. The message was clear. On no account was he to leave the house and he was to await Jasper's return. A prisoner in all but name.

Paul sat staring into his mug of coffee. Radio One filling the kitchen but not catching his attention at all. He needed to be with company, he needed a friend. Not a lover, but someone who wanted to be with him just for himself. Without him realising he was having to come to terms with life as a rentboy. It had not really occurred to him that that was exactly what he was. A saleable item, with plenty of prospective buyers who would pay good money to feel his young, large cock inside them. His dusky skin tones, allied to his well-defined body, plus his willingness to please, made him a very saleable commodity. At ten o'clock on that particular morning there was probably no lonelier person in Birmingham. He would have gladly gone home to his mother, but there

David Keane

would be the problem of "Bad Breath"and maybe the law. Perhaps he would phone her later. Could use the 141 system. Phone Andy. Good idea, he'll come round.

"Hi Andy, it's me Paul."

"What do you think you're doing? Get off the line!"

The line went dead.

Paul was both angry and disappointed. Andy was upset, thought Paul. Perhaps he ought to go and see him and explain that he would talk to no-one. All secrets were safe with him. He must make sure that Andy understood that. Paul wanted to talk to Alex, but he would presumably be in class. Go to Andy; he would understand that he didn't want to stay with Jasper. Andy would help him get his own flat and then he could get back to work. Once he had formalised his thoughts, his mind became clearer and he decided to shower, go into town and talk things through with his friend, Andy. After talking things through they would probably have time to have sex. The thought excited Paul as he stepped into the shower. As the water relaxed his body and mind, his thoughts drifted off to fantasizing about Andy and Alex, having him in so many ways. Sharing him, loving him, comforting him. His erection was firm, strong and demanding relief. He jerked himself violently, the self-abuse arousing his desire as he dug his fingernails into his nipples. Then his free hand squeezed his balls until the pain seared through his legs and up his body. From the shower he could see the handle of the lavatory brush. Switching off the torrent of soothing water he stepped from the shower, grabbed the brush and without any lubrication pushed it into himself. It slid in easlily and he shagged himself with little care. Blood seeped from him and ran down his wet thighs mingling with the water clinging to the hair on his inner thigh. His spunk shot from him in massive gushes and although the orgasm was long and plentiful, his mind still wanted Andy inside him, making him bleed. He wanted to bleed for him, to show him his love. His thoughts concentrated on the ideal of Andy thrusting inside him, whilst he tongued Alex to orgasm. Perfect happiness. He dried and dressed quickly. No time to waste, must get to town and tell Andy how he felt and what he wanted to do. Today would be the day he put his life on track. Get on with it.

The bus trundled into town, seemingly stopping at every opportunity to swap passengers. Would it ever complete its journey? Paul stepped from the bus on New Street. Just a short walk and he would be there. Excitement rose within him as each step took him closer to the flat. He was there. Press the bell button.

"Yes?"

Andy's voice crackled from the mini-wall speaker.

"Let me in, it's Paul."

The door lock buzzed and Paul pushed the door open, and began to run up the stairs to be met by Andy coming down. Andy grabbed Paul by the neck. "What the fuck you doing here? Anybody see you? You bloody fool. Get in the flat!"

Paul was shocked into silence and did as he was ordered.

Thirty Two

Hope had turned to despair. Trust to betrayal. Paul sat on the white settee and Andy approached him. The slap across the face took him totally by surprise, its power irrelevant.

"Don't you ever listen? You were to stay where you were for everyone's safety. But oh no, you couldn't, could you? You make me fucking sick! You put us all in danger but you're too fucking selfish or just too thick to realise."

Andy lunged once more at Paul who took the blow across his face. The physical sting he felt was nothing to the huge inner hurt. He did nothing to fight back as Andy pummelled his head. He knew he had to be punished. Andy lifted Paul from the settee and in one movement threw him to the floor. Andy savagely kicked Paul in the stomach twice. He abruptly stopped the assault and bent down to cradle the wounded youth's head in his arms and they both sobbed quietly. Andy clutched Paul to his chest and then began a slow rocking motion as he kissed the youth's forehead. Paul lifted his head to be met by Andy's lips. Tongues met. As a couple they strove to stand.

"Fuck me please," whispered Paul.

Silently Andy led Paul to the master bedroom. Paul stripped in silence and Andy was shocked to see the raw redness of assault already visible on Paul's stomach. Andy was quickly erect to take his spoils. Apart from a weakly spoken "I'm sorry" from Paul, they pleasured in silence. Condom, no lube. Andy took him with little thought for Paul's comfort. Paul felt he deserved the searing pain. Paul almost dangled from Andy, whose head rocked slightly, his eyes were closed. A deep murmuring issued from Andy's lips and he shot deeply into the ragdoll suspended silently on his cock. As he withdrew, there was a violent knocking on the flat door. Outside stood two police officers, and just to one side, Alex and his father, who had put an unsolicited protective arm around the trembling broken sports captain. Andy opened the door wearing a silk dressing gown. Paul sat up naked on the bed and could be clearly seen through the open bedroom door. The visitors, with the exception of Alex, and his father entered the flat. Fifteen minutes later the flat door opened and the group leaving now had the addition of two more persons. Paul caught sight of Alex and his father.

"Bastard!" Paul spat the word to Alex's face.

The driver of a horsebox parked at the M42 Services. Smiling as he unzipped the jeans of a willing youth, the zip jammed and the youth helped the man gain entry, thinking to himself, let the man do his thing quickly, then he will have paid for his lift. The horsebox driver stroked the boy's neck and the youth recoiled as the man's breath made him retch. The offended man tightened his grip.